JANITORS VS. THE LIVING DEAD

SISTERS OF SLAUGHTER

MICHELLE GARZA & MELISSA LASON

Paperback ISBN: 9781639511891

eBook ISBN: 9781639512140

Published by Death's Head Press, an imprint of Dead Sky Publishing, LLC

Miami Beach, Florida

www.deadskypublishing.com

Cover by Justin T. Coons

Edited by Zoe Lemmon

This novel is dedicated to our biggest supporters and understanders of our weirdness–Bobby, Kiki, Ricky, Kahlan, and Chris. We love you guys!

CHAPTER 1
WHAT VENGEANCE BIRTHS

STEPHI HELD her eye open wide while she brushed her lashes with the growth formula, her pale eye vulnerable and watering in the bright vanity lighting. With each stroke, she focused on getting the expensive lash oil down to the roots before dragging it out to their tips. She tried not to move, tried not to breathe too deeply, knowing any slip could equal a jab to her sensitive eye, a painful mistake.

A door slammed somewhere in the house, causing her to jump and jam the lash formula wand into her eye. The pain was sudden and piercing. She yelped and blinked, her vision darkening to complete blackness in the matter of a few agonizing seconds, a blurry halo swallowing everything. She leaned over and fumbled blindly with the sink before getting the faucet on, quickly splashing water onto her face and into her eye frantically. She needed to see, to know the source of the commotion-though she felt in her stammering heart she already knew-. She blinked and through the tears she could see just a bit but everything around her was still blurred. Her hands shook as she blotted her eye with a hand towel. In the bedroom behind her, thundering footsteps made her jump and wipe at her face in a frantic race to correct her vision, to clear away the darkness and the unknown and to confirm what or who was stomping in her direction.

"Shit," she cursed.

Her vision cleared, and in the mirror she saw the bathroom

doorway darken with the hulking silhouette of her husband. Even through watering eyes she could tell it was him by the shape of his head and how he held his hands at his sides balled into fists, not to mention he was already demanding things of her in his usual grumbling voice.

"I told you to pick up the living room and the bedroom before I got home and you're too busy in here looking at your damn face. You're always blowing my money on face creams and stupid shit. Why do you obsess over your looks so fuckin' much?"

Stephi didn't answer. She wiped the streaming tears from her face with the back of her hand, reminding herself how volatile Teddy could be. She needed to remain quiet and do as she was told.

"Don't just stand there lookin' stupid, run me a bath!" he said.

Stephi nodded and turned to the bathtub while he stomped back into the bedroom. She cranked the handle over to the hot water side and stuck a stopper into the drain. Her anger ate at her, it screamed for her to tell him off.

I stabbed myself in the eye, you stupid motherfucker! Why couldn't you just stay at work? I hate everything about you!

"Look at this place, are you hanging artwork again? Wasting all my money on amateur paintings?" his voice grated on her, it was obnoxiously loud even over the running water of the tub.

She leaned over the sink again and examined her eye in the mirror. It was red and irritated, her sclera bloodshot like crimson spider webs. She dabbed at her eye and barely got it to stop watering when he came back into the bathroom.

He was in his underwear and in his hand he held the hammer she forgot laying on the dresser.

"Put this shit away and take your clothes off."

She turned to face him and he tossed the hammer at her. She didn't catch it; it bounced off her thigh and hit the floor with a loud clank.

"Fuck," she gritted her teeth and gripped her leg.

"Hey! Watch your damn mouth!" he threatened and grabbed her by the shoulder.

Pinching her roughly with one massive hand, he forced her down to the ground.

"While you're down there," Teddy said, innuendo heavy in his voice, and pulled his underwear down. "Why don't you get me started?"

Lately it felt like any sexual interactions between them were predatory or only done as some form of sick punishment to her and she couldn't understand why. They didn't always get along but their sex life was decent up until the last few years, it was becoming like torture to her. Stephi's hand found the hammer and she couldn't take it anymore. She looked up at him, smiling down at her, it made Stephi feel vile. All she could focus on was how lumpy the veins in the side of his head looked, how she hated them, they always bulged and looked disgusting. Her eyes zeroed in on them and all she could envision was a bull's eye tattooed there, a target begging the hammer to find it.

She was faster than him, stronger than he ever knew, and he truly wasn't expecting her to finally realize she had had enough.

Stephi watched Teddy die and it was better than she ever imagined it would be. His naked body convulsed and slumped in the bathtub after a momentary horizontal ballet of grappling and slipping on the blood-slick porcelain each time he tried to escape the water. Finally, after what were only a few minutes for her but eons for him, he gave up and he let himself settle into the bloody tub. His hand went to the agonizing crater in his skull, he mouthed silent words. She wasn't sure if he was begging for help or continuing to verbally abuse her before his life faded away.

Maybe he just had to call her a whore or a bitch one last time.

His body slid further down into the water, his blood rapidly clouding it a deeper shade of crimson. She was happy they selected a larger tub when the house was constructed, his hulking body eased into the warm red bath nicely without his knees being bent. She watched with a quivering hand, the hammer heavy in it. Stephi let him continue to bleed out in the water for a couple hours while she collected her thoughts, and devised a plan to get rid of his corpse.

She was given the handheld electric carving knife as a wedding gift from one of her cousins, she scoffed at the gift when she opened it. She never planned on slicing her own turkey at the dinner table like Martha Stewart. She was relieved she had it once she realized her husband was far too big to carry and there was nowhere to stash an entire body unless she wanted to try burying him in their backyard. Again, heavy labor like digging a hole was not in her repertoire and her nosey neighbors might see her from their second story bedroom window, so that was definitely not an option. She thought of cutting him into pieces and tossing him in the lake but she worried he'd end up rising to the top because shit always floats. A better place came to mind, a place more deserving of a piece of crap like Teddy.

Her husband's head was a pain to cut free, the blade got stuck on his spinal cord several times and she resorted to forcing the blade along with her body weight before it made its way through with a wet crunch and hit the bloody porcelain on the other side. His torso was the real bitch, and when she accidentally sliced one side of his stomach open she almost couldn't go on. She paced the bathroom, breathing deeply, trying to will the nausea away. The smell of his insides was something she would never forget, like wet dog and blood. She couldn't just cut his arms and legs off; she needed him in smaller pieces in order for him to fit in his new tomb. She pieced them out by sectioning them off at each joint. She forced herself through it and reminded herself of the Hell he had made her endure. Cutting him into small pieces with an electric meat cutter and fishing handfuls of his insides out of the tub then shoving them in plastic bags put Stephi's gag reflexes to the test but her hatred for Teddy numbed her gut and her feelings of remorse. The bathtub caught nearly all of his blood, making the clean-up easier for her. Lugging his pieces out in trash bags wasn't so easy. He felt heavier in separate bags than when he laid on top of her in bed, or when he pushed her around and shouted in her face when he was angry. She wondered if his sudden weight gain wasn't just her own conscious telling her what she had done was wrong. She told the doubtful side of her mind to shut up and continued the act of securing her freedom. It was hard but she managed to get it done by lugging him piece by piece out the side door and soon he was packed away on the back of his golf cart.

Serenity Canyon was an exclusive neighborhood and had houses lining each of the streets which circled around the luxury clubhouse in the center, all boasting a quick walk to the best putting greens in

Arizona, many right outside their doors. The plan was created to only accommodate up to twenty large cottages with well-manicured lawns and views of the iconic red rocks of Sedona, Arizona, creating sky rocketing property values and a sense of being totally elite for its residents. On one side stretched the expansive lake and golf course which were built first and became the go-to course in all of Arizona in a few short decades. When the housing development was announced, a rabid war of the who's who of the West Coast started. Only those with the heftiest bank accounts came out as victors and became the permanent residents there in Serenity Canyon. Teddy was one of them, which delighted Stephi at the time, and soon their new home was constructed. But, she quickly learned it would be the most regal prison she had ever seen. The neighborhood came complete with its own security crew who watched over her like jailors for her influential husband.

At the far edge of the golf course and lake she could see her destination, hidden behind a row of tall hedges, almost invisible in the dark. The lights were on at the club house at the center of the development but she didn't worry about being seen, many of the neighbors used their golf carts to haul bags of trash to the dumpsters behind the club. She would just say she had cleaned out her garage if any neighbors greeted her. It was late anyway, many of the residents were well into their golden years and were asleep, and those young enough to be awake were working on keeping their own secrets hidden. If she had learned anything from her well-to-do neighbors while living at Serenity Canyon with all their perfect white smiles and designer clothing, it was how to be a better liar.

The house Teddy bought for them happened to be on the opposite end of the development but he, like all of his neighbors, had only a short ride on the golf cart to reach the course, a selling point for the residents. He bragged to his military friends how he only had a five minute golf cart ride to the first hole. He had no idea when he purchased the place that one night he'd be making that quick, familiar journey in a number of pieces and wrapped in trash bags. Teddy's prisoner was breaking free of her gilded cell and ridding herself of the warden who had left her with bruised ribs and broken teeth on too many occasions to recount.

Stephi's blood-slick hands fumbled with the heavy bags for the fourth time as she stumbled up the pathway from the cart in the dark. She worried one might spring a leak, but just like the commercials on TV advertised, they held his pieces and fluids nicely without losing a single drop of blood. If she could have left a truthful review on Amazon, she would have, but she knew it was out of the question.

She kicked the outhouse door open and heaved two bags onto the floor beside the others. The one with his disfigured torso and innards was too heavy, she had to carry it alone and use both of her hands. It made a wet sloshing sound as she struggled to carry it up the small hill that reminded her of when Teddy hated the gazpacho she prepared for him after he complained about her lack of cooking skills. The bastard took one bite, gagged and dumped it into the trash then made her haul the bag to the trash can immediately. With each sloshing step she prayed the bag wouldn't break because he'd slap her and make her clean it up. It was the last time she tried cooking for him or playing the good wife role, he wasn't worth it. She often wondered why she had ever married him, but each time he was away at work for weeks on end and she was left to do as she pleased in the luxury community she remembered, especially when she used his credit card to pay for drinks at the clubhouse for all her friends. Her life was perfect all accept for him, and now he would be gone forever and she would live life how she pleased.

The outhouse, nicknamed The Shit Shack by the crass cleaning crew, was rarely ever used. It reminded Stephi of the restrooms at a summer camp she went to as a child and it made her cringe. The cramped emergency-use bathroom was built when there was only a golf course in Serenity Canyon, years before the construction of the luxury cottages and new country club with tennis courts and swimming pools. It had a light on a timer inside of it but no lights outside. It was out of place in the ritzy neighborhood but it was hidden out of sight behind a high wall of hedges. Like a blemish beneath a pound of concealer, it wasn't easy to see but almost everyone knew it was there. It was actually only kept around to provide a place for the employees of the grounds to use if they chose to. The lowly folk in maintenance were prohibited from using the neighborhood outdoor facilities, even though they were employed to clean them. The residents of Serenity Canyon were far too high-class to be seen doing their business in an open hole over a mound of feces only concealed by a thin steel trap door, and that's why Stephi figured they would never find Teddy there. His pieces would slowly rot away down in the dark hole amidst an occasional pile of waste deposited by a sick caddy or a hungover gardener.

Finally rid of him.

Stephi turned to look in the cloudy mirror. She was a mess but she was free. If liberation made her look ten years older, she would deal with it until after she cashed his life insurance check and found a good plastic surgeon. She went back to work, holding her breath as she tore the bags open over the reeking toilet bowl. She couldn't escape the stench of Teddy's blood and the mounds of feces beneath it. There was a gaping hole directly under the steel toilet, a mouth of Hell opening wide to receive the bastard she married. It had a wide trap door of sorts, the entire width of the bowl, no water, and a pedal to step on which released some kind of blue fluid, it smelled faintly of mint to mask the horrors below it. It yawned open, a filthy steel maw, before dropping whatever waste someone left in it down into the abyss beneath it, which was a hole about seven feet deep and four feet in length and width, a tomb of water soluble toilet paper, urine, and fecal matter. The steel plate was filthy with dust and dried bodily fluids, the walls and corners of the floor also held a dirty film as if no one had even been inside the outhouse for weeks or months. It was the perfect place to be rid of Teddy.

One by one, she let his pieces fall into the stainless steel commode and stomped on the pedal until they were drowned in blue liquid and then dropped into the black hole. She listened as they plopped down into the godforsaken sludge. His ribcage had to be sawed into six jagged sections, and she cursed as the saw slipped and scratched at the porcelain beneath him. She let them fall into the darkness like pieces of a puzzle she didn't care to ever put back together. The bloody, crooked chunks of flesh and rib bone once guarded his heart, the cold unmoving organ which should have been devoted to her but never was. She smiled bitterly to herself, he deserved to be there. He was such a piece of human waste.

"Who's the cunt now?"

At last, she unwrapped his head, bloody and slippery as a dead fish in her hands. It was lopsided from the blow she struck him with and from the few extra she gave him to ease her perpetual anger. It was nearly flat on one side and though the trap door seemed to accommodate large loads, she hoped it would fit. His face was like a butchered pig's, drained of blood and devoid of life. He still sickened her and frightened her, just by looking at his jaws, always set in a way she thought made him look perpetually bitter, ready to spew hateful words at her. His pale eyes were still wide open in shock. It was the first time she had ever seen fear in them and it was there now forever. The hammer to the side of his head did him in so quickly his face still held a look of confusion, disbelief she would ever raise a hand to him, let alone a hammer. She almost took a picture of it.

"Look at you now!"

She stepped on the pedal but the head got caught in the hole. She was forced to push it down and as it fell she caught a glimpse of his fetid tomb before she removed her foot from the pedal and let the small door shut on him, trapping him. She could faintly see the pale shapes of his bloodless pieces nestled cozily in the putrid piles of human waste and fluttering winged cockroaches.

The phone rang but Stephi didn't hear it at first. She was too busy scouring the condo, cleaning any traces of evidence she may have left behind. When she did hear the phone ring, she yanked it from the wall and threw it down the stairwell.

Probably his mistress, of course beating on me wasn't enough, he had to go and cheat on me too!

Stephi steadied herself and pushed his infidelities out of her mind, they didn't matter anymore. She didn't care who was trying to reach her or him, her life was changing, morphing into the existence she always wanted. The one she deserved. She would just need to put on the distraught face of a woman missing her husband. She would practice it in the mirror until she got it just right and tell the rest of them at the club Teddy went on a hunting trip, and when he never came home she would claim he must have met trouble somewhere on the road. It would be weeks before she would file a police report. It would give her time to construct the perfect alibi, and to work on her acting. Stephi couldn't just pretend, she would *become* a distressed wife, and soon a grieving widow once it was clear he was never returning.

Dr. Abileen shook her head, and hung up the phone.

"Dr. Reinart isn't answering. His cell is going to voicemail and no one is answering his landline."

"Would you consider that unusual for a man like Theodore?"

She looked to the broad man in the black suit and nodded, "Yes, Teddy always answers the phone."

"Teddy?"

"Theodore, Dr. Reinart," she said.

"And do you think he was in contact with the parasite?" a second, thinner man in a black suit asked.

"It's highly likely we were all exposed. He was one of its developers and present when the first patient came back," she answered.

"How did the exposure occur?"

"Our first test patient died, many hours later he came back to life. We were struggling to contain him, and he," she hesitated, "vomited on all of us."

"Vomited?" the agent asked.

"Yes, like in the movie *The Exorcist*. Projectile vomited on all of us," she said, her hand straying to her stomach.

"Who *was* the first?" the agent asked, stepping away from her just a few extra feet.

"A cancer patient. He agreed to undergo Dr. Reinart's testing as long as his family was handsomely rewarded after he was gone. That's all I know about him."

"Why did you conduct this testing on a human and not a monkey?"

"Dr. Reinart said he tested it shortly on rats and didn't want to waste time on testing it on anymore animals, and he had a willing subject," Dr. Abileen answered as she perched on the edge of a desk, her eyes never leaving the agents.

"And you didn't question that?"

"I'm not the one in charge here. I only followed orders," she folded her arms over her chest.

"I see, and let's be frank here. I don't think you mind, in your present state, if I'm brutally honest. This isn't the only operation using humans as test subjects. So, I'm not completely surprised. I just wonder why you didn't anticipate a bad outcome."

"Would it have made a difference if a monkey was the subject, and came back to life and puked on us, exposing us all?" her eyes narrowed

"I suppose not, and Dr. Reinart, did he appear sick when he left?" the broad man asked.

"No."

"Give us his address," his thin partner chimed in.

She scribbled down Dr. Theodore Reinart's address and through a thick glass window before her she could hear groaning. Her heart stuttered in her chest, and in her mind a timer began, one she had no idea when would go off, but she knew it was there and it turned her stomach.

"What is the latency period, doctor?" the thin man asked, looking up through the bulletproof glass. He spun slowly, surveying the almost honeycomb shaped lab positioned on the outskirts of Phoenix in an unassuming industrial complex owned by the United States government. They were at its center and all around them were separate rooms, four in front of them were visible through the wrap around window. The two rooms behind them were for the guards and filing cabinets, there was also an entrance from the outside but no visitors were allowed in. Those rooms had no windows, and only one of them had a door to the lab. No one walking from the street could see in, and if need be, no one could get out, not even the doctors. The four rooms before them were laboratories all interconnected by thick steel doors, perfect for isolating problems. Those rooms were where the "magic" happened.

"I can't say for sure. The first one happened nearly twenty-four hours after death but the second was much sooner," she answered.

"Why was Dr. Reinart allowed to leave?"

"He conducted testing on all three of us who were exposed and it seemed we were all okay. None of us showed signs we were carrying the parasite in our blood. It wasn't until Dr. Entz came back that I began to worry it was hiding within us. If that is the case, it would mean we could change faster than the first subject," she tried explaining.

"How much sooner?"

"I," she hesitated, her eyes flickering to the window the groaning resonated from. "I can't say. This is something we've only just begun to research. It could be anywhere from two to twenty-four hours. It was only supposed to leave the subject paralyzed, not a zombified corpse."

"Did Dr. Reinart have an antidote or something?"

"Not that I know of."

"Seems a little irresponsible," the thin agent said with a smirk.

"Listen, I couldn't contact the doctor. I feared the worst, so I alerted the higher-ups and they sent you. We may be looking at an outbreak if Dr. Reinart ends up like Dr. Entz, " Dr. Abileen's voice rose with impatience.

"How long has it been since you've seen him?"

"Twenty-eight hours, and fifteen minutes," she answered, glancing at the clock on her computer screen.

"So, he could be just like our gurgling, puking buddy in there?"

"Yes."

"And how are you feeling?"

"Tired, but fine," she answered.

"And yourself, would you like to enjoy these hours working, or would you like it over with now before you end up like him?" he pointed to the widow.

A garbled voice moaned and a bloodied hand fell against the glass. In the dark room on the other side loomed the silhouette of a man, twisted and crooked. He was hunched slightly, his abdomen protruded unnaturally, clearly pregnant with something writhing beneath his skin, His cheeks bulged and wriggled, something moved beneath his pale flesh. One eye bulged and receded as if something was building there, ready to burst and force the eye from its socket. Thick mucus hung from his mouth, tinged bright yellow-green with stomach bile. He walked though he shouldn't, he snarled, screeched, and clawed the air though it should have been impossible because his heart was still. He was dead and yet very much alive. His attention turned to the voyeurs at the window, he raged at them. His shrieking voice rang out and it was followed by a yellow shower of vomit against the window pane. It made her tense up, her gut knotted.

"I'm not dead yet."

"Yet."

She recalled Dr. Entz's agony at the moment of his death. It was so sudden. She knew this could be a disaster, if not the end of mankind if it continued to spread. Especially if the parasite had mutated and was able to take a hold of someone quickly, it would be like a wildfire in a summer wind. She wasn't sure if she wanted to endure the agony and the madness of it and yet she held a tiny fraction of hope she could find the off button, the cure.

"I owe it to the world to stop this before it really starts. I will let you know when I want to end it," she spoke.

"We'll leave two men outside the door, they will be given instructions. You have twenty-four hours, unless your change happens sooner, and then they'll blow your brains out."

She nodded and turned back to her work, "Okay."

"Godspeed, doctor."

Dr. Abileen didn't know how to respond, she figured she didn't need to care about polite pleasantries anymore. "Just find Reinart and bring him here if you can, and if not, then destroy him completely before this gets beyond any control…and I mean destroy him completely," she said.

"How long do you plan on keeping the other?"

"Until I decide if he's useful or not."

"And you can handle disposing of him?" the thin man asked.

"I took care of the first one. They can be knocked down by firepower, but the only way to end them is by burning them to nothing, " Dr. Abileen nodded her head to another room beyond the large glass window. In it was an incinerator with its mouth open like a stainless steel monster.

"Besides, I'm already a potential carrier. Why endanger anyone else, why risk having anyone else exposed when I can get rid of him myself?"

"You guys don't fuck around, do ya? With an incinerator like that, I'd say ol' Teddy thought this might happen, that ya might need to perform a hasty cremation?" he said, eyeing it.

"When you work with biological weaponry like parasites and viruses, you need to be prepared. In this case, we were lucky to have it. It was the only way to stop the bastard."

"Looks like we're heading to Sedona, a few hours north of here, " the thin man spoke to his partner as he read the address scrawled on the sheet of paper.

They left the lab, and behind them Dr. Abileen could hear the thick steel bar pushed into place, the containment lock. She was only leaving there once she was good and dead. She needed to make the last of her life meaningful.

In the darkness and filth, the mound of feces writhed with the movement of Teddy's broken body. A cold, bloodless eyelid blinked. His mind awakened to a blank darkness, a curtain hiding something important. It echoed with voices but it saw no faces, it was trapped in some liminal space between living and dead, haunted by a life he once lived but could not remember. A finger twitched on a hand two feet away. It crawled through the stinking waste, dragging its arm behind it like a tail. Toes wriggled like fetid little piggies, as the hand dragged them closer to the lopsided head. Teddy's mouth hung open in a silent scream of animalistic rage as its body fought to reassemble. Long white tendrils snaked out of the ragged wounds left by Stephi's shaky hand and an electric meat cutter from each severed body part. They wormed and squirmed until they found each other and slowly they began winding together and pulling his pieces closer and closer to each other until they started to stitch him back together. His flesh was covered in excrement and crawling with the roaches that had made the bottom of the toilet in the Shit Shack their den. His eyes blinked rapidly, his body a mass of raw nerves, agony unceasing. His body was slowly fusing together. Along the jagged incisions, the skin was coming together in thick, painful swaths of scar tissue, puckered and red beneath his dressing of fecal matter.

Hours passed and his confusion steadily grew to rage, his pain multiplied until it was a driving force, urging him to stand on his trembling legs. Teddy sat up, howling as his insides shifted beneath his healing wounds. His stomach and other organs had been shredded by the miniature saw used to piece him out and as they dragged themselves back into the cavity of his abdomen. He didn't know how he ended up there, who he was, or what the purpose of his existence was now. Within him, commands were sent, his reawakened brain twitched and squirmed. He was confused and frightened but he obeyed and stood in the knee-deep filth, it steadily pulled him downward like rancid quicksand. He looked above him in the absolute darkness and saw nothing but those piloting him urged him to jump. Teddy leaped up with all the strength in his weak body and felt his head and arms connect with something cold and hard. Roaches fluttered down from the ceiling of his tomb, their wings tickling his cheeks. He was commanded to jump again, this time he knew to expect something to be just above him.

He touched the slimy underside of the toilet above him, it knocked him back down again, spraying his disfigured face with blue liquid. In frustration he jumped back up and punched upward with all of his power, even in a debilitated state his strength was ten times what it was when he lived. He had no idea, but the vermin living in the shit hole witnessed it and scurried away for their lives, burrowing into the crap, yellowed toilet paper, and minty blue liquid. His anger was blinding as he leaped and punched the steel above him. His fist knocked the toilet free from the bolts holding it to the floor of the Shit Shack. The commode fell to the side, exposing the hole beneath it.

Above him, the faint light of the moon shone through a tiny vent at the roof of the outhouse.

Teddy jumped and grasped the edges of the abyss he woke up in and pulled himself up into the outhouse. He grappled and fought until he flopped like a newborn foal onto the tile floor, covered in fecal filth. He stood on trembling legs, motionless for a moment, feeling the burn in his muscles. He took a step forward and a motion censored light flipped on, blinding him. He shrieked and grabbed the broken toilet and threw it against the wall. The shack trembled. His erratic motions spattered liquefied excrement across the floor, walls, and ceiling. Teddy froze when he caught a glimpse of himself in a scratched mirror. He was a monster, gnarled, hulking and slick with feces and blue water. He stepped closer to the mirror and placed his palm against it. He was alive, but who was he, why was he here? The squirming in his brain shut down those thoughts, and ordered him to kill, to procreate. Teddy felt a sudden burst of anger surge through him. His limbs moved and not really of his own accord, there was a message, a demand, and his body complied before he gave it a second thought. He was simply informed of what he was going to do and it happened, no questioning; only obeying. He beat the walls of the tiny outhouse, he was reborn to kill, and he would do it.

Puffkins howled at the back sliding glass door. The Pomeranian had been pacing and yapping for hours. Sylvia Brandon stomped down the stairs and into the kitchen. She couldn't stand to have her sleep interrupted, it made her grouchy and it seemed to be becoming a nightly occurrence with Puffkins.

"What is your problem?"

The little fuzzy dog looked at its owner insistently, and then to the door.

"You need to pee pee, don't you?" Sylvia knew in the dog's old age its bladder had become increasingly finicky. The last thing she wanted was to step in another puddle of piddle when she came down to make her morning coffee, or step on a pile of something worse.

The dog barked and howled. It scratched at the glass door with its claws.

"Okay, okay."

The elderly woman wrapped her robe about her and tied it tightly. It was summer but she didn't think it would be decent for her neighbors to see her in her pink silk pajamas. She was a proper lady. Her husband James had died three years before, but she remained loyal to his memory even when other women her age had already had boyfriends, lovers, or husbands soon after becoming widows. She would keep the Brandon name until she was buried beside James in his family plot in Maine. She unlocked the backdoor and slid it open, leaving the back yard light off as to not wake up Claudia next door. A stench hit her nose and she recoiled.

"That disgusting portable toilet is stinking again. They need to do away with it once and for all."

The dog didn't answer her, of course, but stared at her with its dark eyes then blinked rapidly as if it agreed with her.

"Come on, just because it stinks out there doesn't mean you can do your business inside. You picky little thing."

Sylvia made a mental note to complain to Peter about it in the morning. She already had a list of grievances she meant to unload on the property manager about the two housekeeping women he hired to clean her house every Monday.

Puffkins growled and whined, but refused to step foot outside.

"Get out here. I refuse to clean your piddle again!"

She carried the dog out onto the manicured back lawn and set him down. Puffkins cowered at her feet, shivering and pawing at her slipper-covered toes.

The dog squatted and the horrible smell intensified.

"My goodness, is that you?"

The dog sniffed the breeze, yelped, and scurried back to the door without Sylvia.

The old woman came as quickly as she could to the back porch, hurrying to put the rancid smell behind her and get back to bed. Her foot slipped on something in the dark and she tumbled forward. She caught herself on a cushioned chair beside the back door. As she glanced down, she could see the concrete was covered in something dark and slick. Her nose was invaded by the overwhelming scent of feces. She gagged and a mouthful of vomit escaped her. Embarrassingly she wiped it away and fought to stand up straight only to slip again in whatever was defiling her patio. She fell against the wall but managed to right herself.

She carefully stepped forward and stuck her arm inside the house and found the light switch. She flipped it on and for a moment was blinded by its brilliance. She squinted and examined the concrete beneath her feet.

"Is that…?"

She didn't need to finish, her heart and gut lurched when she realized there was a swath of feces tracked into her house. Sylvia loosed a short disgusted cry. Her dog yelped from the darkness inside the house.

"Puffkins?"

She knew it was impossible the small dog was responsible for such a mess.

"What in God's name?"

From inside her house, she could hear the startled yapping of Puffkins, and fear tore through her. She figured there was some animal in her house, and now it was pestering her sweet dog and only companion. She was scared but she wouldn't let her dog be killed. He was all she had left in the world to love and be loved by. It wasn't necessarily bravery urging her through the door, no longer caring whether anything bad happened to her since James died, but Puffkins, she couldn't handle him being harmed or killed.

Sylvia hurried inside, nearly losing her footing on the defiled tile floor. She kept only one light on in the kitchen at night, just enough to light the way to the refrigerator, she regretted it now. The porch was illuminated at her back, but the house was far too dark. The spacious dining room and sitting room looked like a black void, an entire universe of hidden terrors awaiting her. She could see the bottom of the stairs, miles away from her in her horrified mind. Though she considered herself a strong woman, she didn't know if she alone could help her poor dog. She opted for the phone hanging on the kitchen wall just beneath that one blessed beam of light. Its beam called to her, it was her only hope of getting someone to help her through this odd and disturbing situation. She would phone Larry in the security booth stationed at the entrance of Serenity Canyon, but would he make it in time to save Puffkins? The dog was yowling and barking from somewhere in the darkness incessantly, driving her mad. Sylvia ran towards the light, for the phone.

Her hand grabbed the receiver, and a shadow fell across her, blocking the light. An overwhelming smell filled her nose and mouth. Her stomach lurched into her throat. She didn't want to turn around and face the source of the shadow covering the light. A hand grabbed her boney shoulder and spun her around.

She faced it, the stinking intruder, the monster staring down at her. Sylvia tried to speak but all she could manage was a squeaking cry as she looked into the clouded eyes of a dead man. He was covered in human waste and his body crawled, not only with maggots in the crusting filth on his skin, but something beneath his pale flesh writhed. She feebly tried to pull away. She couldn't stand the thoughts of his touch, not with those things beneath his skin. She couldn't breathe enough to scream, her lungs were constricted with terror and disgust. She slapped and batted at him weakly but he never let her go. He looked as if he'd been torn apart and fused back together with putrid sludge.

The creature looked vaguely familiar even though it had a lopsided head and a body frankensteined together with human waste. She knew him. He was Stephi's husband, Dr. Reinart. He always wore a scowl on his face, one that transcended the usual elite air taken on by those with big bank accounts. He appeared to think he was better than *everyone*, including his high class neighbors. It was also whispered in the gossip circles of Serenity Canyon he was abusive to his wife, and Sylvia believed it. Stephi would wear long sleeves in the summer, sunglasses in the evening, and never questioned him when he bossed her around at the club in front of the whole neighborhood. The doctor would raise his voice at everyone and he treated the maintenance staff like dogs. Sylvia could see there was something about him, something dark behind his eyes- his temper always seemed to be bubbling just below the surface- he was a ticking time bomb ready to explode, without care or mercy for even his wife.

By his emotionless eyes and rough grip on her shoulder, she could tell something was horribly wrong. Sylvia knew he was going to kill her. Her heart seized in her chest, sending a burning ache spreading beneath her rib cage. Its wild beating had been replaced by an agonizing stillness which drowned out the barking of her dog and filled her ears with complete silence.

The frail old woman fell to her knees and slumped forward. Teddy caught her by the hair, he no longer knew who he used to be, only an intense rage urging him to kill all living beings. His mind felt like some distant, black, galaxy, and he was lost in its cold nothingness. He craved the intense burst of light and heat which would only come from causing pain and horror. He had never been controlled by something so strongly in his life, no religion, lust, or addiction was as great as the need to destroy gripping him. His arms trembled, his mouth salivated, and all at once he felt a hunger so great mixing with an agony in his gut. As if he not only wanted to devour the old woman, but also a great urge to purge something filling him up inside, knowing it would be nearly orgasmic when released. It hurt and thrilled him to look into her terrified eyes. He gripped the sides of her head and spun it around until she could look down at her sagging ass cheeks, her neck snapping like a dry twig. He let her fall awkwardly to the floor then lifted a waste encrusted foot and drove his heel downward into her backwards head. Her face caved in, her dentures popped out and bounced on the floor. Her eyes stared blankly in her misshapen visage. Teddy's gut churned, he leaned over as a thick, vomitus sludge fell from his mouth into Sylvia's toothless maw. Somewhere in the dark the barking stopped.

Lalo stood at the top steps of the maintenance shop, the break room and lone sanctuary of the janitorial staff of Serenity Canyon. He hesitated to announce who would be the new employee, knowing the crew could get a little rowdy at times.

Rosa and Isabel were talking quietly between them and sharing an orange, they were the source of the most gossip among the crew. They glanced at him and their conversation died. He figured they had blabbed to everyone what they saw when they just-so-happened to open his door while he interviewed Sunny, the new girl.

"Listen up," Lalo said.

"Let me guess, you hired that hippy bitch? What was her name, Sunshine?" The crew member closest to the stairs, Carl, spoke stuffing the remainder of a powdered donut into his mouth.

He choked and coughed, sending hunks flying. White crumbs hung on his lips and fell down on his shirt. His uniform was covered in white powder making him look like he sneezed after snorting a line of coke.

"Take it easy, man," Lalo warned. "There was no way I was hiring Jose's cousin, not with those face tattoos!"

"Wait til Jose finds out. He's gonna be pissed!" Carl said.

"Me vale verga, Jose can go fuck himself," Lalo said as he descended the steps.

Another crew member, Jason, was standing before an arcade game at the bottom of the short stairs. He didn't bother to even look in his supervisor's direction.

"You got a point, boss," he said.

Jason slammed his fist against the joy stick in defeat. He felt his pockets and found no quarters. He left the arcade and went to sit next to Carl at the break room table.

"Take it easy, Tony Montana," Jason said, watching Carl aimlessly trying to wipe the white powder from his shirt and the corners of his mouth.

"What the fuck are you talkin' about?" Carl asked.

Jason pointed at the white chunks resting on Carl's shirt and laughed, "Can you eat any messier? You're always getting shit all over yourself, like the cookie monster, but ugly as fuck!"

"Fuck you, hippy!"

"Whatever, asshole," Jason said.

They smiled at each other and laughed. Jason was youngest among them, but he fit in well with the menagerie of freaks on the crew.

They were nicknamed SCUM by a former employee, old Jim, after the big S.C.M embroidered on their uniforms. The moniker stuck to them all like feces on a bathroom wall, they were definitely looked down on by all the residents of Serenity Canyon. To the hoighty toighty residents, Lalo and his crew really were scum.

Lalo wore a deep crimson Serenity Canyon Maintenance polo and khaki cargo pants, he kept his hair freshly cut and his goatee short to keep his appearance presentable for the upper management but he was a janitor through and through, like his father before him and his grandfather before that. He had a gut of cast iron, he'd seen some shit and he didn't shy away from cleaning vile things, but he was also the boss now which meant he could delegate the worst jobs to those on his crew.

"The new girl starts tomorrow."

"That's fantastic," Carl complained.

"Don't start, Carl. She has experience and she seemed like a good person, better than the other three I interviewed," Lalo said.

Another crew member sat beside a vending machine in the corner. He looked like a catfish with his beady eyes and gaping mouth, and his voice constantly sounded like he was talking in slow motion. His name was Shane, though most of the crew called him Grandpa for his grouchy demeanor and how he complained about everything.

"She'll expect us to do all her work for her," Shane whined.

"Bullshit, she'll work harder than your lazy ass," Jason said.

"Ain't that the truth," Carl laughed, donuts flying out of his mouth and landing in gooey globs on the table.

"She'll be taking my spot on housekeeping with Rosa and Isabel. I'll work with you guys. I'm making new work schedules and you'll get them tomorrow when she comes in," Lalo said.

"And why tomorrow, why not today? That means she's gonna miss the Shack," Shane said.

He looked like an idiot but he definitely was not. He knew what time of the month it was.

Carl and Jason exchanged a worried glance. Rosa and Isabel rose from their seats and made their exit, chattering between each other in quiet voices. They were never put on cleaning the Shit Shack. They had to look and smell impeccable to be allowed to step foot in the cottages to provide their weekly housekeeping duties.

"Draw straws, assholes! It's time to see who cleans the Shack," Lalo announced pulling from his pocket an assortment of fast food straws he had clipped earlier at random lengths. He clinched them in his fist and his crew gathered around him.

"Shouldn't we wait for Jose?" Carl asked.

"I told that dick head what time to be here so he's definitely on duty at the shack. The question is," Lalo paused, "who gets to join him?"

Jason drew his straw, a blue one. He knew Lalo had a deep abiding love of Jack's burger palace and the blue straws provided there were thick and rigid, strong enough to puncture a man's jugular. It was about three inches long and his gut told him he made a good choice. Carl drew next, it was red and significantly shorter.

Shane wandered over and drew his straw, it was comically short. The loser for sure.

Lalo laughed when Shane threw it in the trash can in a huff.

"Your turn in the Shack, white boy!" Carl said.

"Get your stomach ready and wear the suit!" Lalo teased as Shane walked away grumbling.

"Oh, and tomorrow is our yearly O.S.H.A video. Be here a little early."

"O.S.H.A can suck my dick," Shane said as he pushed out the door.

He wanted to challenge Lalo's decision more but he knew better. Beneath his boss's smile was a serious look in his eyes, it was always there, lurking. Lalo had a short fuse, one Shane knew better than to light.

Shane had only seen Lalo seriously explode one time and he didn't want to see it again. It was the night he stumbled upon old Jim in the Shit Shack, sucking back on a bottle of cheap booze. The old man made the mistake of telling his boss where to stick that booze bottle and Lalo went from zero to one hundred in about three seconds. His only witnesses were Shane and Jose. They never told Peter about it because Jim deserved the punch to his gut he received.

Lalo was a little disappointed Carl got to sit out this tour of duty so he devised something entirely different yet just as wretched for him to complete before the shift was declared over.

"You two," he pointed to Carl and Jason. "it's that other time of the year again."

"You gotta be fuckin' kidding!" Jason said.

He knew what that meant. After being on the maintenance crew for two years he knew the task in which his boss referred and it turned his stomach.

"Come on, Lalo! Those cans don't need any cleanin'," Carl said.

"It's starting to smell like someone climbed up on my face and took a dump in my nose. Clean those perimeter trash cans and do it before four o'clock," Lalo answered.

He made his way back up the steps as Jose came strolling into the shop. Late, as always.

"You're on the Shit Shack," Lalo said.

"What the fuck? I did that last time."

"That'll teach you to be late."

Lalo had his hand on the door when Jose asked the inevitable question.

"Hey, what about my cousin, eh?"

"I found someone more qualified."

Lalo laughed to himself as he exited, he could hear Carl as the door closed.

"Some fuckin' hippy girl named Sunflower or some shit! She ain't qualified for shit!"

The air was rank as Shane and Jose drew closer to the set of outhouse toilets stationed on the far end of the lake and golf course behind the wall of hedges.

"I'm fuckin' tired of Lalo actin' like an asshole just because I'm late sometimes. I don't deserve this."

"What about me, motherfucker? I was here on time and I got stuck cleaning it!"

"Shut up, Grandpa. You always act like you're the best worker on the crew and you're lazier than dog shit."

"Suck my dick, Jose!"

Jose knew Shane hated it when he called him Grandpa. He wouldn't get any sympathy out of him after calling him his most-hated nickname. He needed to apologize, and quick, or the day of work beside Shane would be an unbearable pout-fest.

"Okay, I'm sorry. I'm just mad because Lalo needs to clean this shit once in a while."

Shane nodded, his arms crossed over his chest.

"Don't pout like a little bitch," Jose said.

"Whatever, man," Shane said.

The golf carts given to the SCUM crew were the old rundown carts the course gifted them when the club bought newer models. It helped them get around the property quicker, but there were rules they were made to follow if they didn't want to walk. Jose never followed the golf cart safety rules. He drove them like he stole them.

"Jose and Shane," Peter, the property manager, spoke over the radio.

"Go ahead," Shane's slow-motion voice replied.

"You guys better slow down unless you wanna hoof it everywhere."

"10-4, Pito," Jose took the radio from Shane and answered.

"What?"

"I said 10-4, Peter."

The golf cart screeched to a halt. Peter watched Jose and Shane argue for a moment before laughing and continuing onward at a much slower pace.

Lalo was standing at the door when Peter turned around.

"Does Jose have a problem speaking English?"

"No, why?"

"He always mispronounces my name. I don't want to offend him, but my name is Peter, not Peeto."

"I'm sure it's a mistake, sir," Lalo said, stifling a laugh. Jose was essentially calling Peter a dick in Spanish, a nickname the crew often used behind the manager's back. Jose was typically the only one amongst them that had the balls to use it in actual conversation.

"Okay, well did you hire that young lady?"

"Yes, she starts tomorrow."

"That's excellent. Now remember, tonight we have an event in the club. A charity gala. Please make sure the hall is clean and ready, so there'll be overtime for anyone who wants it."

"Sure thing," Lalo said.

As Peter passed by him, Lalo could hardly contain his smile. Jose was a bastard, but a funny bastard.

Shane held his ribs, he laughed just as slow as he spoke and it made Jose crack up. His bad mood eased a bit and he readied himself to get to work.

"He's gonna find out one day what that means."

"He ain't gonna find out shit, just keep your mouth shut," Jose warned, still laughing.

"Dude, I ain't no snitch," Shane said.

"Better not be, pendejo."

The stench hit them like a brick wall and grew worse as they got closer to the Shit Shack. The smell of putrid feces turned their stomachs.

"Que chingados es esto?"

"Man, what the fuck? It's never smelled *that* bad!" Shane pulled his shirt up over his nose.

"I can fuckin' taste it, it's so bad!" Jose jammed the breaks on the golf cart and they sat in disbelief.

"What's goin' on here, man?"

Jose pointed beyond the Plexiglas windshield but Shane's eyes already took in the sight before them. There was a trail of feces leading down the sidewalk from the Shit Shack., black-brown sludge, reeking like an open sewer. They climbed carefully out of the cart, and stared for a long moment at the mess before them.

"If it looks like this out here, imagine the inside. Lalo should have called the shit-sucker to empty this fucker months ago."

"Yeah, but he claims it's hardly ever used. I don't think it's been emptied in years, there's three feet of old turds at the bottom of it."

"How did this even happen?" Jose asked staring at the mess.

"I know, it's like the turds jumped out of the hole and ran away." Shane couldn't help but laugh at the scene, "it's so funky in there even the turds wants to get away!"

"Probably some kids threw an M-80 in there or something."

"Hopefully they got drenched in turds as they ran away. Look at this nightmare, dude."

"We're getting O.T. for this, buddy. This is gonna take forever to clean," Jose said and went to the back of the cart. He pulled out two yellow plastic suits.

"Get your condom on, this bitch is gonna be messy as fuck!" he said, tossing one to Shane.

They pulled the suits on over their clothes and shoes, and grabbed two pairs of goggles and extra thick gloves out of their supplies.

"I used to be so embarrassed to wear these things but then I realized none of these bitches around here would ever give me the time of day anyway, they're too fuckin fresa for a simple dude like me."

"It could be they're all stuck up, like you're suggesting, or it could be that you're ugly as a baboon's ass too, Jose."

"Whatever, pendejo. You wish you were as sexy as me!" Jose slid his goggles on nice and slow then let his hands run down his chest. He gripped his dick through his yellow hazmat suit and winked.

"Oh fuck, let's get to work before I get too jealous...or horny," Shane laughed.

Shane worked on hooking up a pressure washer they kept on the back of the golf cart. He grunted as he carried it over to the metal box in the ground where the hook up to the water system ran. Jose removed gallon jugs of super disinfectant cleaner and brushes on broom handles.

They planned to clean up the outside first, and then work their way into the disaster zone, ground zero for what appeared to be an explosion of some sort. It seemed unreal, but the smell of it reminded them it was no nightmare. It was real and they had to fix it.

"This almost looks like footprints. I hope the little bastards who did this get an incurable disease."

"Just cover it all and let it sit for a while, then I'll blast it. I'm gonna radio Lalo because if we run low on chemicals he'll have to bring us some more from the closet. I only want to suit up once and not unzip this motherfucker until this job is done."

"Word," Jose agreed.

"This place smells like a thousand assholes but it sure has some funny memories."

"If we're ever lucky enough to have them tear it down, we'll have to put a little plaque where it once stood."

Isabel and Rosa stood on the front steps of the Brandon residence. Sylvia hadn't answered the door and Peter gave them precise instructions not to knock more than three times on a door before leaving. Their rounds had been mapped out long before either of them ever joined the SCUM crew. There had been a handful before them but none of the others ever cleaned with such care as Rosa and Isabel. The crew of two women, soon to be three when Sunny joined them, cleaned one street of houses each day of the week. Many houses already had live-in maids but there were still good number of them who took their free weekly deep clean of their houses over hiring anyone else. Serenity Canyon also provided a laundry service, and chef services too, but they were members of Peter's elite employees, they were on a higher level than Lalo and his SCUM crew.

"Toca la puerta una ves mas, y nos vamos."

"Si, si. Relajate," Isabel whispered and knocked on the door, this time a little harder than the polite wrapping she gave it the first two times.

"Mrs. Brandon? Are you home?" She called, trying to keep the annoyance in her mind from creeping through her voice.

The two women waited, listening closely but they heard no footsteps or voices, and strangely no barking. Rosa pinched her nose, a terrible odor was hanging around and it only got worse the longer they stood at the door.

"¡Huele como a mierda!" Isabel complained.

"¡Guacala!" Rosa laughed.

"Hey, amigas!" a voice called from next door.

Isabel rolled her eyes and cursed under her breath, "Pinche, Claudia."

Rosa grinned as the neighbor came trotting across her front yard. She was older than Isabel and usually in a very happy mood as opposed to the younger woman she called her partner. Isabel was only as nice as she had to be to keep her job and nothing more. She had been in housekeeping since she was only a teenager and worked all kinds of cleaning gigs from hospitals to schools to hotels. Serenity Canyon was definitely the best paying and most swanky place she had worked at, but the people they cleaned up after could be back-stabbing fucks, even more than usual.

"Hi, Clau!" Rosa said.

"Hey, girls. I know it isn't my day for cleaning but can you help me around my house a bit real quick? I'm having an after party tonight when the gala ends."

Isabel glanced nervously at Rosa, they weren't supposed to provide extra cleaning but they were ahead of schedule since Mrs. Brandon didn't answer her door.

"Sure. I think we can help you for a little bit."

"Oh, Isa! Thank you so much!" Claudia was always overly polite, which was better than the way some residents treated Isabel and Rosa, but she usually asked way too much of the only two housekeepers employed at Serenity Canyon.

"Oh my goodness," Claudia waved her hand in front of her face, "it stinks out here!"

"Yeah, it's really bad!" Isabel agreed.

"Must be the porta-potty. Maybe you should tell Peter?"

"Do you think Mrs. Brandon is okay?" Rosa asked, her eyes wandering back to linger on Mrs. Brandon's door.

"Oh yeah, I saw a shadow in her window earlier, I'm sure she's fine. Come on. Let's go inside my house where it smells better."

Claudia spun around and waved them along behind her. She was in her late fifties but plastic surgery kept her looking much younger. She had a lot of energy and liked to brag about her days as a professional cheerleader and dance teacher. Isabel didn't hate her as much as she did a few of the other women around the neighborhood, but she still had the feeling Claudia was as gossipy as an old hen. Isabel would know, she was a chismosa herself and it took one to know one. Rosa liked to talk to Claudia while she worked because of the outlandish stories she imparted to her about the neighbors and their families. It was like a telenovela in some of the households, apparently, and Claudia knew all the dirt, all the good juicy gossip.

"Come on inside," Claudia welcomed them in, "I was thinking of making some margaritas if you two want one, and I promise I won't tell Peter."

"Oh no thank you, it's too early for me," Isabel said, carrying the plastic caddy she brought into the houses filled with supplies. She couldn't help but wonder what impossible tasks Claudia would ask for after being so friendly to the SCUM staff.

"Oh, nonsense. It's five o'clock somewhere!" Claudia said with a wink and looked to Rosa with a smile.

"I don't drink, but thank you," Rosa lied.

"Okay, gals. I need you to make sure the whole downstairs looks extra good, as well as the guest bedroom and restroom. We're going to party down so there might be someone staying over. Can you do that for me?"

"Sure."

"And before you go, I'll grab my husband's ladder and you can dust the chandelier in the dining room and the pottery shelves in the living room. After that, I just need you to clean the windows inside and outside on the bottom floor here, and maybe help me change out the flowers in the vases in the entryway. Oh, and make sure there no light bulbs burnt out in the recessed lighting."

Isabel nodded, she was right to feel suspicious of Claudia's offer of booze on the job. The bitch was gonna make them earn their money today.

"That awful stink outside is so nasty. It's been hanging around all morning. I hope it goes away by the time my party starts," Claudia spoke as she walked into the kitchen.

The roar of a blender breaking up ice cubes silenced them before they could even respond but they smiled at each other, knowing Shane and Jose were in Hell cleaning the Shit Shack. It had to be the source of the permeating stench.

Teddy watched out the bedroom window through a crack in the oak blinds. He felt the urge to kill, but his newly resurrected body wasn't at its full potential yet. After a few attempts, he still hadn't managed to crush the small hairy thing which whined from somewhere in the darkness of the house. He wasn't ready to hunt. His escape from the pit of waste was taxing on his new form. When he found the dark sanctuary of Sylvia Brandon's house he was called to it, not only to ease the rage he felt inside his dead heart by crushing her skull, but to allow himself to acclimate to being alive again.

Distorted memories flashed in his living-dead brain. Human faces, laughter, of them speaking their language, and of him responding in their tongue. He was alive once, one of them, now he was something completely different.

His entire form was a pulsing ball of nerves and pain but the remembrance of what he once was filled his damaged brain with agony. He gripped the sides of his lopsided head and grunted. He stumbled to the bed and fell face first onto its down comforter. He hit the blankets with a splat, smearing chunks of half-dried feces all over them. His entire cranium felt like it was on fire, and the memories continued, like a slow moving train through his clotted brain.

The stinking creature he had become could feel pain, it could feel hatred, and yet it couldn't fully comprehend what he once was. It had no idea, no inkling what it meant to be human, to love or feel joy. He only knew the searing in his brain made him want to tear them all to pieces. He slipped into a state much like slumber or hibernation, whatever was powering him back to life bid his body to rest until darkness claimed the land once more in order for them to repair his body as best they could.

He twitched and moaned as his system began to power down and as his body refused to move, but true Hell was unleashed as his brain continued to recall things from his life before…dreams, and none of them eased him at all. They produced the opposite reaction. His anger multiplying with each moment he was forced to see what he once was, how he ate, bathed, fucked and fought. His memories at last climaxed with the vision of his death, like a bloody orgasm of pain and betrayal. It started with a sudden explosion of pain. A hammer was slammed against the side of his head, his skull fracturing until it penetrated his brain. His blood seeped out into the bath, coppery water in his mouth and lungs, filling him up. A burning suffocation he couldn't stop, his body refused to respond to his mangled intellect. And finally, his life fading with the vision of a woman standing over his quivering corpse, and her vengeful smile, his murderess. Remembering his death was like a living nightmare, a horrific movie playing out on the screen of his memory.

The woman, the cold hearted bitch, with eyes just as dead as his became, she did it. She killed him, and in turn she birthed him as a new life form, a monster. Teddy hated this woman, his mother of sorts, he didn't know her name but he wanted to destroy her. His torment wouldn't end until he stripped the skin from her body and vomited into her mangled face.

Downstairs, a shuffling in the kitchen told him the old woman had come back. Her frail body wasn't even worth depositing his larvae into but he had to release them, his body demanded it. A faint moan and the sound of clamoring reminded him her head was now on backwards. What a bumbling waste of flesh, the passengers inside of her would soon flee her unworthy carcass. His first child was a disgrace but he wouldn't be like the woman who killed him and birthed him into his new existence. He would teach the new one how to kill and how to spread their kind. She just needed time, and so did he.

The things inside of him constantly relayed messages to him, almost like a new form of conscious only they weren't touched by the weaknesses of remorse or mercy. At first their multitude of voices, overlapping each other was confusing and frustrating, but now they melded into one, becoming more than a voice, they became instinct. Their sole purpose was to strive, to survive, and to procreate. They told him of their mother, a Goddess he had met once before when he was a living man. They were her children, malformed deities the size of hair strands. They were his new Gods and he would obey them with the frenzy of the embattled pagans of old. He would kill for them, procreate for them, and give his own flesh for them.

CHAPTER 2
VISIONS OF A DEAD BRAIN

DR. ABILEEN FELT a cold sweat forming on her upper lip as nausea churned her stomach. She gripped her desk and swallowed a mouthful of saliva. She was busy studying the footage from each time the dead returned and though she felt her body starting to ache, she didn't have time to die. The world didn't have time for her to die.

The first was the cancer patient that had been sick for days before succumbing to death and it took nearly twenty-four hours for him to return. The parasite was meant to be used by the military to paralyze whole armies, but what it did instead was kill and reanimate the dead, and that was the poor man's fate. He was simply called Charlie, that's the only name Dr. Abileen was ever given for him. He had terminal brain cancer and was given three weeks to live. She had no idea how Teddy found him, or how the morbid contract was negotiated, only his family would be taken care of for the rest of their lives in payment for Charlie's brave sacrifice.

Dr. Abileen was at his bedside when the parasite was administered to him intravenously. Charlie shrieked as it coursed through his veins, his eyes watered uncontrollably and it soon became obvious he had lost all control of his bowels. He went completely stiff and then slowly his body eased. Teddy attempted to speak to his patient but Charlie could not respond, instead he lay wide eyed and motionless. They tested his brain activity and found it appeared much like he was sleeping or in a coma, next they tried his reflexes and found zero response. His vital signs slowly weakened but he clung to life for days. Dr. Abileen wondered if he was cognizant of what was taking place. If he knew he was slowly fading away, if he was terrified of at last finding out the greatest mystery of mankind. He was sailing the vessel of his soul into an oncoming hurricane and when he emerged would he be in Heaven or Hell, or would he just cease to be? Was he still producing thoughts, or was he simply just being pulled slowly into darkness without a care?

Teddy watched Charlie day and night, hoping for him to awaken but he never did, at least as a living human being.

Charlie was unrestrained, laying on a stainless steel gurney, nearly a full twenty-four hours after his demise. The period of paralysis at first delighted Teddy with the thoughts of success, but when Charlie slipped into death he grew introspective and despondent.

Teddy leaned in over Charlie, and was beginning to examine the corpse. He believed his paralyzing agent had simply killed the man. He was lost in thought, calculating what may have gone wrong when Charlie's eyes popped open. He thought it was just natural relaxation of the eyelids but Charlie's hand lunged up and grabbed the doctor by the throat. It was then Teddy knew he was horrifically mistaken. The dead man's hand was unbelievably strong, tightening around Teddy's windpipe, cutting off all air. His eyes went wide, his mind raced, he couldn't comprehend what was happening.

Dr. Entz screamed and stumbled backwards but Dr. Abileen grabbed Teddy by the arm and yanked him back. Charlie wouldn't release him. Instead, he sat straight up and continued to squeeze the doctor's throat until his face went violet. Teddy beat the corpse's arm but he wouldn't release him. He was becoming frantic with each breathless second.

Finally, Dr. Entz snapped out of his paralytic terror and grabbed a scalpel. He jammed it into Charlie's left eye and he released Teddy. Charlie yanked the scalpel from his eye and leaped off the gurney and came for the three doctors. A gurgling hiss escaped him, his good eye fixed on the three with ravenous anger.

"Dear God," Dr. Entz said.

Dr. Abileen managed to grab a stool and bash Charlie over the head, but that didn't stop him. He rose to his feet as they scrambled for the door. They screamed for the guards who were posted beyond the examination room, not to protect the doctors from the instance of living dead attack, but to protect the top secret information inside the laboratory beside the exam room.

"Open the fuckin' door!" Dr. Abileen screamed.

Dr. Reinart was typing in his code to unlock the door when Charlie belched loudly and unleashed upon them a shower of sour vomit.

Dr. Abileen remembered how badly it stung her eyes and burned her nostrils with its acrid stench. When the guards finally came with their guns drawn, she realized she had been holding her breath. The sound of gunfire in the small room thundered in her ears. Charlie fell onto his back but continued to writhe and screech. They emptied the clips of their handguns into him but he didn't die. They reloaded and continued to fire on him, coagulating blood and stomach juices ran out of him, his bowels loosed a spray of black waste, but he rolled away from their bullets and tried to redouble his attack.

"Shoot him in the head!" Dr. Abileen screamed, her memory recalling every zombie movie she ever watched. They obeyed her command and each fired for his cranium, bullets left his face disfigured and the back of his head blown out, but he still lurched towards them.

She picked up the steel stool and jabbed Charlie backwards with its four legs, like a lion tamer in some fucked up nightmare of a circus. He was weakened but still fought with vigor. Dr. Abileen shoved him with all of her strength until she had backed him into an adjacent room.

"Lock him in!" screamed Dr. Entz.

"No! I'm ending this!" she answered.

Charlie swiped and lunged at her, yet she managed to keep him away. He growled and frothed at the mouth, bloody spittle filled with the remnants of his meager stomach contents flew onto her lab coat, tainting its pristine white with blood streaked bile. He was too close for comfort, like a rabid dog hell bent on tearing her limb from limb. Her arms trembled and it sent a shockwave of alarm through her.

"Help me!" Dr. Abileen cried over her shoulder.

In the split second when she looked back, she could see Teddy, the defeat in his face. He was questioning everything they had done, his research had failed him.

The two guards ran forward and drew their batons and beat him in the face and helped her shove Charlie back until he was at the mouth of the incinerator. Charlie made one final move. He hunkered down and pushed the three of them back. She thought he would either get the best of them or escape, but the guards drew their pistols and fired. One bullet cut a swath across his cheek as he attempted to dodge it, splitting it wide open. A second shot severed his ear nearly completely and left it dangling by a thin slice of greying skin. Blood spattered across Dr. Abileen's chest but she lifted the stool once more. He faced them, seething with rage. He winced, and the wound in his cheek began to pull back together; wriggling tendrils of flesh at his ear began to reconnect. Dr. Abileen refused to let him live any longer. The horror he had become was nowhere near human. She rammed him back towards the incinerator.

"Come on, push him inside!"

It took the strength of Dr. Abileen and the two young guards to force Charlie into the furnace. She punched the button, slamming its door shut like a hungry mouth.

"Wait!" Teddy cried, but it was too late.

Dr. Abileen quickly pressed the button and watched the horrifying spectacle of him being consumed by flames. This time the ability to heal himself was not strong or fast enough, his cries confirmed his second death was near.

It was slow at first, not instant death, but she could see through the tiny glass window how he still fought, right until his body was charred so badly it fell apart. She left him in there until his pieces crumbled to dust.

"What did you do?" Teddy asked.

"He had to be cremated, no other force would kill him. They shot him in the head and he was still walking," she said, the thoughts of it frightened her beyond belief.

"Why did you kill him?" Teddy scolded her for destroying his work, but she could see in his eyes he knew Charlie could never have been tamed enough to keep for observation, and they didn't have restraints strong enough to keep him bound forever. Charlie had to die…again.

Dr. Abileen pulled up the video of the time surrounding the death and return of Dr. Entz. She didn't want to watch anymore after reliving what happened with Charlie, but she knew she had to. Her gut told her Teddy wasn't coming back, at least not alive, it twisted her heart with sadness and fear. If he came back, just as Charlie did, how many would die before he was stopped? How far would this spread before it was contained? Dr. Abileen pushed herself away from her desk and puked into the trash can beside it. Through teary eyes she examined it, it appeared ordinary, she saw no traces of blood or white squirming tendrils or anything alarming. She hoped it wasn't the beginning of her end. She needed more time. She wiped the vomit from her chin and the tears from her cheeks and went back to work.

In the recording, Dr. Entz was studying the samples of blood they collected from Charlie prior to him dying the first time. He sat in a chair not far from Dr. Abileen. He was hunched over the microscope, intent on the sample and any mysteries there might have been in the dying man's blood. Dr. Abileen had her back to him. She didn't notice his jerking movements and how he'd tilt his head side to side as if his neck ached or how he swabbed sweat from his forehead with a tissue from his pocket. He wasn't feeling well and didn't say anything to her. It was evident in the way he kept rubbing the back of his neck, but even if she had noticed it, at the time she would have most likely figured his neck hurt from being bent over a microscope for hours on end. She trusted the blood panels conducted by her superior, they betrayed no traces of parasite in any of their systems.

Dr. Entz gripped his chest and fell forward. His face smashed into the microscope, flattening his nose on impact, blood exploding from either side of his face like stomping on a ketchup packet. Dr. Abileen's response was instantaneous, after the rising of Charlie her body hadn't eased. She was on her feet immediately. She constantly felt on high alert, ready for another attack, she could see herself hesitate, the fear in her eyes on the video. She had approached him cautiously, repeating his name but it was quite clear to her he was dead. Dr. Abileen called for the guards who came in with weapons drawn. They too hadn't forgotten about having to force a zombified cancer patient into an incinerator, they were ready to kill. She felt for a pulse, and found none. Dr. Abileen motioned for the guards to help her lay him on the floor where she performed chest compressions. It was only for five minutes by the time stamp on the recording but she recalled it felt like an eternity, a grueling exercise in futility. Numerous attempts to get his heart beating again, and nothing, there was no life in him, it had fled faster than a bullet from a gun. She never gave him mouth to mouth. She wondered if she should feel ashamed, but she couldn't bring herself to get so close to his violet lips. They reminded her too much of Charlie's, the gaping lifeless maw of a dead man. She sat with her head in her hands and ordered the guards to lay him on the floor of the room beside the incinerator room and seal the door.

She attempted to call Teddy several times after the sudden death of Dr. Entz and got no response from him. She and Entz had been left there when Teddy claimed he needed to go back home for a day or two to retrieve a notebook he kept there with a few notes of importance. They were still under the assumption they were in no danger of becoming like Charlie.

Dr. Abileen hit fast forward on the video and watched time leaping forward in great increments until the lifeless body of Dr. Entz suddenly sat up. She halted the video, a cold terror filled her. It had only been an hour after his death when he rose. Watching it all take place through a recording made her feel like an entity, a ghost reviewing her past life and soon she knew she would be, a ghost…or at least she hoped so. She didn't want to live again after death. She didn't want to become a vomiting, stinking, creature. She felt tears sting her eyes, her breath caught in her throat. The painful beauty that was humanity, all its triumphs and failures, she didn't want to let it go. She hit rewind and wished she could do the same in real life. She would never have accepted working on the project if she had known the disastrous outcome. Through the tears she watched herself moving in reverse, Dr. Entz was filled with life again. He wasn't gripping his chest, he was just silently working, quiet as a mouse as he always was but he was alive. Dr. Abileen hit play and watched him hovering over his work, intent on helping her through their problem. Though he was never incredibly personable, his steadfastness was a comfort to her. Now she was completely alone. She squinted when she watched him, studying his face in those last moments, the way his wrinkles deepened at the corners of his eyes when he was really focused.

His hand went to his chest, gripping at the fabric over his heart. Dr. Abileen leaned closer to the screen, her eyes focusing on the blurred image. No, it wasn't his heart. Her view focused on the shirt pocket his hand hovered over and watched as something fell from his hand and rolled beneath the desk seconds before she spun around. She paused the recording, it was a small plastic container. She had never seen it before. Curiously, she got to her feet and entered the lab. Dr. Entz, in his new state of being, beat the door as she came closer to the room he was locked in. She quickly got to her knees and climbed under the desk, but kept her eyes on Entz and the door. It was made of reinforced steel, the military didn't fuck around, but he still rattled it with the full force of his rage. She felt around with one hand, stretching as far as she could manage without taking her eyes off her living-dead colleague. Entz was bashing himself against the door wildly, his monstrous shrieking filling her ears made her heart stutter. His screeching turned to wretching and she knew he was unleashing another gut-full of bile. Her fingertip brushed something made of smooth plastic, she fumbled until she had a hold of the object. She scrambled to exit the room and once more went to her desk. Entz came to beat the glass observation window behind her computer but she felt safe enough to open the small plastic box. Inside of it were tiny white pills, her eyes went wide. She recognized them. Her father had to carry them for years before he died of a massive heart attack.

"A heart attack?"

Dr. Abileen looked up to Dr. Entz and wondered, "Did he have a bad heart? Was his death natural?"

She went to her computer. She knew where to find the answer. She opened the user screen and typed in a familiar name, Teddybear123, and a password she had memorized, Studmuffin69. Secret girlfriends were privy to so much more information than wives.

The desktop was filled with files but she clicked on the one labeled team profiles. She scrolled down to *Doctor David Entz* and opened it up. There were a few pages of his accomplishments and on the final page his personal data, and there among his height, weight, age and race was what she sought, his medical history. She wasn't surprised to see he had a heart condition, not after finding his nitroglycerin tablets, but she had to be certain. It made her question as to how Charlie actually died; did the parasite kill him or did he naturally succumb to the tumors eating his brain? If that was the case then was the sand really running out in the hourglass of her existence or would she live to be ninety-four years old and die in her sleep only to return as a toothless, feeble, puking creature?

Dr. Abileen found herself facing even more questions than answers but she had hope, if being exposed to the parasite didn't mean gradual zombification then it was possible Teddy, and herself, could be cured of the agent before their natural deaths came and their unnatural second lives began. She closed Dr. Entz's file but couldn't help but do a little more snooping. His inbox had an email he had yet to read. She felt a little guilty about going through his messages but she figured if it meant possibly saving lives she should do it. She opened the email and began reading it, her jaw dropped.

"You fucking bastard."

Teddy had went home to speak freely with someone in the defense program about the new chemical weapon he had developed, and not a paralyzing agent like he originally proposed, but an agent to kill their enemies and turn them into weapons against their own people.

He also offered up another human test subject, a female, young, healthy, and intelligent. He offered up Doctor Sarah Abileen. The hours the email exchange took place were during the times she had called him in frantic hopes he would rush to her rescue, what a fool she was.

She originally suspected he had only gone home because his needy wife had been getting suspicious he had a girlfriend, which he did, but to her surprise she learned he was also making secret deals, agreements that would surely earn him a big payday while offering her up as a sacrifice. His betrayal cut her deep. She had been willing to be his mistress, but she wasn't willing to be a guinea pig or an accomplice to creating a weapon so devastating to the entire world. Such things weren't meant to be in the hands of men because they were all fuck ups. The parasitic worm would be used for evil no matter what nation wielded it.

"Fucking bastard."

Dr. Abileen signed out of Teddy's profile and sat for a long moment. She felt used and tainted by the man who claimed to be producing a death-free weapon. Now she was more than likely carrying an agent in her body which would zombify her upon death, like some horrific STD. She couldn't believe she ever trusted Teddy, and that she ever believed in him and his research. He was willing to kill her and resurrect her as some undead creature, a walking time bomb, as an example of his new weaponry. She felt an anger swelling in her gut. It was only tempered by the constant nausea residing there too. The weakness previously settling in on her was morphing into something she would stoke into a fire. It was hatred. She had to hurry, her work was only just now beginning.

"Guards!"

They came rushing into the room, this time their guns were trained on her. They both were equipped with respirators and hazmat uniforms. Those yellow suits and guns, the incinerator, they would be the last thing she'd see in this world if she failed. Dr. Abileen recalled the thin agent's orders he left with them and she grinned bitterly.

"It's not time yet, hopefully not at all if I can get the answers I need. I need help subduing Dr. Entz."

The sun was setting over the scenic view of Serenity Canyon. It lay on the outskirts of Sedona, Arizona. The cotton candy sky was broken up by the crimson silhouettes of the legendary red rocks. They were mythological in a way, tourists flocked to see them and feel the energy they held. Some even said they held mystical powers. Amidst the picturesque landscape beyond Stephi's window she could see a man bent over a trash can, and half his ass was hanging out of his sagging pants. A young man stood beside him, holding a water hose between his legs pretending he had an enormous cock. The custodial crew, SCUM as she and other residents had referred to them many times, was a blemish on the upscale neighborhood's appearance. Stephi grabbed her cell phone, she had Peter's number on speed dial. She halted. She couldn't afford to have Peter asking her any questions about Teddy. She would have to live with the indecent display taking place right outside her window. The younger custodian kept inching closer and closer to the older man, mimicking as if he was going to ass ram him while he was distracted with cleaning the inside of a garbage can. She never considered herself a prude, but she definitely didn't move to Serenity Canyon to be around low class assholes.

"That's enough!" she yelled and beat her fist against the window.

Stephi was feeling stronger since getting rid of Teddy. There were moments of intense paranoia and dread about getting caught but they were wiped away when she roamed her house freely, not concerned with whether or not she was going to upset him in some way and suffer for it.

She turned to the vanity in the bedroom and took a long look at herself. The white of her one eye was still red, it made her smile. She was changing, becoming a whole new woman, and she refused to be anything other than fierce. She walked into the bathroom and gazed at the tub. Flashes of what she did to Teddy played out in her memory, though some of the gorier parts had been erased by her consciousness mercifully. She knew it wasn't for any feelings of guilt or remorse, she had none of those for her former husband, it was more to preserve the way she saw herself. She only wanted to remember the moment the hammer made contact with his skull, that glorious explosion of power, and not the slippery, stinking minutes when she was elbow-deep in him, fishing intestines out of him like slimy eels and shoving them into garbage bags. Those didn't fit the heroic image she had of herself.

Stephi sat on the edge of the tub. The porcelain was once again sparkling white, she was proud of the work she did and was confident the cleaning ladies would never know what took place there. For just a second she could still smell Teddy's cologne and made a mental note to get a new air freshener. She wanted nothing of him left in the house, not a picture, not a memory, not even a smell to remind her of him. She was reclaiming herself and all she was.

Stephi stood up and turned the water on in the tub. She ran a bath and stripped naked. When she stepped into the water she sighed and sat in the very place her husband bled out.

This is my house, not yours, and soon it will be like you were never here at all.

Jason jumped and the hose fell out from between his legs.

"I fuckin' told you to stop actin' like a dumbass!" Carl said, pulling up his pants over his ass crack.

He stood back a moment to wipe the sweat from his forehead and catch his breath.

"I didn't think anyone would be staring out the window at us."

"How many years have you worked here? Come on, that's all these uppity fucks do is sit around and watch us!" Carl fumed.

"Hopefully she doesn't complain to Peter."

"Yeah, that's all we need. I'll tell him to shove this job up his asshole."

"Sure you will," Jason teased.

"I'm closer than you think, asshole."

"I bet!" Jason said.

"This bitch and her husband, he's a military doctor or something, always walking around the club like their shit don't stink. I hate to tell that bitch but it does stink just like a poor man's."

"Her husband is weird. He's always staring at me like he wants to start a fight," Jason said, looking back over his shoulder to make sure no one was listening, "or fuck me!"

"I bet you money he's a serial killer," Carl said.

"No fuckin' way," Jason laughed.

"I'm dead serious, boy. I ain't talking about some Richard Ramirez type, where you know just by lookin' at him he's a freak. I'm talkin' about the Ted Bundy type that no one expects until they find bodies buried in their back yard!"

"You're crazy, Carl!"

"The fuck I am? You wait and see, he's got some skeletons in his closet."

"Whatever man, let's get this work done. I get the feeling that bitch is still watching us."

"She's probably watchin' our sweet asses, wantin' a little piece of our toned bodies after bangin' that saggy older man for so long," Carl said.

Jason chuckled, picked the hose up and squeezed the nozzle. He sprayed the inside of the can Carl just scrubbed with a brush. A river of rancid brown water drained out of the upturned can and soaked into the grass. It smelled like sour milk and dirty feet.

"Jeez, what the fuck do they toss into these things, rotten corpses?"

"You ain't new around here, you help me dump these. They throw food and coffee and dog shit in these and then they leave it to rot in the sun for us to take care of."

"I know. I just like to bitch about it," Jason said.

He dragged the can into a sunny spot beside four other cans and turned it upside down.

"How many more do we have?" Carl asked, wiping the sweat from his face again with a stained hanky.

"You okay?" Jason asked.

"I'm fine."

"We're about halfway through the neighborhood cans, then we gotta get the ones out by the management office."

"Fuck that. Let Peter do some work for a change," Carl complained.

"That ain't never gonna happen, bro," Jason said.

"I'm serious, his gingerbread man lookin' ass just walks around kissin' ass all day. He don't do any goddamn work. I'm gonna tell his ass about it," Carl said.

"I'm sure that conversation would go over like a fart in a whirlwind," Jason pulled a pack of cigarettes out of his shirt pocket and lit one. "Hey, Peter. We left you some trash cans to clean, and he'd be like, hey Carl and Jason, you're fuckin' fired."

"Give me one of them," Carl said.

"What? Fuck off. You're always bummin' my smokes. Besides, you look outta breath, old man."

"Come on, don't be a dick. I left mine in my lunchbox at the shop. I promise I'll give ya one of mine when we go on break. Besides your ass needs to quit before you end up wheezin' like me."

"I'll give you one but I don't want any from you. You smoke those cheap pieces of crap that taste like I lit a tire on fire and I'm breathing the smoke."

"You stuck up little bitch!" Carl laughed until he wheezed, accepting one of Jason's smokes.

"Do you think she'll bitch about us smoking?" Jason asked, turning his head towards Stephi's window.

"We had that battle back when old Jim first worked here, and they agreed we can smoke as long as we take the butts with us. What the hell can they say when half these old hoes walk around puffin' on menthols and letting their dogs shit everywhere?"

"That's true. Fuck em'," Jason laughed.

"That's right, boy. Fuck em'."

The two smoked and joked but the feeling of being watched never left them.

Jason bent down to put out his cigarette and to collect the butt, a blur in the bushes near Stephanie and Theodore's house caught his attention.

"Did you see that?" Carl asked.

"Yeah, what was it?"

"Looked like an animal, maybe it's a gopher or somethin'."

They walked over to the bushes and kicked around. A yelp and a snarl proved Jason right, "It's a damn dog."

The little dog ran from the bushes, his hair filthy and matted.

"Damn, did you smell that?" Carl asked.

"Yeah, that dog was caked in crap! Talk about animal abuse, these rich fucks think they're better than me but at least I bathe my pets!"

Jason watched the dog dart into the hedges of the neighbor's yard.

"Should we try to catch it?" he asked taking a step towards it.

"Hell no! That thing was running seven hundred miles per hour, we'll never catch it. We ain't got time for that. Let's tell Claudia and the whole neighborhood will know in five seconds."

The stack of trash cans was drying in the sun behind the management office. Carl and Jason made sure not to fuck around because they were certain Peter would be lurking. They rounded up their supplies and were ready to head to the parking lot when Lalo stopped by.

"Hey, guys."

"What's up, boss man?" Jason asked.

"I just wanted to let you know we have O.T. this evening, there's something going on in the club."

"Seriously? I had a hot date with Jason's mom planned, I guess I can reschedule."

"Fuck you, Carl!"

"You're gonna have to take her out a different night. Just meet me over there when you guys are done," Lalo said and walked away.

"Hey, let's go tell Claudia about that dog."

"I don't want any bitch tryin' to claim we're being creepers."

"What about the poor dog? Its owner is probably worried sick about it."

"You're only worried about Claudia's cleavage."

"You may be correct!" Carl laughed.

Jason's hesitated, "I think I need to take a piss before we do anything else."

"Oh sure, you always gotta go to the bathroom when it's time to put all the supplies away."

"Don't be a dick, Carl. I can't go in the shit shack and Rosa just cleaned the bathrooms in the custodial shop."

"Okay, fine, " Carl nodded.

"I just gotta make it past Peter so he doesn't accuse me of wasting time."

"I need to talk to Peter for a minute anyway. You go and I'll try to keep him busy while you do your business, " Carl said.

Sunny and her mother Adriana moved to Sedona two months prior to her finally landing a full time job. Her mother wasn't happy about her accepting a job as a housekeeper, but it paid decently and it provided decent health benefits she couldn't get working in a shop or restaurant. Besides, she couldn't keep accepting money from her uncle Anthony. He had a big heart and she felt like she was only taking advantage of his kindness by letting him float her loan after loan, it was time to support her and her mother on her own. Serenity Canyon was her ticket to finally settling down in their new town.

She had stopped by her current employer, a shop called Chrystal's Crystals, and resigned. She didn't like feeling as if she was letting anyone down with quitting so suddenly but she knew it was in her best interest. Luckily for her, there was no animosity when she broke the news to her boss. Instead, the older hippy manager gave her a hug and wished her the best. It was an amicable split, which eased her mind a bit.

Sunny had gotten all the way back home when she discovered she forgot her wallet in the office she was interviewed in at Serenity Canyon. She dialed the property manager's phone number, he had given her his card as she left without knowing she was hired. She felt anxious during the two interactions she had with the strange red head. He felt off somehow. The way he shook her hand, his palms wet with sweat. The way his eyes roved over her body, and he didn't particularly try to hide it. She just hoped the job would keep her so busy she wouldn't be around him much.

"Serenity Canyon, the ultimate in luxury living, where the red rocks touch the sky. This is Peter."

"Hello, this is Sunny. I had an interview earlier and I didn't realize it until now but I left my wallet in the office when I filled out my employment data," She spoke quickly.

"Oh, yeah. I remember you. You're the blond girl. I heard you got hired. Congrats!"

"Thank you."

"So, how are you?"

"I'm okay but I need my wallet."

"Oh, you poor little thing. Listen, if you want I can drop it off at your house?"

"Oh, no that won't be necessary. Can I come pick it up?"

"Well in that case, you're more than welcome to come grab it. I will have it waiting in my office for you. I'll stick around to make sure you get it."

Sunny hung up the phone and felt a twinge of anxiety, it rolled around in her heart as her mind contemplated just leaving the wallet until the following day which was her first day on the job anyway. She despised pushy men. She worried she would end up losing her job before it even started if he tried to get handsy with her.

At last they breached the doorway of the Shit Shack. Shane gagged and backed out quickly but Jose was too macho to follow him. He stayed, pretending to be strong even though a cold sweat was beading on his forehead.

"Get your pasty ass back in here. We gotta finish this up and get outta here," Jose said.

"I'm comin', let me get the hose."

Jose was shocked by what he witnessed inside the old outhouse. It looked like the stainless steel commode had exploded.

"Those little fucks must have thrown a bomb down the hole," He said.

"Jesus fuckin' Christ, there's shit everywhere," Shane said, dragging the pressure washer hose in behind him.

"What do you think they used? An M-80 or somethin'?"

"Dude, they must've thrown at least a couple cherry bombs in there to cause that kind of damage. If I didn't have to clean up after it, I'd be impressed," Shane marveled.

There were feces on the rickety wooden ceiling, on the walls, and on the mirror a stinking brown hand print. It was big, too big to be left by some twelve year old rich kid looking for excitement amidst puberty in the boring golf course neighborhood. Jose held his hand up in comparison, it was bigger than his.

"Look at that, that ain't no kid's hand, dude. This was a fuckin' adult."

"An adult? That looks like a fuckin' Sasquatch's handprint. Looks like Swamp Thing wiped his ass on his hand and smeared it on the mirror."

"Motherfuckers, they're tryin' to fuck with us. They did this on purpose just to make us clean up their shit," Jose fumed.

"They're probably outside somewhere laughin' at us from their ten thousand dollar golf carts, the cock lickers!" Shane said.

Jose pushed passed Shane and he dropped the hose to follow him. They stepped out onto the sidewalk and looked around. The golf course wasn't far away, it was mostly empty but for the tall thin shadow of a resident by the name of Pastor Crumm. He was mid-swing when Jose hailed him.

"Hey, you pee pee touchin' asshole!"

The pastor was startled, and luckily, was also hard of hearing.

"Take it easy, Jose. I don't wanna lose my job."

"Take it easy? Fuck that!"

"Dude, come on. This is royally fucked but you know Pastor Crumm didn't do this. Look at him, he's a feeble old fuck."

Jose stared at the old man, who in turn was staring back at the two maintenance men decked out in yellow plastic suits.

"Are you okay, son?"

"No. I'm not okay. Did you see this fuckin' restroom?"

"Take it easy," Shane said and grabbed Jose by the arm.

"What did you say? I couldn't hear you," Pastor Crumm approached them with a slow, hobbling gait.

"He said the restroom is kinda dirty, so don't use it."

"Oh, hi Sean."

"It's Shane."

"Oh, right. Don't worry. I never use that old thing. I thought it was only for your crew?"

"Yeah it is, but someone not on our crew went in there and fucked it up!" Jose said.

Pastor Crumm nodded, the fake smile falling from his face, "I'm sorry to hear that."

"When I find out who did this, they're gonna be really fuckin' sorry."

There was an awkward pause before the pastor responded, "Right, well you boys take care."

He went back to his game.

Shane slapped the back of Jose's head, "You can't say stuff like that, man!"

"The fuck I can't. He'll go back to his buddies in the club and soon the word will spread they can't mess with us."

"No, the word will spread to Peter that we were using profanity to some old asshole and we'll get shit canned."

"I'd like to see Pito try."

"Man, cut it out and let's get this cleaned. I wanna go home on time tonight."

Their laughter faded and they readied themselves to get down to business again.

Lalo approached the golf cart. The news he carried would be taken either with glee or dismay. Knowing both Jose and Shane, he figured it would be the latter. The smell coming from the Shack was abnormally awful. He hesitated, and thought maybe he'd wait until they returned to the shop to inform them they had to stay later to help with the charity gala taking place at the club. He didn't want to get roped into helping them. He had paid his dues in the shack and now they had to too. Shane came walking out of the Shit Shack, Lalo could tell it was him by the way he walked, like if he made his way slow enough the work would be complete before he went back inside. It was too late to turn back. He would have to tell them about the gala, and he would be damn lucky if he escaped without lending them a hand.

"Shane, get Jose. I need to tell you something."

"Oh, god. What is it now?"

Lalo knew from his reaction Shane would definitely complain, Jose would be a roll of the dice. He claimed to need overtime in the past, but he was also notorious for asserting he was the only person on the crew who actually worked hard and needed days off to rest. Rosa and Isabel already heard about the overtime and both were surprisingly agreeable with working some extra hours.

"The shack was literally destroyed, man! We won't be done for at least another hour or more," Shane said and went back to call for Jose.

"What?" Lalo asked and dared to go check out the damage.

"Looks like they blew the fuckin' toilet up."

Jose stepped just beyond the doorway, "Come check this bullshit out."

Lalo had never seen such destruction committed at Serenity Canyon. He worked for years in schools, and saw some serious vandalism, but the Shit Shack looked like a grizzly bear had awoken in a crank-induced rage from hibernating and tore it to pieces.

"What the fuck happened?"

"Exactly. We can clean it but the damage will have to be repaired, or tear this fuckin' thing down once and for all," Shane said from behind him.

"I'll let Peter know. Just clean it and lock the door. There's nothing else we can do." Lalo scoffed under his breath, "fuckin' little rich bastard kids."

"There was a shitty handprint left on the mirror and it was bigger than my hand. It had to be an adult," Shane said.

Lalo looked over his shoulder, his eyes tightened, "An adult?"

"Yeah, this wasn't the work of any teens."

Lalo usually kept his cool, but he had a short fuse and when he truly went off even Jose kept his mouth shut. Shane could see the rage in his boss' eyes. He had a momentary flashback of watching Jim's wiry old body being tossed against the Shit Shack wall.

Lalo's mind was replaying every time he had been disrespected as a janitor. His lips tightened into a snarl, it was the final sign.

"Chingada madre!" Lalo kicked the bathroom door.

"Take it easy, bro. We'll get this cleaned up."

"What else did you have to tell us?" Jose asked.

"There's a fuckin' gala happening tonight at the club and we're all working late."

"Sure thing, Lalo," Shane said, there was no way in hell he was going to complain after knowing how close Lalo was to unleashing his true rage.

Lalo looked to Jose who nodded, "Sure. I need some extra cash."

"Good. Meet at the club in two hours, and clean yourselves up before you show up because if Peter says one fuckin' word to me about my crew I'm gonna smash his fuckin' ginger head."

Lalo left them to continue their work. He was fuming at the state of the Shack. He believed Jose and Shane, they wouldn't lie about the handprint and they definitely weren't exaggerating the state of the shack. It had been intentionally destroyed and left in disgusting disarray by one of the residents of Serenity Canyon.

Lalo had a list of them he hated, and he knew there were a few who hated him too. He let them all know on many occasions what his crew were responsible for and what they weren't. Peter had threatened him once if he didn't use more tact when turning down unusual work requests he could be in serious trouble, he could even be let go. Lalo couldn't believe he had it in himself to not bash Peter's brains out with a mop handle when he threatened to fire him for refusing to have Rosa and Isabel wash cars upon request. He should have earned an award for walking away that day, but Lalo wasn't so sure he could walk away again, especially with the disaster in the Shit Shack. He was sick of the club members being so demanding and the management office refusing to hire enough workers. They were lucky the picky bastards agreed to one new employee when in reality they really needed at least three. The SCUM crew was working their fingers to the bone on a daily basis and the only thanks they ever received were usually disingenuous or ploys to get them to do extra work. He stopped in his tracks and took a deep breath. He needed to calm himself before speaking with Peter. With each deep inhalation his nostrils were assaulted with the stink of the foul black sludge from the Shit Shack. He fought with his anger. He cracked his knuckles and felt the scars of so many fist fights, some were warranted while others not so much. His radio crackled and broke his concentration.

"Lalo, there have been many reports of a horrible smell. We need that taken care of ASAP before the gala tonight!"

It was Peter, his voice like a shrill old woman's was a lit match getting closer and closer to Lalo's short fuse.

"Lalo, do you copy?"

Lalo lifted his radio to his lips, "I need to talk to you about the smell."

The seconds went by, Lalo wanted to scream into the radio at Peter but he held it inside.

"Okay, come to my office and make it quick."

"10-4…Peter," he replied, wrestling back his rage.

He took one step forward and nearly stepped on a small object. It scurried away yelping. Lalo followed it into the bushes beside the sidewalk and bent down. He stretched his hand out to a small, filthy dog. He recognized it as being Mrs. Brandon's Pomeranian. He recalled it had a stupid name only rich white women give their dogs.

"Here, Fluffystuff," he coaxed softly.

The dog trembled so violently he thought it would fall over dead. Its hair was matted with filth and it smelled horribly.

"Guacala! You stink!"

Puffkins came nervously forward and sniffed Lalo's fingertips. He licked them and whined. Lalo didn't know what to think of the state of the poor animal, but after witnessing the Shack he wondered if the same asshole who destroyed the outhouse had done something to Mrs. Brandon's dog. Lalo reached into his pocket and pulled out a pair of gloves, he never went anywhere around work without them. He slipped them on and slowly petted the dog's crusty fur.

"Come on, Fluffystuff."

The dog allowed him to pick it up. He couldn't cradle it because he didn't want to dirty his shirt with the filth stuck in its hair, but he knew just who he would leave in charge of taking it back to its owner.

"Peter, I have something for you," he laughed, his anger finally abating.

The beast which once was called Teddy twitched and shifted on the king size bed. He was witnessing a nightmare, a memory from not long ago, of watching one of his kind being charred to nothing but dust. His skin crawled with maggots and roaches were nesting in a hole in his skull. He was used to the feeling of their many legs tickling against his skin, in a way they were comforting to him. They were the only living thing he could abide now. Inside of him twitched, not a heartbeat but a writhing, especially around the wounds he received at his death. It was his new Gods, the tendrils which pulled his pieces back together. The squirming things, they were piloting his body, urged his bruised brain to bide his time, to recuperate his strength. His eyes never closed when his body fell into the slumber-like state, they remained wide open and only his dead mind wandered somewhere between being asleep and being awake. Something in him told him he would never truly sleep again. He would just kind of lose power on occasions when his form required rest. His memories were still plagued with visions of himself from before but nothing he recalled left an ounce of joy in him. He was dead now and he hated all living things. One thing he was aware of was his former intellect, pieces of it remained, it was superior to any human the Gods had entered. He was special.

Dr. Entz screeched as the guards tightened the straps holding him down to the gurney, one at each wrist and ankle. He appeared to be asleep when they first entered the room he was locked in but soon found out subduing him was quite the task, especially with the pools of puke and waste he had loosed on the floor. It only reinforced in Dr. Abileen's mind just how indestructible the creatures were, and how vile they could be. She wanted to test his powers of resurrection and self-healing. She also needed to know if the parasitic worm actually killed him or only went into effect once natural death had already claimed him.

"You two stand outside the door, but watch from my lab window. I can't afford for him to escape if he gets loose."

They followed her orders obediently and for a second she thought just how crazy the situation was for them. They signed on to be military men, but to deal with a reanimated corpse? That takes a whole other level of loyalty to their country.

Dr. Entz writhed beneath a bright flash of light as Dr. Abileen prepared to examine him. She wasn't sure if it was actually an examination, or an autopsy, or a vivisection. All she knew is she would cut the answers right out of him. She'd split him from his chin to his foreskin if she had to, even if he spit and shrieked the entire time her scalpel and forceps were at work.

She hit record on a small recorder and spoke, "Dr. Abileen, the fourth of April, twenty eighteen. Examination of Dr. Entz. His death occurred more than nine hours ago, and yet he…lives."

His gut rumbled. She knew the significance of it and grabbed a wadded towel she had ready for him. She felt a surge of fear as she struggled to shove it into his mouth, disgust crawled up her spine as she duct taped it in place, silencing him and hopefully clogging him up from any vomitus eruptions. He was no longer alive, she had no humanly compassion for him or any concern for his suffering while she did her work, she just wanted it over. Dr. Abileen went into a robot-mode, that's how she always thought of it and it helped her through the opening of cadavers in Med. School, and through the after-party clean up at her college dormitory. Vomit, snot, blood, crap, piss, puss, bile, they were all just random liquids and substances when she initiated robot mode. She picked up a pair of scissors and began cutting the clothes from Dr. Entz. He had already freed himself of his leather shoes when they fought to get him under control, but the rest of him was swathed in bloody, waste covered clothing. His pants were still damp with bodily fluids which ran down his legs each time he got riled up and left puddles on the floor in the room he was held in. Dr. Abileen wore thick gloves and under those were three pairs of latex gloves, even if she had already been exposed she still didn't want his feces, blood, and vomit anywhere near her hands. She cut the legs of his pants away, the scissors nicking his flesh as he writhed, leaving a deep gouge in his thigh. She hesitated and watched in horrific wonder as thin worm-like fibers squirmed out and fused with each other stitching the jagged hole back together. She quickly grabbed a pair of tweezers from a steel tray of tools beside her and fished one of the fleshy tendrils out of the wound. It squirmed beneath the white light bathing it.

"What are we dealing with, a parasite?" She opened a glass vial and deposited it inside.

She ran her fingertip over the sealed wound, only a scar remained, "The body heals itself through means I have never witnessed, and I don't believe anyone else in my field ever has…"

Dr. Abileen took a step back and stared down at Dr. Entz, he hadn't stopped fighting to break free, she didn't think he ever would.

"The patient's flesh and eyes hold the tell-tale hues of death and yet his is not rigored and it appears he never was. He is just as agile and strong as he ever could have been, or possibly more so."

She didn't know what secrets Teddy kept in his handwritten notebooks, or how he discovered or created the parasite, but she knew he must have had no idea the true outcome of what he believed to be his most grandiose work.

She went back to removing the clothing from Dr. Entz until he was completely naked. She took up her scalpel and sliced him from shoulder to sternum on each side and then sternum to groin, the typical Y incision reserved for corpses. His flesh was easily peeled back to reveal muscle and bone. She noticed his bindings cutting into his flesh at his wrists, making bloodless wounds, and she hoped they would hold. A beast like him would rip his own hands off just to be free.

She hovered over his chest with a bone saw. He squirmed as she set it down into his flesh and attempted to cut in as straight a line as possible. She was in a hurry but her perfectionist side cursed when he jump and the saw went sideways. She removed it and watched him while he thrust himself upward and tried to break free, his flaccid prick flopping side to side. She was overcome with disgust and fear she would soon be tied to a steel table with her body exposed to some scientist.

"Be still, you bastard."

Dr. Abileen was beginning to sweat in the layers of gowns and plastic and latex she dressed in to protect herself from his blood and other bodily fluids. Her nerves were on edge and she couldn't quiet the howling voice in the back of her mind telling her she was a corpse.

The bone saw had filled the air with blood and bone dust, it clung to the plastic face shield she wore. Wiping it clean with a paper towel, she grabbed a pair of rib shears. She jammed them into the opening she already made. It took all the strength in her weakening arms to cut through his ribs, each cracking and snapping as she went through them with a meaty crunch. Peering inside of him gave her chills and she wondered who would be examining her once she was dead. She prayed it wasn't for many decades to come. The hole she created squirmed at its edges with thin white worms no thicker than eyelashes yet much longer and they moved quickly and with purpose to examine the gaping intrusion she had created. She took a step back and gagged at the sight of them writhing and reaching for the flesh at the opposite side of the opening. She cursed and picked up the saw again, slicing at the parasites, clearing her line of sight. She gazed into his yawning abdomen where his stomach and organs were already taken over by pale threads, all moving and weaving themselves around the liver and kidneys, and wriggling around across the exposed intestines, exerting their dominance of his whole being. They seemed to be focused on his digestive tract. Dr. Abileen turned her attention to the area of the heart and lungs still shielded by his ribs she had sawed and scissored through, knowing she needed to get a good look at them before making any conclusions.

She was tired but she gripped the roughly hewn rib bones and cracked him open further and stared down at his still heart. Its walls had ruptured, she could see an abrupt slit-like tearing, the flooding of blood being pumped uselessly to everywhere it didn't need to go.

"Not a trace of them."

There were no signs of the strange worm-like tendrils repairing it. Each wound inflicted upon him since his return had already been fused back together by the parasite, but his heart had not been.

Dr. Abileen moved to stand at his head, hastily sawing the top of his skull off. The worm-like tendrils kept fighting to pull it back together. She sawed right through them unmercifully. His skull cap fell away and hung by a piece of his scalp. She involuntarily shuttered, her skin crawled just looking at them work. She stepped back, disgusted to see his brain was encased in the squirming tendrils, crawling in and out of holes the size of pin pricks, taking over his brain completely and rapidly repairing signs of trauma inflicted by the guards.

"His heart is destroyed and there is no sign of the parasites rebuilding it. He was dead before the worms took hold of him. It waits for the body to die before taking control over it and only reconstructs what it deems necessary to survive," she spoke to record her findings in the case she didn't survive.

Dr. Abileen shuffled back as a thousand tendrils snaked their way across Dr. Entz's open chest, some as long as her arm but hair thin. He was filled with them. She trembled as they began pulling him back together. She wished she hadn't burned Charlie, then. She would have liked to see the number of the things inside of him, maybe she would know why Entz hadn't taken as long to reanimate.

Dr. Entz was nearly completely sealed when she snapped out of the hazy nightmarish daydream her mind wandered into for the few moments, of a world populated by humans infested with writhing parasites.

"Guards!"

The two men rushed into the room. Their pistols permanent fixtures of their bodies now, extended and ready to kill.

"At your command," one of them said after it was clear she was still human, "where are we taking him?"

"We're gonna burn this motherfucker."

Dr. Abileen was tired, right down to her bones. She was relatively sure even if she was exposed to the parasite, if it was hiding in her body, she wouldn't change unless she died. Her fear of Dr. Entz morphed into anger. She refused to let his disgusting ass be the reason she was killed and came back to constantly mess herself. She used the rib shears to clip through the straps used to hold him to the gurney. Dr. Entz shot up and shrieked, she nodded to the soldiers and they opened fire on him. Bullets impacted his freshly opened chest, rocking him backwards. He scrambled off the head of the gurney and backed away as they continued to fill him with lead, his wounds feverishly squirming as the parasitic worms attempted to heal him.

The soldiers halted to reload and Dr. Abileen grabbed a heavy fire extinguisher from the wall. She ran straight at Entz. She swung it with all her strength and hit him in the jaw, his neck snapped and he tumbled back into the waiting incinerator. She forced his legs inside and as he regained his footing, he found himself a spectator of his own cremation. She pressed the button to slam the door shut. Entz was trapped; vomit flew from his mouth, showering the tiny viewing window on the incinerator door. In it were tiny white things like sesame seeds, eggs. She felt like vomiting but swallowed it back fearing the guards would force her in next to Dr. Entz. She slapped the on button and watched as it heated up, a quick roar, but the flames ate him slowly. His skin sloughed away in black sheets, revealing his parasite riddled flesh just before it charred to. His lungs were roasted; he could no longer issue his shrill battle cries. His esophagus was fried all the way down and his stomach split open, spilling the seemingly endless supply of puke into a steaming cloud in the intense heat. He fell to his knees as his body fell apart. Dr. Abileen refused to look away until there was nothing left of him.

CHAPTER 3
WELCOME TO THE NEIGHBORHOOD

SUNNY AWKWARDLY STOOD on the other side of Peter's desk. He opened his desk drawer and pulled out her wallet.

"Kept it in there so it would be safe," he winked.

"Thank you."

She reached for it and he teasingly pulled it away. She hoped her face wasn't betraying her inner dialogue.

Don't fuck with me, you freak.

He handed it to her and she shoved it down into her purse and spun on her heels, ready to get out of his office.

"Hey, where ya headed?"

"Home. I told my mom I'd buy groceries."

"Too bad I'm busy or I'd go with 'ya. I need some stuff for my house too; the cabinets of a bachelor can get pretty bare."

She smiled and nodded, "Yeah too bad."

"Ya want a tour of the neighborhood before you go?"

"Uh, sorry. I'm in kind of a hurry."

"Oh, right," he smiled.

"Okay, well, see you tomorrow," Sunny said and made her way to the door.

On the other side she could see Lalo approaching while carrying a small animal out before him. She hurried to open the door for him and was hit by the smell of feces as he walked in.

"Peter, this is Mrs. Brandon's dog."

"I'll take it back to her, but what happened to it?"

"I'm not sure but the shack was destroyed, looked like someone blew it up. There is crap everywhere, and now this."

He handed the dog across the desk, and before Peter could refuse, he forced it into his hands.

"Are you saying this dog is covered in shit?"

"Can't you smell it?" Sunny asked, too interested in seeing Peter get crap on his hands to leave. He deserved to get contaminated after being a constant creep. She smiled, knowing Lalo had hastily shoved the dog into Peter's hands just toy with him.

"No, I was kicked in the head by a horse as a child and lost most of my sense of smell."

"Oh, here's some gloves," Lalo said as he removed his own and fished a pair out of his pocket to toss at Peter.

"Gee, thanks!"

"No problem. I gotta get to work at the clubhouse. Let me know how that all turns out."

"Are you sure someone vandalized the outhouse?"

"Vandalized? More like blew it the fuck up!"

"I'll call and report it to the police," Peter said, fumbling with the dog as Sunny followed Lalo out and closed the door.

"Wait!" he tried to stop them.

He dropped the dog and rounded the desk to chase after her but Puffkins yelped and scurried away, disappearing somewhere beneath his office chair and desk.

"You little shit!"

For a moment he was pulled between harassing Sunny some more and doing his duty as the property manager, but his need to be an ass-kisser outweighed his perverted urges. He needed Mrs. Brandon's approval and praise. The dog would be his ticket. Besides, if the new girl wouldn't pay him any attention, he would turn on the charm and maybe hook himself a sugar mama. Sylvia was a widow, after all.

He slipped the latex gloves on and knelt down.

"Come here, Puffkins. I know your name. I always see you out walking with your mommy. She's gonna be my mommy soon."

Peter reached under the desk and dragged the dog out. It yelped and bit at his gloved hand but he didn't let go. He carried it out his office door and down the hall to a janitorial closet. Inside it there was a large floor sink, which was used to dump mop buckets in, and copious amounts of soaps and cleaners. He sat the dog down in the sink and Puffkins immediately tried jumping over the two foot porcelain wall surrounding him but to no avail. The sink was like a miniature bathtub and he was stuck at the mercy of the red headed man with a crazy look in his eyes. Peter dowsed the dog in hand soap, it smelled faintly of lavender, then turned on the hose attached to the faucet.

"Let's make sure it's warm, little buddy," he said, grabbing the end of the hose and letting the water run over his wrist like one might do to test the warmth of a bottle of milk for a baby. It was warm but not hot.

"It's just right."

He turned the hose on Puffkins who yowled and trembled.

"Soon, you'll be good as new! And your mama is gonna love me. I bet she's been lookin' all over for ya!"

Peter dried the dog with hand towels and set it free in his office while he went to the restroom to make himself look nice for playing hero to the widow. He took a comb out of his pocket and quaffed his red hair. He sniffed himself to make certain none of the awful smell had attached its self to him but, of course, his diminished sense of smell made it nearly impossible to tell. He went back to his office and opened his desk drawer. He dug around until he found a small bottle of cologne he was gifted for Christmas by the old skank Claudia. He couldn't deny she was attractive but she was far too easy for his taste, he liked his ladies demure. He twisted off the cap and splashed some in his palms. He rubbed it on his neck and across his chest. He was ready.

"Puffkins, come on let's get you home."

The dog squatted in the corner of his office and anxiously relieved itself.

"You little shit!"

The dog scurried to get away but he had nowhere to run. Peter caught him and stomped out of his office carrying Puffkins under his arm.

"Can I ask you something before I head out?" Sunny asked, walking beside Lalo.

"Let me guess. Peter tried hitting on you?"

"How did you know?"

"Look at the guy, he's a fuckin' weirdo."

Sunny laughed, "You ain't kiddin'."

"Are you ready for tomorrow? I hope Peter didn't make you change your mind."

"No. I need this job, " she looked about her at the expansive property and smiled.

"Oh good. I didn't want to have to interview Jose's cousin again," Lalo laughed.

"Well, you don't have to worry. I'll be here. I refuse to lose this job to a guy with face tattoos."

Lalo veered in his path and she followed.

"Walk with me to the clubhouse. I'll grab a few uniform shirts for you from the storage closet by the kitchen."

"That would be great. Before I left the first time Peter said he would have to order some for me."

Lalo shook his head, "He doesn't actually know anything. Peter just sits in his office and acts like he's the boss."

"Oh, I've worked for people like him before."

"So, if you ever need anything just ask me or one of the others on the crew and we'll hook you up. Then you won't be stuck in Peter's office again."

"Oh thank God!"

"You'll get a little bit of a tour on the way of the splendor of Serenity Canyon," Lalo laughed and swept his arm out in an exaggerated gesture.

"I need to know as much as I can before tomorrow."

"What you need to know first is all the residents are basically rich bastards. You can't take it personal."

"I understand, we're just employees to these people," Sunny nodded, and on cue two old men on a golf cart rode by without even acknowledging their existence.

"And you'll be treated like one by most of these pricks," Lalo pointed at them.

"Of course!" Sunny giggled and said, "Now, tell me about the property."

"The club is the center of the property and around it is the neighborhood, there aren't that many cottages out here. It's supposed to be exclusive so they don't allow just anyone living here, or visiting either so we can't have anyone come to see us. My wife was almost arrested when she brought me lunch one evening."

"Oh, man!"

"Other than people being pricks, it's a good place with great benefits," Lalo said seriously.

"That's why I'm excited to get to work here," she motioned to the grand property, "tell me more about my new paradise."

"The golf courses are maintained by an outside company, just like the kitchen, and we are responsible for cleaning and maintaining the property. We have two golf carts but they're being used right now so that leaves us walking," Lalo said.

"I'm not afraid of some exercise."

"But tomorrow you will be on a golf cart, along with Rosa and Isabel. They're both chismosas but they will take care of you." He shook his head, "I'm sorry, I mean they're gossipy."

"No, it's okay. I know some Spanish."

"You'll be fine, then."

"What's happening over there?" Sunny asked, pointing to the opposite end of the golf course where in the distance Shane and Jose stood by a golf cart in yellow suits.

"They're cleaning the Shit Shack," Lalo paused, "uh, the outhouse."

"Outhouse?"

"Don't worry, that won't be your job. Plus, it got so messed up we'll probably have to have it closed for good."

"I can't believe a swanky place like this would have one of those."

"Oh, it's been here since the golf course was first built. It's reserved for the maintenance crew, none of these rich fucks would step foot in there."

"Doesn't surprise me!" Sunny laughed.

They continued their stroll to the club, Lalo imparting advice to her along the way.

Teddy emerged from the bedroom into the dark hallway and made his way downstairs. The newborn, the old woman, was starting to make a ruckus in the kitchen. He wanted to calm her, to help the pilots squirming inside of her get accustomed to their new form. He issued a low screech and the sounds of clattering pots and dishes halted. He stepped into the kitchen and she stood in a gooey puddle of bodily fluids. She was facing him which meant her back was to him and her arms were reaching out behind her, feeling blindly around the home which she once inhabited as a human. Teddy gripped the sides of her head and spun her head back the way it should be. Her body dropped to the filth stained tile. She lay there motionless for a while, longer than he approved of but the vessel he spat his larvae into, her body, was feeble. He watched her as tiny tendrils rose to the surface and writhed just under her paper thin skin. They were repairing her spinal cord and esophagus in order for her to be mobile and for her to regurgitate her larvae into other hosts. Her fingers twitched and her arms began to move. It was the closest thing he felt which mimicked human joy, watching her begin to crawl across the floor and pull herself up at the countertop. Mrs. Brandon, as she was once called, stood there for a moment before turning around. She hissed softly and he knew her body was repaired.

The back sliding glass door was still open and he knew the hairy thing, the dog his human side of his memory recalled the name of, had escaped. It was a shame. He was hoping his new child would get some practice in killing by tearing the hairy little thing to pieces. The sun was setting, the sky outside ablaze with red and orange. The darkness would steal over them soon and he would leave the refuge of the stinking house in hopes of making new children and filling his gut with those who weren't worthy. He looked to the old woman and contemplated eating her for just a moment but then the memory of the woman, his killer, filled his head. The agreement he made with the squirming Gods inside him came to his dead mind, he would spare his children and only dine on living flesh.

In the stillness of evening outside he heard a sudden blasting cacophony, like howling winds. Music, his human memory recalled. The racket killed the moment of peace he felt watching his newborn. His rage was reignited. His purpose screamed in him, he was born to kill the living. The old woman heard it to, felt it reverberate in her flesh. She hissed, her toothless mouth drooling. Teddy came to her side, his child was hungry too. He heard the empty pit of her stomach wailing, the egg-filled bile inside of her broiled. He put his filthy hand on her shoulder to calm her. She needed to be eased until night fell and the darkness would conceal them while they hunted. He felt her tension fading, but she trembled. He knew she would never be strong enough. She wouldn't be able to carry the hosts and their eggs very long, but he refused to kill her.

A sudden dinging sent her scrambling over the counter. It rang in his skull, rattled his brain and sent him into an instant fury. It rang out again, this time it was followed by a knocking at the front door. The doorbell, he remembered now, someone was there just beyond the oaken door. What was once Mrs. Brandon crawled around the side of the counter on her hands and knees on the floor and crept through the living room toward the door.

"Mrs. Brandon. I have something for you!" a man's voice called.

Teddy would teach his child to hunt, after all.

Teddy had been so tempted to pull the door open earlier, when the voices of women were on the other side of it, but his body was shutting down. This time, he would have his way. The Gods within approved of killing this man, demanded it. They were a hungry scourge, requiring flesh to feast on in order to reproduce and advance their kind. He would obey them.

He crept forward with the old woman in tow. His muscle memory from being human did certain things like opening doors without making him puzzle over them. He reached out his filthy hand and touched the doorknob. On the other side of the door, there was a commotion of barking and a man frantically trying to calm a dog. The little hairy thing had returned and he brought with him food, or a possible carrier for Teddy's children. It pleased him.

"You little shit. Calm down," the man whispered.

Teddy stood with his mangled head pressed against the door, listening.

"Stop biting. Mommy will answer the door soon."

Teddy twisted the doorknob and slowly cracked the door open a few inches.

"Hello, Mrs. Brandon. I have Puffkins, he must've escaped!" the voice called.

After a long pause without a response, Teddy watched the door easing open. He pressed his back against the wall and let the opening door conceal him as the silhouette of a man stepped over the threshold.

"Mrs. Brandon, I'm coming in. I have your dog…are you okay?"

The little hairy dog squirmed and yelped. Its teeth found the hand of the man squeezing it under his arm. He dropped the dog and it ran out the front door for his life.

"Jesus frickin' Christ!"

The red headed man took a step towards the door but halted as he glanced back over his shoulder. The old woman was standing in the entryway to the darkened kitchen, her silhouette outlined against the single light on behind her.

"Oh, I'm so sorry, Mrs. Brandon. I'll catch Puffkins again. I'll be right back."

He turned to exit but the door slammed shut in his face. His gaze fell on Teddy's new form.

"Dr. Reinart?"

He just froze there, trembling for a moment. The stench of Teddy hit him like a punch in the gut—rancid, vile— it made Peter's stomach knot with nausea. The doctor was filthy, his eyes fixated on Peter, unblinking for far too long. Beneath his cheeks something squirmed in thin lines and the side of his head looked like it had been bashed in then smashed back together. Peter realized Teddy was not himself and then he screamed. It was high pitched, and died suddenly when the old woman ran up behind him and pushed him to the floor.

"What the fuck?!" Peter stammered as he tried squirming away from Mrs. Brandon.

Teddy stood over her, and watched as she hastily tried bashing the man's head against the floor but her strength was lacking. Teddy lifted his filthy foot and let it fall on the side of the man's head; it bounced off the tile floor. He cried out again, and Teddy knew he must be silenced before they were discovered.

"Theodore, Mrs. Brandon? What are you doing? Please, don't hurt me!"

Teddy pushed the old woman away and bent down over his prey as it tried to fight back, kicking and punching, but it couldn't escape him. He was far too angry and far too hungry. Teddy lifted his fist and let it fall into the man's nose, crushing bone. Blood squirted out each of his nostrils like in miniature crimson fountains, driving the old woman mad. Beneath her skin squirmed the hosts, her demanding Gods. They urged her to feed and to give birth. She crawled onto the man's chest and attempted to bite into his throat but she had no teeth. Teddy was getting impatient. He forced her back and punched into the man's gut with all his strength, cockroaches scurried from his arm and across Peter's chest. Teddy felt the wind being forced from his prey's lungs, silencing his cries. Teddy halted for a moment, his human memories flooding through his thoughts.

Peter. The red headed man's name was Peter.

He recalled hating him even when he was a human, though he wouldn't have stopped even if he had liked him. He was no longer Teddy. He was beyond humanity and death, a new life form birthed to destroy mankind. Peter's mouth hung open as he fought to breathe. Teddy shoved his fist into Peter's mouth; he forced it down into his throat. He could feel Peter fighting to breathe, his gag reflex made his stomach jolt. He reached up and grabbed Teddy's arm and clawed at it as he forced his fist down deeper. Peter's face was violet; he was losing his struggle to live. Teddy felt his bottom jaw snap downward as he thrust his fist even deeper as Peter's body quivered, he was seconds away from dying. Teddy's gnarled fingers twisted, his jagged nail finding purchase in the soft warm flesh. He gripped the inside of Peter's esophagus and yanked it like the slippery innards of a jack-o-lantern. He ripped a small fistful of meat out as he withdrew his bloody hand from the dead man. He tossed it the old woman and she swallowed it without gumming it. It slid right down her throat. She was ravenously hungry. Teddy decided he would teach her to lay eggs on another victim, they both needed to feed on Peter to gain the strength to fight the other humans he was sure were in abundance just outside the front door. He quickly shredded Peter's clothing from his body, leaving his Serenity Canyon polo in tatters on the floor of Mrs. Brandon's luxury condominium. His old memories whispered of the place he once lived, Serenity Canyon, of the neighbors inhabiting all the cottages. He remembered flashes of their gaudy furniture, their wives filled with plastic and the way they smiled like dolls. It sickened the new Teddy. He couldn't wait to kill them all.

Peter's mouth gaped open, his jaw dislocated by the girth of Teddy's arm. Teddy gripped one of Peter's fingers and tore it free from his hand like separating a chicken wing from its drumstick. He tossed it to Mrs. Brandon. She caught it and suckled at the blood running from it. She used her manicured fingernails to start stripping the flesh and skin from it. There was a deep opening left from Teddy ripping Peter's jaw away so he gripped it with both hands and began splitting Peter open until he was torn apart all the way down to his Little Peter, exposing a buffet of organs and meat. Teddy began to feast, he was starving but he made sure to toss soft handfuls of intestines and stomach to the old woman who gorged herself until her stomach bulged and she was bathed in blood. Teddy knew she would soon need to empty herself, the eggs and larvae inside of her needed to be deposited into another living being. They would finish dining and then he would take his child to the source of the music he heard earlier and there they would both impregnate the entire community of Serenity Canyon. They were the new species of man, an apex predator driven by the squirming passengers in their brains. Their Gods would rule through them.

Lalo led Sunny though the back of the kitchen. It was swarming with men and women dressed in white linen uniforms, their minds fixed upon the task before them.

"What's on the menu tonight, Sandy?" Lalo asked a short woman with her grey hair braided and wound into a tight bun at the back of her head.

"Rich people shit," she answered, not even glancing up from a tray of hors d'oeuvres.

Sunny laughed, she liked the old woman already. Lalo stopped before a door and unlocked it, "What size shirt do you wear?"

"I think a medium, but give me a large so Peter doesn't oogle me while I work."

"You got it," Lalo said and pushed the door open.

Inside were shelves and cabinets, it appeared well stocked.

"Is this your secret stash?" she asked.

"Yes, and now that you're part of the crew you're allowed to come and grab supplies as you need them. Peter doesn't know about it either, he doesn't really know jack about anything, actually. You can hide here from him if you ever need to. He's afraid of Sandy."

"She's my kind of girl," Sunny said.

He opened a cabinet and rifled through a stack of dark crimson colored shirts. He handed her five of them and closed the cabinet.

"There ya go. You're all ready for work tomorrow, but there's one more thing."

"What's that?"

"You gotta meet the crew," he said.

"I'm nervous. I hope they don't hate me," she teased.

"I wouldn't worry about that. You'll be one of us, don't worry."

Lalo walked through the kitchen and out a door. It opened to a fancy room lined with long tables. A chandelier hung from the ceiling and the massive windows were draped with deep red curtains.

"Fancy shmancy," Sunny said.

"This is the main hall. Peter calls it the ballroom but that sounds too elegant for me."

Sunny marveled at the dinner tables set with too many forks and spoons, crystal champagne glassed sparkled in the light of the chandelier. There was a small orchestral group near the two massive doors she guessed to be the main entrance. They were only practicing for the real party, but their tune sounded magical. Sunny thought she would feel like a princess being invited to such a swanky event.

"Do they have a lot of events?" she asked.

"At least four or five times a year. You should see it at Christmas, talk about rich fucks."

"Wow, and we clean up after all of them?"

"That's right. It's kind of a pain in the ass but we get overtime for it."

"I'll be happy to get some overtime."

"At least you're happy about it. I had a few complaints today."

Sunny gripped her work shirts and waited, anxious to get to work at a place so regal.

"You want somethin' to eat before the kings and queens arrive?" Sunny looked back towards the kitchen as a sudden voice spoke. Sandy was walking towards them with trays of elegant finger foods, smiling as she approached. Her white uniform was embroidered with a silver crown over the breast pocket and the words Royal Dining.

"Yes, please," Sunny answered, her stomach empty.

"You better be sharing!" Shane's voice echoed from across the hall.

"He can smell free shit, especially food, from miles away," Lalo said.

"Only if you don't smell like the Shack!" Jason said running in from a side door, hurrying towards Sandy and the free food like a shark pursuing an injured seal.

"You better grab some, honey. These guys will swallow this whole tray in a matter of seconds," Sandy said and Sunny could see she wasn't kidding.

Sunny grabbed a few things to eat but was nearly bowled over by

Jason and Carl who made it to the tray before Shane did. Sunny backed up a few steps and watched as her other three coworkers came strolling in.

"This is Shane, Carl, and Jason. And here comes Jose, Isabel, and Rosa," Lalo said.

The three men stuffing hors d'oeuvres into their mouths like fiends nodded and waved but continued to eat.

Jose, Rosa, and Isabel were busy with a lively conversation. The two women were laughing and pointing at him as they approached.

"¿Lalo, es verdad? ¿El Shit Shack explotó?"

"Si, es verdad," He laughed, the rage he felt earlier subsided.

"I feel like I smell like a walking pile of crap!" Jose said.

"This is our new crew member, Sunny," Lalo said as an introduction to Jose and the chismosas.

"Hello," Rosa said and offered her hand.

Sunny shook it and was relieved to see the smiling face of the older woman. She didn't know what she was expecting from any of her new crew but her anxiety was fading as she watched them joke and share food. She felt like she would get along just fine with them.

"Hey, Carl. What about the cans?" Lalo asked.

"Don't worry, boss man. Me and the kid took care of em' for 'ya," Carl answered.

"Did you hear about the Shack?" Jose asked.

"It looked like someone blew the damn thing up," Shane said.

"What?!" Jason asked.

"Maybe old Jim did it for revenge for getting fired?" Carl said.

"Damn, ya think so?" Shane asked, turning serious.

"Come on, after getting fired the only thing he blew up was his liver with a bunch of cheap booze. Jim didn't do that," Jose shook his head.

"Dude, you remember the hand print. Maybe he did it in a drunken rage. Think about it," Shane said with his mouth full of food, "who else would even know its back there?"

"That's true," Lalo agreed, "this place is too far out of the way. Who comes way out here to destroy an old outhouse? Plus, we have a security guard at the gate, no one gets by him. And the adults in this place wouldn't go in the shit shack if they were giving away free money and Starbucks in there."

"So, you don't think one of these uppity fucks did it just to fuck with us?" Jose asked.

"No, I don't think so anymore," Lalo said.

"What are you gonna do? Tell Peter?" Jason asked.

Lalo thought about it for a while, "I already told him about the shack being destroyed but I don't think I'll mention Jim's name unless we can prove it was him."

The grand entrance door opened and the neighborhood residents began piling inside. The SCUM crew was forced to exit through the kitchen, scurrying like roaches when a kitchen light is flipped on.

"Keep an eye out, if you see Jim around then let me know. I really hope it isn't him causing a problem because I'll have to report him," Lalo said.

"Only after me and Shane rough him up. It's fucked up we had to clean up the Shit Shack if his ass was responsible."

"We still don't know he was, but keep your eyes peeled, " Lalo said.

They exited together out the back door as the orchestra began to pick up, and voices filled the grand hall. The gala had begun and now it was time for SCUM to waste a few hours before it was clean up time.

"Same stuff as we always do?" Jason asked.

"Yup, keep outta sight until this shindig ends. Make yourselves look busy or Peter will complain," Lalo instructed them. "I'll walk you to your car, Sunny. It's dark out here now and I don't want you gettin' lost," he said.

Rosa and Isabel separated from the group and made their way towards the pool house. In the back room reserved for yoga was a television. Lalo knew they were off to watch the news or the latest telenovela and gossip but he didn't stop them. They knew to stay out of sight until it was time to clean up after the gala. The whole crew would have to find their own hiding spots and hope Peter was too busy sticking his nose up all the richy-rich resident's asses instead of seeking them out.

The whole neighborhood was headed to the gala, most of them

driving their golf carts, but some drove their shining cars down to the reserved parking lot outside of the club. There was a small list of guests invited from outside of Serenity Canyon; they were the investors who came in from other states, business associates, and realtors looking to possibly expand the community to accommodate more cottages, big wigs only. No ordinary people were ever invited into the community or the club and it made the residents feel elite. Jose and Shane had already disappeared, knowing the routine. They both had their own hiding places, Lalo wasn't even sure where they went and he didn't care as long as no one complained about them.

"What's this even for?" Sunny asked.

Lalo, Jason and Carl were walking along with her toward the parking area.

"The gala is being held to raise money for a new inner city sports club they want to build in Phoenix," Lalo said.

"But mostly it's a chance for all the residents to get together and brag about all the nice things they have and to cry fake tears for those less fortunate than them," Jason added.

Sunny laughed, "Sounds like some people I've worked for in the past."

"Oh, good. Then you're used to working for a bunch of fake assholes." Carl felt his shirt pocket and looked at Jason.

Jason shook his head and fished his cigarettes out of his pocket, "You're gonna owe me big time."

"I thought I already earned these smokes when I saved your ass from Peter!"

"What happened?" Lalo asked.

"This little motherfucker was sneaking into the management office to take a leisurely piss in the fresh, air-conditioned men's room, and along comes Peter, but who came to the rescue?"

"Super Carl!" Lalo said.

"That's right! I took the heat while he escaped."

"You're a good man!" Sunny laughed.

They were walking towards the front gate when a set of headlights blinded them from the other side. The guard, Larry, stood at the driver's side window for a few moments and let the car in. The gate rattled as it rolled back, allowing the black car into the inner sanctum of Serenity Canyon.

"I was told the guests would all be here already, I wonder who that is?" Lalo said.

They had to step back to allow the car to pass them. It came to an immediate stop and two men climbed out. One was a hulking man in a black suit, the other was slighter of build and he took control of the situation.

"Good evening folks."

"Good evening," they mumbled in reply.

"I would like to speak with you all for a moment."

"I'm sorry, but I'm on my way home," Sunny said, she didn't know who the hell this guy was but she needed to be heading back into Sedona or her mom would definitely worry.

"No, I'm afraid not," the thin man pulled an I.D. from his pocket and showed it to them with a smug grin. His partner did the same and it was clear they were more than police officers.

"I'm sorry, who are you?" Lalo asked, squinting in the gathering darkness.

"Agents Boze," the thin man answered, taking two exaggerated steps closer to Lalo before nodding towards his partner, "and Jackson. FBI."

"Okay. How can we help you?"

"Jackson, have the guard follow us," Agent Boze said to his partner.

"You all need to come with us, answer some questions, and if everything shakes out okay, then the little lady will be allowed to go home."

"What is this about?" Carl asked.

"Leave the questions to us, like, for instance, where can we go to interview you all?"

"We can go to the management office," Lalo offered.

"Great, just a moment and then you can lead the way," Agent Boze said to the group of stunned janitors, watching Agent Jackson as he hurried towards the guard at the gate.

Larry didn't seem to like the idea of abandoning his post but when the badge was flashed in his face, he too obeyed.

Lalo felt his nerves twisting his guts as he showed the two FBI agents to the management office. There had to be a major problem if the men in black had shown up to Serenity Canyon.

Peter's torso was hardly anything more than bloodstained bones with a single lung. His right eyeball bulged in its socket in his savaged face. He was left with few strips of skin on the soles of his feet and his palms and his mop of bright red hair still clung to his skull like a toupee fused to his brain. Teddy felt his gut squirming and heard the old woman's preparing to back up her throat. The squirming Gods inside of them were preparing them to lay their eggs. They needed hosts, and they needed them right away. Mrs. Brandon hunkered down over Peter and unleashed a mouthful of bile and larvae into his face but Teddy knew he would be a feeble vessel, an impotent one. His brain could house a few pilots but his stomach and intestines were gone, leaving no place for more of their children to gestate. He pushed her back from Peter's corpse, refusing to let her waste the larvae on such a runt.

Beyond the opened back door, an orchestral hum drifted on the evening winds. It was calling to him. He stepped over to the front door and turned the knob, his waste-crusted hand was slick with Peter's blood. The night air smelled fresh, invigorating, it would be a good night to slaughter as many humans as he could. Behind him came Mrs. Brandon, her stomach gurgled loudly. She would need to be emptied completely as soon as possible. Two voices drew his attention and he ducked back around the door. Two young humans were walking down the sidewalk outside, his mind raced with thoughts of how they would make incredible incubators for his young. The squirming Gods would be pleased with him. He grabbed the old woman and threw her to the ground just outside the door. She screeched and fumbled to stand but Teddy hissed at her and she laid her head back down on the concrete.

"Mrs. Brandon! Are you okay?" a voice called.

Teddy felt a jolt of exhilaration. They would be his.

Andrea and Kim stood on the sidewalk, confusion and fear rippling through them.

"Oh my God. I think she's hurt!"

"Come on. Let's go help her."

The two college students had come home for a weekend at the club. Their mother, Claudia, was boasting how she had a huge party planned for after the gala which meant they would both get really drunk and have the possibility of meeting Mr. Denny's grandson, Eric, who was rumored to be the hottest young bachelor visiting Serenity Canyon. They wouldn't have missed it for anything. They downed a few margaritas with their mom and gossiped a bit about the neighbor lady, Mrs. Brandon, then decided they would walk down to their old friend Skylar's house to see if she would be at their mom's party. Skylar always managed to find the best coke in Sedona, so she had to be in attendance. They hadn't walked more than ten feet beyond their driveway when they watched the old woman fall. They were never really friends with Mrs. Brandon, they always thought she was boring, but their mother stayed on good terms with her, so they couldn't ignore her when she was obviously in distress.

Kim trotted towards Mrs. Brandon with Andrea in tow. She had her cellphone in her hand so she handed it to her younger sister.

"Here, get ready to call 9-1-1. Mrs. Brandon," Kim coughed and gagged.

Andrea glanced down at the old woman. She was lying face down, her feet were filthy, and there was yellow-brown puddle leaking through her thin pink pajamas.

"Oh. My. God. Don't touch her, Kim! She's disgusting!"

"What's wrong with her?"

"She must be wasted or something. Here, let me call mom instead of an ambulance."

Their eyes were on the gut-churning mess of Mrs. Brandon. They didn't notice Teddy lunging out the door until he already had them by the hair. They screamed as they were dragged into Mrs. Brandon's house but most of the neighborhood had already headed to the club, their cries for help were only heard by the two creatures who wanted nothing more than to destroy them.

Teddy threw Andrea against the wall, cutting her scream off with a sickening thud. Kim tried to run only to be caught by her long blond ponytail. Teddy wrapped it up around his fist and lifted her off the ground. She kicked and cried, her eyes darting between the door to freedom and the crumpled body of her sister. Teddy shoved her head first into the corner of Mrs. Brandon's stone fireplace, splitting her forehead open. A bloody river ran into her wide eyes and she fell unconscious. Teddy released her onto the white sofa, her blood seeping out in a crimson stain into the expensive material. He breathed deeply the coppery scent, knowing her life was ebbing away by the sound of her labored, shallow breaths.

He grabbed Andrea by one ankle and dragged her over to lay her beside her sister. He shrieked and Mrs. Brandon came to stand at his side. It was time for her to become a mother, to birth her children into the healthy bodies of the sisters lying on a sofa.

Teddy lifted Kim by her hair, her neck was crooked but he knew she still lived. Gripping the sides of her head, he ended her life in one vicious jerking motion. He handed her over to the old woman, who still wasn't strong enough to hold the dead girl. It was frustrating to Teddy to see his first child be so feeble. She clawed at Kim's mouth until it hung open, and then began regurgitating mouthfuls of vomit, eggs and larvae into it. She did it with a ravenous need to empty herself, he was pleased with her eagerness.

He grabbed the other girl and gripped her bottom jaw, as a test of his own strength and also to show off a little bit, he tore it from her face with a wet shredding sound. Leaning her back in his arms, as if she were an old lover, he vomited his children into her.

The children of the great Goddess were growing, mutating, maturing, bent on survival. Each time he procreated, they would come back much sooner than he did, especially those with healthy bodies to house the squirming Gods. The tendrils would work quickly within these worthy vessels, to claim them completely and then to urge them to do their bidding. He wondered how many more with such healthy corpses would be at the place with the music playing? Even if they were all as old as Mrs. Brandon, they would still be reborn in a matter of hours or possibly minutes by the way the children of the Goddess were growing in strength and numbers. It made him think again about himself and his own creation. Even when his pilots fought to keep him from remembering, there were moments when visions slipped through.

He was dressed in a white lab coat, and one of his brethren was before him. There were two other humans there with him, a woman fought to force the male of his kind away but he kept fighting to destroy them. In Teddy's new perspective he could tell the reanimated man had once been deathly ill, his body wouldn't be a worthy host for very long. The squirming Gods within him were quickly trying to abandon his diseased flesh and that's when it happened. It spat its young into Teddy's face, it was his father. He felt an odd sense rising in him, a lonesome hollow feeling. He could recall the woman, the murdering bitch, like the one who ended his human life, she forced his father into flames. If he had the chance, he would rip her head off and spew his progeny into her gaping throat.

Night had claimed the sky over Serenity Canyon. Teddy and Mrs. Brandon left the two women on the floor, their bodies already shifting and wriggling with ecstatic parasites. They headed towards the gala, making their way into the darkness of the golf course to keep from being seen. The orchestral music drifted on the winds, and with it the laughter of humans and the stench of cigars and rich foods. The sounds and scents turned his gut and made the squirming Gods scream, his brain was on fire with their demands and the need to appease them. Teddy could recall the days and nights he spent in the club surrounded by the very people he sought to hunt. Their dazzling white smiles, as fake as their friendships, their lilting laughter, now it sounded psychotic in his mind, he couldn't believe he ever actually belonged among them. His hatred for the living was magnified each time he recalled his past life, the fraud that was a happy existence. He almost hated himself for being like them, but then he would get glimpses of his true self as the man he once was. He secretly harbored nothing but loathing for such ignorant specimens, he was always a scientific man, an observer. Teddy knew his supreme intellect had carried over even after death, he had always been a predator and just as he hid himself in the darkness as he approached the gala, his past-self kept his true disdain hidden. They were dim and self-centered, focused only on their wealth. While Teddy, he thought of himself as the father of a new age, a Dr. Frankenstein birthing a new monster, one he became himself. While they focused on liposuction and the stock market, he was creating something grand and frightening, a weapon none of his neighbors could comprehend.

Teddy and Mrs. Brandon halted on the edge of the course, obscured by the darkness and bushes. The people were lively inside the clubhouse. They could see their silhouettes in the windows. The squirming Gods demanded he strike, and loose his children in them all in an endless cycle of procreation leading down from countless mutating and evolving lines. He felt the nervous twitching of the old woman beside him, she was receiving the same command. They would both obey.

While Teddy and the old woman silently rounded the building, back in Sylvia's living room the miracle of recreation was taking place. Claudia's daughters began to twitch, their healthy flesh had been quickly taken over, their brains hijacked and recoded, all in less than an hour. The children of the Goddess were becoming too proficient, hell bent on the mastery of the human race.

Andrea sat up, her jawless mouth constantly dripping saliva. Her gut bulging with a writhing creation and a brain riddled with commands quickly translating to each of her extremities, she was reborn. Her sister, Kim, hissed as she awoke. They wouldn't ever recall who they once were or being blood sisters, they weren't as advanced as Teddy, but they would know in their new existence they were kin. They would be told in their subconscious by the squirming Gods they are sisters and all humans were food and places to house their young. The commands filling their minds would be something they could not disobey, their limbs would move without their consent to fulfill the motives of the parasites taking root inside of them like marionettes constructed of flesh and bone.

They got up on trembling legs and advanced. Kim stumbled forward, towards the door and its filthy handle, their father had opened it, they would too. Beyond the door was a nervous cough and then a knocking. It caused them both to hiss, startled by the sudden intrusion. A voice called from the other side of the door, drawing them close to it once more.

"Mrs. Brandon? It's Pastor Crumm. I came to see if you needed an escort to the gala tonight."

Kim moved back to the door and placed her hand on it. Her arm felt numb, she fought to open the door, tapping and scratching on it at first until her pilots ordered her to turn the door knob. She obeyed and an old man stood politely on the door step, he had his head turned toward the house next door. They didn't remember but it was once their house where they lived with their mother.

"I hoped someone with class would agree to sit with me, and not these types next door," he was half-whispering, his face still turned to regard Claudia's house, "I'm sure that woman will have another one of her parties, tempting half the neighborhood with her cleavage."

What used to be Kim looked upon him with curiosity and hunger, like a hunter might watch a doe in the forest before sending an arrow through her side. He turned his head back, expecting to see the old widow but instead he was face to face with a bloodied young woman.

"What in God's name?"

Andrea lunged past Kim, her jawless mouth constantly agape. She caught him by his throat as he started to scream, strangling it down into his throat. She dragged him inside and Kim didn't even close the door. They fell on him, teeth and nails ripping into skin. His throat was torn open, a massive hole which bled him out in only minutes. Andrea couldn't chew his flesh so she simply ripped slices of his flesh from him and shoved it down into her throat, gagging it down into her perpetually hungry stomach. Kim had migrated down to his abdomen and though he wasn't a very large man he still had a ring of fat around his midsection which was soft and chewy. She delighted in it and when they had both had their fill, they sat on the floor, stomachs distended and rolling for a while, looking at his corpse as one might a slice of cake after they had too much dinner. The squirming Gods in their brains ordered them to empty their gurgling, churning stomachs into him. They reacted quickly, almost instinctually, to obey the orders filling their minds, their bodies moving involuntarily-as naturally as breathing now. Kim barfed onto the gaping hole she feasted on, unleashing a churning, squirming mass of larvae and eggs into him. Her sister in both life and death, Andrea felt the urge to empty herself from the other end so she stood over his face, one foot on each side of his head, and released young onto him. They felt lighter, more energetic. The night was calling, along with the distant sound of humans, they would hunt.

CHAPTER 4
THE FROZEN GODDESS AND HER CHILDREN

DR. ABILEEN COULDN'T SHAKE the nerves eating away at her stomach lining and making her hands shake violently. She was in a race with time, and she knew she was at a disadvantage. She went to Dr. Reinart's research room and gazed at the filing cabinets lining the right-hand wall. There were only three of them but she knew they contained thousands of sheets of paper. Teddy kept a lot of information on the computer but she had also noticed him filing many things away, and she wondered if it wasn't because he already had a suspicion the parasite would be fatal to those it was administered to. She also knew he kept a handwritten journal, one he refused to let her read even after banging him. There had to be more answers somewhere.

She pulled out a top drawer of a desk at her right and fished out a small set of keys, they would open the file cabinets, but she had no idea if she would actually find any answers within the mountains of files. She took a deep breath, gripped the first key, jammed it into the tiny key hole and turned it. When she pulled the cabinet open, her heart lurched. It was packed with files full of paperwork. She slammed the drawer shut and screamed.

In seconds the guards came rushing through the door with their guns pointed at her.

"It's not time for that, assholes. I just got discouraged. I'm looking for answers, and this just seems hopeless," She motioned to the filing cabinets.

They stood without speaking for a moment before one of them said, "What do you need us to do?"

"I'm looking for a black notebook. If we can't find it then we'll have to search through all of this shit, and I don't think we have enough time. I just hope those agents have the situation under control, because we're lookin' at some serious trouble if they don't."

"Open the cabinets, if the notebook is here, we'll find it."

"And if it's not, if Dr. Reinart took it with him?"

"Then we'll read every fucking file in these cabinets. We don't have the luxury of throwing in the towel, Dr. Abileen," The second guard said.

She nodded and began opening the cabinets, fighting the constant nausea rolling in her stomach. She was still unsure if it came from the horrific knowledge of what Dr. Reinart's team had unleashed, the parasites waiting in her body, or the fact she hadn't slept or eaten in more than a day.

Dr. Abileen and the guards dug through the filing cabinet drawers and left stacks and stacks of loose papers littering the floors and desktop. As they handed her papers, she examined them to see if they held any answers and each time her hopes were dowsed in gasoline and set afire. With every drawer they pulled open, she prayed to find the notebook, but all they found were mountains of white papers. They still briefly pored over every page numerous times, praying they would find even a small clue. Her eyes burned and her head spun, every word ran together, and her heart ached. She couldn't help but let angry tears slide down her face.

"This is fucking useless!" she said.

"Doctor, we can't give up."

"What the fuck are we going to do?" she asked, kicking a pile of paperwork.

She picked up a coffee mug and threw it against the wall. It bounced off and broke into two pieces and landed on the floor, splattering cold coffee against the walls and desk, leaving a stack of papers absolutely indecipherable.

"Fuck!"

"We have to keep going."

"I can feel it in my bones," she wept, "we're fucked."

"No, we're not."

"How can you say that, you know what we're up against! You saw Entz and Charlie, we're all gonna wind up like them. Fuckin' walking, puking shit bags!"

"Look," the guard grabbed her by the arm and dragged her to the desk and the coffee mug, "that vent its loose. The mug knocked it free, it shouldn't be that easy to open."

Dr. Abileen fell to her knees and picked the broken coffee mug up and beneath it the vent covering was pushed aside. Her pants were soaking up old coffee but she didn't care; the vent hadn't been used for heating and cooling, it was a secret stash. Someone had intentionally removed the screws holding the vent cover in place. She shoved it aside and plunged her hand into the small compartment beneath it. Her hand grazed over something cold and smooth and she cried again, this time with the blossoming swell of hope in her chest. She pulled the notebook free and turned to the guards who nodded.

"We found it! He didn't take it with him!"

"Get to work, Dr. Abileen. We'll bring you a cup of coffee and something to eat."

She ran to her desk, gripping the notebook tightly. She anxiously sat down and opened it, her eyes immediately recognized Teddy's handwriting. This time the scrolling letters weren't writing her a hidden message about how he desired to kiss her thighs, instead Dr. Abileen found herself reading a mixture of diary and research notes. She flipped to a passage dated three years earlier, and it took her to the frozen Arctic wastelands of Siberia, and a hole dug into the ice and permafrost.

12/03/2016

The winter here is unrelenting, never have I felt a cold that eats you to the bone. The specimen brought to the laboratory made the agony of enduring the incessant winds worth my torment. She was a beautiful woman in life once upon a time, her facial structure was delicate, and her dark hair was still relatively strong even after the ravages of death and the passage of time. After countless millennia, her hand woven burial cloth was still well intact. The permafrost in which she was buried had preserved her quite well and I could tell she had been burned. I almost hated to dissect her, but the imaging reports were inconclusive as to whether the fire killed her or something else entirely. She bore no broken bones, or evidence of trauma to her body other than her blackened skin, which pointed to the possibility of disease and that is my specialty. The others speculated she was a witch or a criminal of some sort to be set on fire, they questioned if it were a religious ritual, or an accident. All I could tell was she had been loved, or she would have never been caringly wrapped in her burial cloth. Opening her body revealed the true cause, her insides were riddled with an unknown parasite. Small white worms, nearly as delicate and thin as hair, had infiltrated her entirely, completely filled her every fiber, organ, and orifice. My colleagues' suspect she was burned in order to stop the spread of the worms. In my eyes it seemed logical but whoever lit her on fire didn't let her burn long enough to wipe out this worm, this Goddess of all parasites. I have extracted a sample of the parasites from her brain to study in order to determine what they are.

Dr. Abileen flipped the pages madly searching for any other information, entries about his personal life intertwined with his study of the parasites which seemed to take center stage in all of his work efforts. She felt a turning in her gut of nausea as he described how he had only been able to revive one of the worms, the others hadn't survived the frigid temperatures.

12/13/2016

I declined to join the team who travelled to Antarctica. They clearly don't understand the meaning of what I am trying to accomplish. The fools destroyed other specimens possibly holding her kin. The Goddess parasite is unlike any I have ever researched, more intelligent and resilient. She survived being frozen for more than thirty-thousand years. Her purpose is still a mystery to me but I intend to unlock it. Her children would not resuscitate, they were still just wisps, like white eyelashes, newly-born when the host died by fire and was buried. The Goddess squirms and as I watch her closely I can tell she is fighting to survive, to reproduce. I plan to introduce her to a living specimen.

Dr. Abileen flipped the pages again, watching his handwriting change from a steady, scrolling script to a frantic chicken scratch. She was reading his descent as it took place.

12/24/2016

I set her free in a lab rat. Already, she is thriving within it, baring her young within its twitching body. The rat seems none the wiser to the Goddess within it. Fatality of the host does not seem to be her goal at this point, a symbiotic existence is what her kind strives for at the moment, but there is only so much room to blossom within such a small animal. She will seek a larger host, no doubt.

01/19/2017

The rat has not died. It is lethargic and refuses to eat, yet it lives on. It seems impossible for such a prolific parasite to not end up killing the host, but the woman in the permafrost was filled with the children of the Goddess and yet she was ultimately killed by her own kind, by fire. The Goddess endured, like a Titan, destined to birth a multitude of Gods, she refused to die. There are moments when it's like I can hear the Goddess crying for a new home, a warm place to populate with a million squirming threads of herself. She tells me I am superior to the others, that I am the perfect vessel.

01/28/2017

The Rat has succumbed to the parasite and lies in a paralytic state. It has been this way for nine straight days and has not died. It is truly amazing and puts my mind on thinking about the possibilities. The Goddess, though, cannot be content with her home, her vehicle of flesh and bone. I can hear her day and night, whispering in my mind, imparting to me her true power. She has yet to reveal to me her plans but I feel I can use her in some way. She is the key to something great.

02/14/2017

I was contacted by the higher ups, they have plans for me and I believe I have finally found the destiny that the Goddess and I share. I have frozen the rat, and with it the Goddess and her children. They will undoubtedly survive the short trip. The Rat will not, he will be burned, but he will one day be written about in the annals of scientific history. We are heading back to the United States. I have written a proposal and I believe it will be accepted after I meet with a dear old friend of mine by the name of Charles. He has been very ill lately. I believe he is in need of meeting the Goddess and the Gods she can spawn.

"He put the Goddess in Charlie," Dr. Abileen whispered.

Dr. Abileen knew the results of the failed parasite experiment with Charlie, or Charles as he was written about so affectionately by Dr. Reinart, why had it never paralyzed any humans as Theodore hoped it would? Was it the Goddess parasite was mutating in order to survive in the new world it was awoken in? Dr. Abileen guessed it was, and rapidly, which frightened her beyond belief. The "Gods" she had spawned were adapting rapidly to survive. She couldn't believe Teddy hadn't known this could happen. She could only guess his own egotistical complexes of becoming a creator and a destroyer had blinded him to the truth, and with it doomed the Earth.

"You, frozen bitch. I must have burned her along with Charlie, but her offspring they live on, and they'll continue to mutate."

The guards entered with a cup of coffee and two donuts.

"Did you find any answers?" one of them asked.

"No. Unfortunately, I've found nothing of use, really. Nothing about a cure, or a way to stop this other than burning a host to ashes."

"What do we do now?"

"If I can't find a way to destroy the parasites, then anyone in contact with it must be brought here for study, or killed on sight if they are already too powerful and violent," she said, feeling her mouth water with nausea at the smell of the coffee.

"Parasites did all of this? Like worms?"

"Yes, a parasite that hasn't been active on Earth in more than thirty-thousand years."

"Worms that can turn people into zombies?"

"Yes," she said, a cold feeling filling her up inside, squirming just to remind her how close she was.

"Should we contact Agent Boze?"

"Yes, immediately. Tell him to quarantine any and all in contact with Dr. Reinart. He lives in a gated community so hopefully they keep it contained within those walls. I don't want the entire city exposed to this. I will need a few hours, maybe more, to see if any treatment we have will get rid of them. Give the signal to the big men in big offices, the Army will need to lend a hand."

"Do you think you'll be successful?"

"This bitch of a parasite hasn't been tested by our modern medicine. That alone gives me hope."

Dr. Abileen retreated to the laboratory and rolled up her sleeve. She needed to see how rampant the parasites had gotten inside of her own body since she burned the last two subjects she could have gotten samples from. She felt foolish for believing in Teddy when he performed one blood test only hours after being exposed and told them all they weren't carrying the parasite. She really knew better, but at the time she wanted to believe him so badly.

"You got hypnotized by his dick, dick-notized, girl. You fell for every lie he ever told you," she berated herself as she drew a sample of blood.

"Now you're fucked in more ways than one."

Once it was done, she grabbed a plastic cup and hoped she could provide a decent stool sample after having nothing to eat for more than twenty-four hours. She felt completely empty but for the churning of acid in her stomach. She didn't even touch the donuts offered to her by the guards. She went to the staff restroom and gazed at herself in the mirror. The whites of her eyes looked yellow, they were also bloodshot from not sleeping. She was still young, she didn't want to die yet. She imagined herself a ragged, unkempt, zombie, shitting itself and barfing everywhere to spread her young, tiny white Gods looking to inhabit other hosts. She couldn't help but think about why couldn't she have at least cut her hair and had it colored before her demise so she didn't look quite so haggard when she went about spraying her victims with acidic vomit and crapping down the legs of her trousers.

"Okay, let's do this," Dr. Abileen said to her reflection, attempting to put on a brave face and failing. Her eyes grew misty and she choked down a lump in her throat. She leaned forward and pressed her forehead against the cold mirror, it felt nice. She took a deep breath and felt a calmness edging in on her sickening nervousness. She turned and walked into a cramped bathroom stall, pulled down her pants and underwear and sat on the frigid toilet seat.

Once she was finished she washed her hands and hurriedly carried the sample back to the lab. The guards luckily didn't walk in while she was holding a sample of her own feces, she wasn't sure if she could have handled looking them in the eyes while she pitifully inspected it. Even after everything they had been through, she was still trying to maintain an ounce of her humility.

Her mind kept returning to the journal entries. When Teddy returned to the United States was when they first met. He was a tall, handsome man, completely unlike any of the clichéd stereotypes spread about scientists. He often spoke to her of his disdain for his neighbors in the community of Serenity Canyon, how his wife forced him to buy the house there. They were shallow, greedy people, completely unaware as to what life and death were actually about. She felt sorry for him being trapped amongst so many fake people, she became his companion. He complimented her on not only her looks, but her intelligence, and she always got the sense his wife was lacking in that department. He wooed her with not only flowers but books and long conversations. For a moment she missed those early days of their secret relationship. He always made it very clear when they worked together she would still be his subordinate, he wouldn't play favorites with her just because they spent passionate nights together, but she wouldn't have it any other way either. Dr. Abileen wasn't looking to further her career by sleeping with Teddy, she truly cared for him. The daydream of their happy times died quickly as she remembered his emails, and how he would have happily sacrificed her to the squirming Gods he unearthed from the permafrost frozen body.

She readied some slides and held her breath as she looked through the microscope at each of them. The blood smear test showed signs of the parasite and her feces were laced with tiny eggs. The parasite was hiding inside of her, probably in her gut by the way it churned with nausea and the eggs came out in her stool. Since they were now prevalent in her blood it only meant they were multiplying and biding their time. It brought tears to her eyes in a sudden burst of emotion, of anger and sadness, of feeling used, of knowing she was damned.

She wiped them away, telling herself she already knew she would find them inside of her. She had been exposed, just as Entz had, by Charlie, and if her hypothesis was true then she wouldn't become a ravenous zombie bitch unless she died. If Teddy was still alive, he may be able to be saved, just as she may be. She kept repeating to herself the parasite, even though Teddy called it a Goddess who spawned Gods, was nothing more than a pest who required a host to remain alive. It hadn't waged war with modern medicine, and she would hit it with everything available to her. Dr. Abileen went to the door and called the guards. She required a cocktail of drugs, luckily her job gave her access to anything she could ever want.

The guards hurried in, this time they rested their hands on their holstered weapons and it touched her in a strange way. They had been through some horrible things in a relatively short time. They didn't want to kill her unless it was absolutely necessary, it made her feel uplifted.

"I am either going to cure myself or kill myself. In the case of the latter, please burn me until I'm ashes. Call the higher-ups. Agents Boze and Jackson will more than likely need assistance from them to keep this contained. They may be tasked with making an entire gated community disappear."

The guards nodded, looked to each other and then she added, "It's been a pleasure, boys."

"Good luck, Doctor," one of them said.

"I know you can do this," the other added.

"What are your names?" she asked.

"Donald Freely, ma'am," one guard said, his face looking like an overgrown child. It was the first face to greet her at the Phoenix laboratory.

"My name is Trent Carver, my friends call me T," the second guard answered. He was shorter and had a few years on Donald.

"Thank you. You can both call me Sarah."

"It was a pleasure, Sarah," Donald responded while T simply smiled sadly.

She nodded and ushered them from the laboratory before making her way to the pharmacy room on the other side of the incinerator room. She wondered if the pills she was about to load her body up on would have saved Charlie or Dr. Entz but she reminded herself they were both already dead before they even changed into raging zombies, perhaps if they had been administered before the two men died then they never would have come back after dying. The thoughts of it made her hate Teddy even more, both men were transformed into inhuman creatures devoid of life, mercy, or dignity, all for Teddy's selfish purposes.

She collected what she needed, finding it telling that their pharmacy was stocked with a few parasite destroying drugs.

"He knew all along this thing wanted to kill us all. Somewhere in the back of his mind his conscience was still trying to awaken him to the truth. The Goddess hadn't blinded him completely but still he walked right into her trap."

She carried them back to the lab and found herself a seat. The first one she planned to administer was intravenous because she wanted to start killing those insidious worms hiding in her body as quickly as she could. She didn't have the time or patience to swallow a pill and wait a few days to see if it did its job. The world needed her to find a solution, at least Serenity Canyon did, and immediately.

The gala was as swanky as always. The small orchestra played while the residents of Serenity Canyon rubbed elbows and boasted about business deals. The women were draped in their finest jewelry and gowns while the men wore expensive suits and smelled of money. At least, that's how Sandy would describe it. She stood at the service door, watching through a small window as the rich folks danced and dined.

"They better not complain this time," she said and the only answer she got was the steady clanking of pots and pans.

Her crew was at work cleaning up after their marathon of cooking and preparing the finger foods and an exquisite banquet. Dinner and appetizers had been served and now all that was left was to let them all get drunk on expensive booze and then she'd serve them fruit and sherbet as a dessert. They'd love it and claim she was some master chef, when it was mostly frozen garbage the catering company purchased. The poor fools were so rich they never tasted a microwavable dinner or dollar store ice cream rip off, they believed everything served to them was the finest quality. She had gotten one complaint previously but it was four years prior, she still held a grudge over it, and sometimes spit in their food when she was in a sour mood. She retreated to the sink and washed her hands out of habit, they were already clean but she felt the need to get the stink of goose liver pâté off her skin before she went outside to catch a quick smoke.

"Sandy, when is dessert gonna need prepped?"

"Give these assholes an hour or so. They need to get drunk before they demand the sweet stuff, that's how it always is with these people. They don't eat it anyway, just nibble on it and leave it for us and Lalo's crew to clean up."

Sandy strode to the back kitchen door and pushed it open. She was met by the soft breeze and night sky. She hated Sedona most of the time, but on nights like this, she was reminded of why she moved there and took the job as a head kitchen manager for some rising star of the catering business. She pulled out a menthol cigarette as she walked over to the dumpster and lit it, it was smooth and cool as it traveled down into her lungs. She had heard people who smoked menthols get crystalized lungs but she was never sure if it was true, she figured if it was then at least she'd be sparkling on the inside when the coroner cut her open after she was gone. She took another long drag and exhaled a cloud of smoke into the air, it danced against the blackness of the sky above her and for a moment she almost felt content. Sedona was an expensive place to live, her wages were far more than what she made in Phoenix, but she was barely making it up in the magical red rock country. She only came back because of her husband. They had both grown up in the area, around Sedona, Page and Cornville, they wanted to retire there and be buried there.

Her cellphone vibrated in her pocket but she ignored it, thinking it was probably Jim again. The lazy bastard had lost his job and now her paycheck would have to be stretched to pay all the bills again. She didn't know why she married him. She figured it was because he was ruggedly handsome when he was young and a great lay, but as he aged and the liquor stole parts of his personality and the life from his eyes. She just wished he would fuck off forever, especially after getting fired for being drunk and lewd behavior on the job. He was damn lucky they didn't call the police and charge him or he would have been a registered sex offender. Jim always blamed his behavior on some unspoken trauma he experienced being in the military, she never prodded him about it and she did feel terrible he had been scarred but she still wished he would just get his self in line. She was thankful Lalo didn't mention Jim to her, it would have been far too embarrassing for her. She had been the one to land him the job in Serenity Canyon and he completely fucked it all up with his drinking and foolishness, though she never believed he was actually jerking off. She knew in her heart the old booze hound had probably just whipped out his dick to piss away the cheap vodka he kept in a flask in his pocket and some uppity rich bitch caught a glimpse of the shriveled worm in his dirty hands and cried wolf. She sighed, the weight of the world seemed a thousand times greater when she thought about Jim.

She had the cigarette hanging from her lips as her mind wandered deep in thought. She didn't even notice the shadow creeping up along the side of the building. She couldn't smell the foul odor of dried feces and puke over the stench of the juices leaking out from beneath the rusty green dumpster; they trailed out in a sticky river everyone avoided when they dumped the trash. It wasn't until she heard a gurgling belch and felt the spray of something warm and acidic against the side of her face that she turned.

She frantically wiped the burning fluids from her cheek and eye, her one clean eye taking in the sight of two things staring at her. A hulking beast which was once a man and a short, shriveled old woman dressed in soiled pajamas with a bulging gut and vomit hanging from her gaping mouth, their eyes fixed on her like hungry predators. Sandy let out a startled scream and scrambled sideways in an attempt to get around the creatures. They stepped between her and the back kitchen door, her only safety. The monsters looked slightly familiar to Sandy, they were people she had seen before at the galas, but they were obviously no longer human. The old woman's stomach rumbled loudly and she opened her mouth a wave of vomit flew from her mouth and hit Sandy directly in the face. She fell backwards as the smell of rot and stomach acid invaded her nose. She could taste the rancid throw up on her tongue and it made her gag. She couldn't breathe. She felt her heart ignite with a burning so intense she lay on her back and gripped her chest, breathlessly begging for mercy. The hulking filth-crusted monster placed his foot on her stomach but she only fought weakly.

He slid his foot up to rest on her chest, through her ribcage he could feel her struggling heart lurching. He leaned over and regurgitated a mouthful of viscous yellow vomit into her face. She didn't even have the strength to block it from falling into her tired eyes.

Sandy's heart had been weak for a decade but she never quit smoking as her doctor advised. She never stopped dropping by Greasey's and eating a double cheeseburgers on Friday nights, or drinking some cheap booze when the feeling struck her, and it did a few times a week. The situation with Jim being jobless sent her into a dizzy spiral of anxiety, from the moment she opened her eyes in the morning until her head hit her pillow at night all she did was worry. Jim didn't make it any better. He was belligerent every second of every day, especially since he was no longer employed on the SCUM crew. Her heart was destined to fail that night, even if Teddy and Mrs. Brandon hadn't come upon her standing by the dumpster in the dark, she was on her last leg. She knew it, and as their shadows hovered over her, and their vomit bathed her, she was already quickly slipping out of this world and into the next. Her days of worrying about old Jim Beam were over, and though it was frightening, a peace slipped over her as the squirming God children found their way into her.

Teddy watched her body twitch. The children of the Gods within him were changing rapidly, they would awaken her soon, just as the two young women he left incubating his young on the floor of Mrs. Brandon's cottage. The old woman was creeping away from him, towards a door. She hesitated before it, listening to the voices beyond it. He joined her and the clanging of pots and pans spawned an image in his mind of a kitchen. He readied himself, calculating if just he and the old woman could take out the handful of workers on the other side of the door. The squirming Gods assured him they could, and that the mother worm, the Goddess he pried from a frozen brain, would demand he honored her. Teddy felt his hatred of the living fill him with rage. He grabbed the door handle and ripped the steel door from its hinges.

The humans inside were huddled in a panic, as if they thought the door had been blown up. Their eyes widened when they realized it was no explosive or gun which decimated the door but a monster covered in dried feces. He ran inside, the old woman came in directly after him, and the humans scattered like rats.

The kitchen was a mostly open floor plan, with three rows of stainless steel prep tables in its center and near the front ran a line of ovens and fryers. Along its walls were a few sinks, the door to a freezer, a closed custodial closet, and an alcove equipped with a dishwasher and sanitization sink. On the farthest end from the backdoor was a set of double doors leading to the dining area for carrying out large dishes and a small window for plates to be passed out to servers one at a time on ordinary dining nights. This was no ordinary dining night, the gala had the cooks and servers frantically working and cleaning up in an almost robotic fashion-until the door blew in and everyone inside could do nothing but run for their lives.

Mrs. Brandon was faster than he had anticipated and it pleased him, her body wasn't as useless as he first thought. She scurried over and leaped onto the back of a woman who was making a run for the door leading to the dining area. They fell to the tile floor, the prey screeching in terror. Mrs. Brandon silenced her with a fist to her teeth. Blood rocketed out and tears ran from her eyes, she swatted wildly at the old woman but it was no use. She soon got a mouthful of vomit as Mrs. Brandon wretched down into her bleeding face.

Teddy caught two men by the throats as they attempted to hide beneath the prep tables, one in each hand. He lifted them from the ground and watched their feet kicking for a moment before slamming their heads together. When they collided, Teddy could feel the fracturing of skulls. Their blood came quickly boiling out from their wounds and their feet stopped kicking. He held them there, suspended above the ground, and squeezed their throats in his hands. Watching their faces growing violet, and knowing they prayed silently to their weak human God for a single breath, it made him feel invincible. He had always been a large man, and powerful, but the rage the squirming Gods pumped through him made him nearly unstoppable. The children of the Frozen Goddess urged him to feed and to spew his children into fresh corpses. Teddy slammed their heads together over and over until their heads were misshapen and then dropped them at his feet and squatted over them. He unleashed a hot spray of fetid fluids onto them as they died, filling their gaping, bleeding mouths and nostrils with his young.

After a commotion, Mrs. Brandon found the hiding spot of the other kitchen workers next to the dishwasher and sink. Scurrying like cockroaches from the tiny alcove, they screamed and tried their hardest to fight back with dirtied pots and pans. One of them landing a solid blow to the side of Mrs. Brandon's head but when the old woman in stained pajamas still grabbed them by the neck, they knew there was no hope for them.

A woman attempted to flee for the freezer door. Behind her she could hear Teddy's heavy foot falls and feel them pounding against the tile floor. In desperation, she grabbed a kitchen knife on the prep table to try to stab him, slashing a line across his forearm. But even leaving gashes in his skin did nothing to thwart him. She spun to run away but he grabbed her by the bun in the back of her hair. Yelping a short, defeated cry, she clawed at the massive hand tangled in her hair.

He gripped her shoulder with his free hand and ripped her scalp from her head, she dropped the blade. Blood poured down her back from the destruction of her raw scalp. He held the dripping remnants of her hair out before her eyes. She wept and screamed, helpless to stop the brutality being afflicted upon her. Her terrified screams echoed in the kitchen but were drowned out by the incessant orchestral music coming from the gala.

Mrs. Brandon was blocking the door to the dining hall, refusing to let her prey escape. Teddy herded the remainder of them towards the old woman and trapped them. They wept for fear of their impending violent death at the hands of Teddy who was monstrous and covered in excrement and an old Mrs. Brandon who was still dressed in filthy pink silk pajamas.

"Mrs. Brandon?" a woman asked, trying to appeal to the old woman's human side.

She had no idea Teddy was the only supreme vessel. He was the only one who had any remainder of humanity. The others would only be mindless killers, completely detached to what they once were. Mrs. Brandon eyed the woman who continued to attempt to reason with her, though she could see her own reflection in the woman's wide, terrified eyes, she didn't know herself, felt to remorse for what she was about to do. The demands made by the squirming Gods within her were all she knew, all she obeyed, all that mattered anymore.

"Mrs. Brandon. Please!"

The old woman shrieked and cut off her weeping pleas with a snarling growl. The woman fell silent and stared at Mrs. Brandon in disgusted terror. The old woman lunged forward, knocking her prey backwards onto the floor. The woman's head bounced off the greasy tile, leaving her stunned and confused. Blood poured out of the back of her head, but she could only weakly lift her hands and try to fend off the monster attacking her, leaving her wound to weep out onto the floor. Mrs. Brandon over powered her and sat on her chest. The dampness of her soiled pajamas soaked into the crisp white linen shirt the kitchen worker wore. The woman had her hands up, they pushed against the old woman's chest but Mrs. Brandon couldn't be forced away. Boney hands found the struggling woman's throat, and with unexpected strength from such frail arms and hands, a squeezing like a vice tightened until her airway was closed shut. Her eyes felt like they were bulging, as if they'd pop out of her skull, her vision held the horrifying image of the old woman drooling and shrieking in her face until everything went black. She was released but as she feebly tried to gasp for air, a hot liquid filled her mouth and throat, choking the rest of her life out of her.

Mrs. Brandon climbed off the dead woman. Her stomach rolled with larvae and eggs, all awash in ever-churning stomach acid, she felt hungry again. The scent of rich human food didn't appeal to her but the smell of perfumed flesh and cologne tainted meat made her mouth salivate. She lurched towards the service door and peered into the ballroom through the small window. Men and women danced to the irritating whine of violins, their bodies glistening in chandelier light. Mrs. Brandon had always been one of the oldest in the community, but she couldn't recall that. She was focused solely on the prey before her, her rancid breath fogging up the windowpane. Teddy came to stand beside her. He pushed her away so he could get a look at the room full of fresh meat. His body tensed, she could feel the rage building in him with every second he stared through the window, and then he spoke. His voice was a gurgling growl.

"Stephiiiiiii."

Mrs. Brandon scrambled back, confused by his human speech. She hissed at him and swiped at his arm, her fingernails raking over his filthy skin, and instantly regretted it. Teddy spun, his eyes narrowed with intense anger. His fist caught her in the nose and her head snapped back on her already damaged spinal cord. She fell and fumbled to get back to her feet.

"Stephiiiii!" he raged and kicked the old woman, his child.

Her ribcage caved-in on the right side beneath the power of the impact. Mrs. Brandon crawled across the floor, fearing he would kick her again. She could feel the squirming threads inside of her attempting to correct the damage Teddy inflicted. She sat in the corner of the kitchen beside the sink and held her side. Teddy advanced on her and she understood to never challenge him again, he was far superior to her. The Gods inside of her, rebuilding her, told her so. She averted her eyes and lowered her head, knowing if she looked him in the eyes he would rip her body to pieces.

"Stephiiiii," he repeated and left his broken child to mend itself.

He pushed the door open, led by rage and the whispering commands of the Gods within him.

Lalo led the agents into the management office and pointed to a board room close to Peter's office, the same they used for interviews. The light was still on and he wondered if the property manager had stayed late to play ass-kisser again.

"We can talk in here."

"Thank you. All of you take a seat, we have a few questions but the first one is very important," Agent Boze said.

The group sat in the chairs around the table and waited, wondering why the FBI had come all the way to Serenity Canyon.

"Do you know Theodore Reinart? Dr. Reinart? Teddy?"

"Well, yeah, he lives in the community," Carl said.

"Have any of you seen him recently?"

They all shook their heads.

"We were just over by his house today. We saw his wife, but not him," Jason said.

"What's this about?" Lalo asked.

"It's very important we find Dr. Reinart, so important that no one can leave until we locate him," Agent Boze said.

"Is he like a serial killer or something? You're kinda freaking me out," Jason said.

"Let's just say, it's a matter of public safety," Agent Jackson said, looking to his partner.

"Is this your whole crew?" Agent Jackson asked.

"No, we have a few more workers out organizing supply closets," Lalo lied.

The thin agent's phone rang and he answered it. He stepped outside to speak to whoever had called him, it was a conversation of less than a minute before he returned. The questioning paused while he was away, the SCUM crew stared at each other in confusion.

"I don't give a shit what they're doing, call them in here. Now," Agent Boze said.

Lalo pulled his cellphone from his pocket and began dialing Isabel's phone number. He turned to Carl, "Call Shane." He pointed to Jason, "Call Jose."

They went to work trying to get in touch with their coworkers, but from beyond the exit door outside of the interview room the faint sound of screaming caused the agents to run. They dropped their phones and looked to Lalo.

"What the fuck is going on?" Jason asked.

"I have no idea, but I'm not leaving," Sunny said.

"Do you guys think Old Teddy is a terrorist or psycho killer? Why would these FBI boys be here looking for him?" Carl asked.

"I don't know," Lalo said.

He lifted his phone and began dialing Isabel's phone but Carl's phone rang loudly and startled them all.

"Jesus Christ!" Jason said, gripping his chest.

Carl hurriedly swiped and the screen of his phone, "It's Jose!"

"Hello!" Carl spoke into the phone.

Lalo and Sunny stared at Carl as his mouth fell open and his eyes widened at the sound of Jose screaming into the phone.

"What the hell are you sayin'?" Carl barked.

The phone went blank, Carl pulled it away from his face and tapped the screen.

"It says I have no service."

"What did Jose say?" Lalo asked.

"I have no idea, he sounded upset about something then the phone cut off."

Shane hit the roach he left hidden in a faraway closet, it burned his throat and made him cough but it wasn't strong enough to leave him whacky. He sprayed the closet with air freshener, and looked to Jose. He held the roach out but Jose waved his hand and declined the hit. Shane left Jose sitting in the janitorial closet. He had his phone against the side of his head and talking in a low voice. Shane knew it had to be Jose's girlfriend, he always acted extra hard when he spoke to her, like he had to be a super macho guy at all times. Shane didn't feel like sitting around and listening to their conversation so he crept out into the night. He thought maybe Sandy would have some more leftovers he could scavenge. He headed back towards the kitchen, feeling his stomach rumbling hungrily. The weed didn't hit him really at all, just made him slightly hungry. The haunting sound of orchestral music floated out to him as he walked in the darkness, it would have been creepy if he didn't know the source of it. Instead, it made him curse under his breath.

"Rich fucks! Always treatin' us like freaks, like we're the scum of the Earth."

He hunched over and mimicked walking like Igor or the hunchback of Notre Dame, "Yes, masters. Yes, rich fuckers, let me clean your poo poo!" he said in a garbled voice.

It made him cackle wildly.

"Maybe this weed *is* takin' effect."

He took a sidewalk leading to the back kitchen door. The dumpster was in sight, the stench of it drifted on the breeze to his nostrils.

"Fuckin' gross."

He halted for a moment beneath a lamppost when his cellphone rang. He pulled it out of his pocket and glanced at the screen, Carl was calling him.

"This shit ain't over yet, we still have a few hours until it's time to clean."

He let the call go to voicemail, thinking he'd get another handful of finger foods before calling Carl back. He hurried to the dumpster and walked around it and froze. The music had died, he wasn't exactly sure when, but the orchestra had fallen silent. It made him worry the gala was over and it would be time to get to work. When he heard the screaming, he knew there was something terribly wrong. Shane rushed forward but his feet got caught on something in the dark. He fell to the black top and rolled into a pool of dumpster juice.

"What the fuck?"

He got to his knees, nursing a bleeding elbow and attempting to wipe the stinky dumpster fluids off his shirt. The screaming inside the gala continued and he wondered if it was the reason Carl was calling him. He didn't see or smell fire, he didn't hear gunshots, he had no idea what was happening, he didn't know whether he should run for his life or offer to help in some way. He looked back at what caught his foot and gasped. Sandy was there on her back, covered in vomit. She looked dead.

"Oh my fuckin' God!"

Shane yanked his phone out of his pocket. His hands shook as he attempted to call Carl. His phone screen was cracked in his fall and the phone was basically useless. Shane got to his feet and turned his back on the screaming, they didn't pay him enough to play hero. He went to run back the way he came but something caught his foot again and this time he fell harder than the first time. He belly flopped onto the hard blacktop behind the kitchen. His jaw snapped shut, sending a wave of pain up his cheeks. His teeth felt like they were cracked and he tasted blood in his mouth. Rising warmth lit his bottom lip on fire, it was followed by a stinging discomfort, and he knew he had busted his lip open. He didn't have the luxury of nursing his wounds; he was terrified about what unknown tragedy was taking place within the clubhouse. Shane pushed himself up and was trying to get from his knees to his feet when he heard a wheezing. He remembered the old woman he tripped over, he thought she was dead, but she was not, she couldn't be making noises like that.

"Sandy?"

He stood and spun around, thinking he could at least help the kitchen manager. She had sat up, her hair was disheveled now and he hated to admit he didn't want to touch her because she was covered in vomit.

"Are you okay?" he asked.

She didn't answer, she just kept wheezing. It gave Shane an uneasy feeling, the hair on his arms rose.

"Sandy, are you okay?"

Shane stepped toward her. His mouth and elbows dripped warm blood. He came close to Sandy and leaned over her, fearing she was having a stroke and couldn't respond to him.

"Hey, Sandy."

He waved a hand in front of her face. She sniffed and seemed to snap out of a trance. Her hand shot out and grabbed him by the wrist. She yanked his arm downward and dug her nails into the open wound on his elbow.

"What the fuck?"

He fell forward onto Sandy who rolled over, still gripping his arm. She wrapped her legs around it, and bit into the skin at his wrist. Shane screamed and punched her with his free hand. He had no idea where the sudden violence came from, why was she attacking him, and he no longer cared. He just wanted to free himself and he would do anything to break free from her. Her teeth were buried deep into his flesh; she jerked her head to the side and pulled away a mouthful. Shane was frantically kicking and punching at any part of her body he could hit. She was unmoved by his attempts to get her to release him. He panicked and brought his free hand around the side of her face, his fingers finding her eyes. He plunged his fingers into them in a quick jab and she finally crawled off of him. Shane clamored to his feet but Sandy was already on hers. She backed up a few steps and hunkered down, ready to pounce on him again.

"Stay back, bitch! I don't know what the fuck is wrong with you but stay away from me," Shane warned her, backing away.

With each step he took backwards she advanced one step forward. She didn't intend to leave him alone. Her face was red with rage and his blood, her right eye was already swelling shut from him jabbing his fingers in it. It bulged in its socket and white thread-like worms squirmed over it. It was clear Sandy was no longer Sandy. Shane backed up until he felt the cold rusty dumpster looming at his back.

Shane stepped to the side and Sandy made her move. She came for him, swinging her arms wildly, her fingers curled, ready to claw him with her nails. He lifted his arm to block her attack and was startled by her strength, and the way she didn't relent. He jabbed her in the nose with the butt of his hand, breaking it with the force of his blow. Blood spurted down her face and she halted. For a moment he thought she would awaken from whatever psychotic fit she was in, but she just stood there bleeding. Her stomach rumbled loudly, like a slow moaning from her guts. He was shocked by the entire experience. She opened her mouth and projectile vomited right at him. Shane brought his hand up, blocking his face, but the spatter of the acidic spray coated his shirt and speckled his face and mouth. He nearly puked too but he was concentrating on finding an escape.

"You fuckin' bitch!" he screamed and scrambled around the side of the dumpster and down the sidewalk.

Shane ran for it. He had a physical job, but he wasn't the type of guy who ran or jogged for pleasure or exercise. He ran as a crow flies through the darkness, towards the custodial closet he left Jose sitting in. Behind him, he could hear Sandy chasing him. Her winded, cigarette damaged lungs caused her to wheeze like an asthmatic yet she didn't slow down. Shane worried he wouldn't make it and she would catch him before he reached the door to his favorite hiding spot, but suddenly Sandy stopped chasing him and turned her wide, unblinking eyes back towards the clubhouse. Shane didn't stop to see what had drawn her attention; he was keeping his eyes on his only salvation.

To his right in the darkness, two shadows lumbered, both figures were shrieking. They were a good distance away but Shane recognized them in a glance as they passed under a street light. They were two college-age girls from the neighborhood, Claudia's daughters, but he also realized they were both wide-eyed, bloody, and looking bat shit insane, just like Sandy. Their stomachs were bloated and distended beneath their tight t-shirts. They spotted him and started running toward him.

"Oh fuck!"

He pushed himself to run faster and reached the door to the janitorial closet. He pounded on it like a madman. He hoped Jose would open the door because his hands were shaking so violently he didn't think he could fit a key into the lock. The door flew open, revealing Jose's frustrated face. Shane was so relieved he almost hugged his coworker but instead he yelled, "Let me the fuck in!"

In the small room off the side of the pool, the two women made their selves comfortable. Rosa had her feet up and her shoes off. Isabel was busy trying to get a good signal on the television hanging on the wall. They couldn't miss the final episode of Mujeres Fatal, it was finally going to be revealed if Aurelio was the father of Anastsia's son or he was fathered by the dastardly Pepe Cazares. Isabel glanced at her wrist watch and cursed under her breath, the show was going to start and still she couldn't get the static lines out of the picture.

"Puta madre."

Rosa had her phone sitting on a table with the speakerphone on while she chatted with her husband; she trimmed her fingernails while he told her about his day.

"Una pinche ruca no me pagó."

"¿Qué? ¿Por qué?"

"Pinche ruca coda."

"Dile que chinge su madre," Isabel said over her shoulder, still fidgeting with the antenna on the TV.

The phone cut out and the call was dropped. Rosa dropped her fingernail trimmers on the table. She picked up her phone and tapped the screen in frustration.

"¡Ay, pedazo de mierda!"

It wasn't unusual to lose cell reception in Serenity Canyon, especially in some of the out of the way places. Rosa's husband didn't try calling back; he couldn't count how many times their calls had suddenly cut off. Rosa slipped her phone into her shirt pocket and went back to grooming her nails and turned her attention to Isabel and the problem with the TV.

"Apurate, Isa."

"La pinche tele no funciona," Isa said.

Through the waving static Aurelio could be seen, shirtless and lounging on a bed. His eyes were staring out a grand window to the night sky.

"Ay, miralo."

The more Isa moved the antenna, the worse the reception became, Rosa booed.

The sound of a closing door sent Rosa scrambling to dust her nail clippings off the table and pull her shoes back on.

"¿Quien es?"

Isabel put her finger to her lips and shushed her coworker. She turned off the TV and motioned for Rosa to stand up. Together, they snuck into the empty pool complex. It was dark but for the wavering aqua colored lighting coming from the pool. The sounds of the pool pumps hummed and a gentle sloshing of the water occasionally echoed in the empty room but there were no other sounds. The two remained absolutely quiet as they crept around the edge of the pool, trying to make it to the side door to escape before they were caught slacking on the job.

A shadow filled the doorway, blocking their escape. Rosa and Isabel flattened against the wall, looking for another way out before getting spotted. Isabel pointed to the locker rooms and Rosa nodded, they quickly made their way in the direction of the wide entrance. They went to the right and found themselves in the ladies locker area.

From the pool room came a strange, high-pitched screech, drawn out, and almost animalistic as it reverberated off the walls and across the water lapping lazily against the tile steps of the shallow end of the pool. They hurried to the far end of the locker room, gripped by uncertainty. Rosa looked terrified but Isabel was starting to wonder if it wasn't Shane and Jose coming to play a joke on them. They had hours to go before the gala was over and it wouldn't be the first time the two jokesters came to bother the two women while they tried to unwind and watch some ridiculous drama on TV.

"Pinche Jose?" she whispered and walked back toward the locker room entrance.

"No, no, no te vayas," Rosa whispered, still worrying it could be Peter. Her husband had already been fired and she couldn't afford to be sent home jobless.

Isabel held her finger to her lips and smiled. She refused to let Jose and Shane make her look like an idiot, she would scare them instead.

She grabbed a dirty towel out of a laundry bin and stood by the entrance. She peaked out enough to see the pool was calm and its lights were wavering on the walls. The shadow was nowhere to be seen, all was silent but for the usual pool noises. She ducked back and remained still and quiet, knowing sooner or later Shane and Jose would make themselves known. She glanced up at Rosa across the room. She was seated on the bench lining the wall beneath the lockers. She still had a fearful look in her eyes but Isabel rolled her eyes. Peter wouldn't have let his presence be known, he would have crept up on them like a redheaded cat. From somewhere on the distant side of the building came a hissing and Isabel nodded her head, spinning the towel around until it became a stinky whip in her hands, "Ven, putos!"

The sounds grew louder until they echoed off the walls in the pool building, a breathless shrieking, like someone trying to scream during an asthma attack. Isabel halted her silent giggling and listened closer. The shrieking was drawing closer to her location and Isabel decided to risk looking again since she wasn't completely sure anymore Shane and Jose were responsible for the racket. She looked to Rosa who was rising to her feet, her face looked serious. Isabel hurried towards Rosa, trying to be as quiet as she could. The high-pitched racket was just outside the door when she reached Rosa. She held her finger to her lips and took Rosa by the hand. They made their way along the back row of lockers when a figure hobbled into the room. They couldn't see anything but a long shadow but they could hear it and it was shockingly obvious it wasn't their coworkers.

Isabel and Rosa rushed to the other end of the row and ducked around the corner as the unknown figure came crashing into the lockers. Rosa held her hand over her mouth as they froze there for a moment. The ruckus at the other end of the row of lockers grew louder, someone or something was screeching and slamming against the metal locker doors. Isabel couldn't stand not knowing any longer and she silently hoped she would get a glimpse of some sort of animal that unwittingly wandered into the pool complex. It wouldn't have been the first time, they had witnessed bobcats and Javelina roaming on the golf course more times than they could count. It frightened her to think of a frightened bobcat on the loose in the locker room, it would be dangerous for them to confront.

She poked her head around the side of the lockers and saw a bloody figure grappling wildly with a locker door which had popped open. It was mostly bone and raw flesh around its abdomen, it was pale white, and atop its skull was a wild fluff of red hair. It wore a shredded Serenity Canyon shirt. Her breath caught in her throat and tears filled her eyes, she was looking at something purely evil. It halted in its fruitless attack of the locker and turned its hideous face towards her, one eye hanging from its socket. She ducked back around and Rosa took one look at her and knew they were in serious danger.

"Corran," she whispered frantically.

Isabel pushed Rosa along, knowing they had to run for their lives. There was a fire exit in the locker room but the thing with red hair was between them and it. She hoped if they made it into the pool room they could cross over to the east side and either try to hide in the custodial closet there, or use the other fire exit close to it to escape into the night.

As they ran down one end of the locker room, the screeching picked up, Isabel looked down the row and made eye contact with the creature. She screamed and it ran toward them. It moved faster than she thought it could and Rosa was nearly paralyzed in terror when she finally saw what Isabel knew was following them. They sprinted and had to turn and run up the row to make it to the exit door. They rounded the corner and made it to the dark pool room, its waters lapping at the tile walls. Behind them came the screeching creature, hobbling quickly, its arms reaching out to claim them. Rosa screamed, her cries echoing loudly in the once serene pool room. Isabel was ahead of Rosa, they rounded the edge of the pool, and a scream followed by a splash caught her attention. She looked back to see Rosa had tripped and fallen into the water.

The bloody thing jumped in after her.

Isabel screamed and ran to the edge of the pool, watching as Rosa surfaced, coughing up mouthfuls of water. The older woman looked over her shoulder to the bloodied pool water and the creature breaching the surface as well. Rosa turned and frantically tried wading towards Isabel who was urging her to hurry. Rosa was not tall and she had landed in the four foot deep area of the pool and was unknowingly walking into the deeper end of the pool in her terror, soon it was apparent she would need to swim but her clothing and shoes were weighing her down. Isabel looked around her helplessly searching for a way to help her friend. She pulled her cellphone out of her pocket but reception in the pool complex was notoriously horrendous, she had no signal. She shoved it back into her pocket and remembered the pool skimmer they left in the custodial closet for moments when children lost toys, items of clothing, and sometimes their bowels, in the crystal pool waters.

She ran for the closet. Her hands shook so badly, she fumbled with her keys in nightmarish slow motion. Finally, she managed to unlock the door and hurrying to one corner she found the extendable skimmer. Skimmer in hand, she ran back to where she last spotted Rosa. She hesitated, not wanting to get too close to the edge of the pool and the bloody thing in its waters.

She untwisted the long pole the skimmer was attached to and pulled it out longer in quick, frantic motions. She inched it to the edge of the pool and straightened the skimmer pole out but as she hovered it over the water she could see the creature had Rosa by the hair, they were both fighting with each other and trying to stay above the water. She was already too late. It was obvious to Isa that Rosa was no match for the raging monster attacking her. Her heart sank as a swell of terror and anguish filled her, drowning her in hopelessness.

"¡Mierda!" she cursed to herself and felt tears run down her cheeks.

It was dry heaving over Rosa's face, but no vomit came from its mouth, only bloody drool. It changed its tactic of attack by biting into Rosa's throat like an apple. It tore a huge chunk of her soft flesh away and blood spurted into its face. Rosa screamed and inhaled a mouthful of water. She slipped below the surface and the creature went with her. A cloud of red spread out in the pool. Isabel dropped the skimmer and cried. She felt a dizzying terror, her legs hesitated to respond to her brain.

The creature popped back up out of the water but Rosa did not. It started swimming feverishly towards Isabel, thrashing at the water with ravenous impatience, its body and undead mind unaccustomed to the act, and finally her body woke. She spun on her heels and ran. Glancing back as she found the door, she could see the thing pulling itself out of the pool. She hit the fire exit door, it flew open and she found herself in the darkness.

The air was cooler than the humid pool room, fresh with the promise of escape. She wanted to live, she didn't want to become torn to bloody pieces like Rosa. She ran, even with her legs trembling and her lungs burning, she knew she couldn't stop. She had to find someone, anyone.

A scream in the distance caught her ear and she knew it was Shane, his voice was unmistakable. She remembered he and Jose liked to hide in a distant custodial closet and smoke mota. She made her way toward it as the screeching, bloody, thing came barreling out the same fire exit she ran from. Isabel cried as she ran, and pushed herself to move faster, praying to make it to the closet before the screeching abomination caught up to her.

"What the fuck?" Jose asked, sliding his cellphone into his shirt pocket.

Shane ran past Jose, yelling, "Close the fuckin' door!"

Jose did as he was told. He had never seen Shane in such a panic, the stoner seemed to constantly be stuck in slow motion.

"What's goin' on, man?"

"Dude, there's fuckin' zombies out there!" Shane said.

"Shut up. Stop playin' with me, motherfucker."

"I'm not playin', Jose. Don't open that fucking door!"

Jose saw the fear in Shane's eyes, true terror. What he was saying, no matter how crazy it sounded to Jose, Shane believed every word of it. He could see Shane trembling, his arm and mouth were bleeding, his shirt was covered in something atrocious. Jose felt his gut knot up.

"Carl tried to call me but my phone got broken. Call him or call Lalo!" Shane said.

"Okay, calm down."

"Tell them to stay away from the club and call the damn police or the fuckin' Army."

Jose pulled out his phone and swiped the screen, it rang in his hand and they both jumped. Shane screamed and stumbled back against a plastic chair.

"Chill out, it's Carl."

"Tell him what I said!"

Jose answered the phone as a scratching at the door sent them both scurrying to the far corner of the closet.

"Fuck! They found us, man!"

"Carl, listen. Shane got attacked by something. He said we need to stay away from the club."

"We need the cops, there's fuckin' zombies out there!" Shane nearly screamed.

"Hello?" Jose held his phone out and slapped it on his palm,

"What?"

"It says I have no cell service."

"What the fuck?" Shane said.

The scratching at the door became feverish pounding. Shane held onto Jose. Jose tried pushing him away but as the door rattled on its rusted hinges he too clung to his coworker. A sudden scream cut through them followed by a familiar voice.

"Let me in! ¡Abre la pinche puerta, te lo suplico!" Isabel cried.

Jose shook Shane away and ran to the door.

"Don't open it!" Shane cried.

"I'm not leaving her out there!"

Jose grabbed a hammer from his opened tool box on the table by the chair and unlocked the door, He said a prayer and pulled it open. Isabel fell inside, she was trembling and crying. Jose was pushing the door closed when a nearly skeletal hand grabbed the door. A mangled head topped with bright red hair tried to squeeze its way inside. Jose bashed it back with his hammer and barely managed to get the door locked again.

"Was that Pito?"

"I think it was Peter," Isabel wept.

She was rocking and holding herself, nearly catatonic.

"I told you, man. We're fucked!"

"I just hope Carl understood what we said before the phone cut out," Jose said.

"Isabel, give me your phone!" Shane said.

She dug in her pocket and handed it to him with a trembling hand.

"You gotta be fuckin' joking."

"What is it?" Jose asked.

"She doesn't have service either."

"That's impossible!"

"Not if our service was blocked on purpose," Shane said, his face pale white.

"Why? How?"

"It's either the government or this is an alien invasion, and I'm not kidding about either of those options," Shane said.

CHAPTER 5
SYMPHONY OF SICKNESS

STEPHI WAS WEARING her favorite blue ball gown. It hugged her curves but left a little to the imagination. She didn't want to draw too much attention to herself, she wanted to blend in. She didn't want to give her neighbors any reason to suspect there was something different about her, like she was a murderer who ditched her husband's dismembered corpse in the stinking shithole of a portable toilet. She would pretend like Teddy had gone on a hunting trip, nothing unusual, and in a few days pretend she was concerned and then as the weeks went on she would play up the grief stricken wife roll before finally donning her widow's mask and tell everyone he was never returning.

She held a glass of champagne but only sipped at it. She made sure to smile politely at everyone and engage her usual neighborhood friends in conversation so they could all say they saw her the night of the gala and she seemed normal. She only picked at her food, pushing the meat off to the side of her plate. The rare beef looked a little too much like Teddy's meat in places where she sawed him into smaller pieces, chunks small enough to be flushed down with blue liquid and deposited on a heaping pile of feces. She smirked at the thoughts of him rotting there but quickly dashed the smile away. She didn't want to look overly happy. She glanced down at her hands, it was a miracle she ever got the blood to wash off her manicure. She could remember washing the chunks of Teddy from under her finger nails. Not one of her neighbors had asked where he husband was, not even to be polite. They all secretly hated him, she was sure of it. It would make her rouse easier to uphold, no one would question her because no one cared about Teddy.

To her right was Claudia who wouldn't shut up about wondering where her daughters were.

"Kim and Andrea should be here, where are they?"

"Maybe they decided to hang out at home and wait for the real party?" Joel from down by the lake said, smiling and eyeing Claudia like a hungry wolf.

Joel was an older single guy with lots of money, a fake tan and even faker teeth. His hair was also a toupee. He usually hung around Claudia at the galas because the more she drank, the more flirtatious she became. She hadn't invited him to her after party yet so he was laying the compliments on thick in order to gain access to one of her infamous gatherings.

"I told them they had to be here!"

"Oh, Clau," Stephi said, trying to make her voice sound interested in the conversation, "I'm sure they will show."

"I really hope so. They haven't been to the club in ages. I want to show them off!"

"They get their good looks from their mom," Joel said.

"Oh, you're so flattering!" Claudia giggled.

Stephi wasn't sure if Claudia was drunk already or if she was just pretending to be but she was already growing tired of her overly energetic attitude.

"I'm going to get something stronger," Stephi said and left her champagne on the table.

"Bring me a shot of tequila!"

"One for me too!" Joel said.

"Sure," Stephi said and excused herself.

She walked around the edge of the dance floor where the women and men of Serenity Canyon danced close to one another. Stephi never particularly liked dancing, Teddy never made her do it either. She guessed that was one good thing about him, he wasn't into the fanfare most of the residents wallowed in. The small orchestra played an old melody, one she recognized but couldn't name. It made her feel a twinge of loneliness, not for Teddy because he was a bastard, but for someone to wrap her arms around. She wondered how long it would be before it was socially acceptable to find a boyfriend. She refused to be like the old widow, Mrs. Brandon, still proclaiming a fierce loyalty to her dead husband. Stephi would play the field until she found herself a good man, a young banker or lawyer, someone to fill her bank account and spoil her like she thought she deserved after enduring the Hell of being married to Teddy.

Stephi was at the opposite end of the dance floor from her table and she could still hear Joel's annoying voice, even over the music, complimenting Claudia. She took a deep breath, unsure if she could handle staying the entirety of the gala.

"Don't forget my tequila!" Joel hollered at her.

She smiled and waved, cursing him under her fake smile, "I'd like to leave you in an outhouse too, you pushy fuck."

A roaring scream echoed from behind her, everyone froze. The soft orchestral music died in a lurch of forgotten notes and dropped instruments. There was a hesitation, a collective disbelief before everything erupted in a frantic explosion of terror. Stephi didn't have time to turn around, the reaction of the people around her told her to run. She didn't look back as another scream tore up her spine and twisted her stomach. Something monstrous was screaming and it sounded like her name.

"Stephiiii!"

Stephi was swept up in a group of fleeing residents, their couth forgotten, pushing and shoving to get by each other without a single care for the elderly falling by the wayside. Men were no longer gentlemen as ladies stumbled in their elegant shoes and cartwheeled over softly padded chairs to the floor. Stephi didn't turn back, she didn't fight the tide of terror she was caught in, she only went with it and tried in vain to keep up.

"He wants you!" She felt a nudge in her back, hard and fast as Joel went scrambling by.

She stumbled as another one of her neighbors from two streets over elbowed her as he desperately tried to escape. Her ankle twisted painfully in her high heel and snapped. She fell sideways against a table holding trays of food. She dared to glance back at the source of everyone's terror. Her heart faltered and her mouth fell open in a silent scream. It was Teddy, filthy and raging, a dead man walking. She crawled under the table, dragging her injured foot behind her. She held her hand over her mouth as she cried.

"She's over here, now leave the rest of us alone!" Joel screamed.

"Stephiiiiii!" Teddy roared and stomped in her direction, his eyes fixed on her.

It was impossible, she didn't want to believe he was free from his fecal matter tomb, but he was there and the look in his eyes told her he was ready to kill her. He was flipping tables and throwing musicians. He even overturned the piano and crushed the skull of the pianist with his barefoot on his way to his former wife and murderer. Stephi wept and screamed. She tried to move but the bone in her ankle was protruding from her skin, leaving her in absolute agony.

From behind Teddy scurried a woman she recognized as the old widow, Sylvia Brandon, but she too looked disheveled and disgusting. Her head flopped on her neck and her ribs were pushed in beneath her form fitting silk pajamas. The old woman wasted no time in attacking everyone she could get her hands on, tearing pieces of their hair and scalps from their heads, and leaping over tables as she pursued them like a malformed wild cat. Joel tripped on an overturned chair and fell on his face. Mrs. Brandon jumped onto his back. He lifted his head to scream for help but of course no one came to his rescue and the old woman buried her fingernails into his eye sockets. She pulled them out, slurping the eyes off each fingertip like children do to black olives on party trays at graduation parties. She halted for a moment to open her mouth and unleash a shower of vomit on people screaming.

The crowd was rushing towards the entrance door in a hasty exit from Teddy and Mrs. Brandon, but from the door Stephi heard people screaming and a high pitched shriek. She looked frantically to see they were all trapped, the crowd was unable to get away because three women had run in on them. Her heart broke when she realized two of them were Claudia's daughters and the third was dressed as a kitchen worker, the manager Sandy. They were covered in feces, vomit, and blood. They began attacking the finely dressed men and women, and the first was Claudia who fell at their feet and tried reasoning with them.

"Andrea, Kim, please. What are you doing?" she cried.

The three women fell on her and began tearing her to pieces. Claudia's soft skin was torn away from her neck all the way up to her scalp on one side, ripping her cheek away and leaving her eyeball falling from its socket. Blood poured onto the shining floor, her screams died in a shrill cry of pain as her face was disfigured by the hands of her own children.

A handful of men attempted to fight the three women only to be drowned in waves of vomit. Claudia's daughter, Kim, shat down her legs and it rained down into her mother's open wounds. The gala had erupted into bloody chaos.

Watching Claudia die made Stephi realize Teddy, Mrs. Brandon, Claudia's daughters and the kitchen worker were no longer themselves. They were monsters. She knew Teddy was dead when she threw his pieces down into the old outhouse toilet. The only explanation for him walking, screaming her name, and swiping at men who were attempting to get to a side exit door until he broke their necks, was he was now the living dead. Teddy was a zombie and so were the others attacking the gala goers. They were all going to die, they were all fucked.

"Stephiiiii."

Tears streamed down her face. Her death was imminent. She just prayed it wouldn't be too painful.

The table she was hiding under was flipped over, she grabbed a fork from the floor. Teddy stood over her, reeking of death and glaring down at her. The orchestra had died long ago but the night was filled with a symphony of screaming, Stephi felt Teddy's retribution was nigh. Her body trembled, her skin went cold, and the searing pain in her ankle was forgotten.

"Teddy, please..."

His hand shot down and gripped her by the throat, strangling her plea to nothing but a whimpering gasp.

"Stephiiii."

She kicked feebly as he lifted her high into the air. She stabbed the fork into his arm but he didn't react, he wouldn't release her. Any ounce of hope in her was snuffed out.

From behind him, the service door to the kitchen flew open again and zombified kitchen workers joined the fray, decimating any hope there was for a few men and women to survive. They spread out, attacking Serenity Canyon residents and the last of the small orchestra who had come to play the music for the evening. Stephi wondered when at first she dumped Teddy's body down into the waste hole whether she would go to Hell and now she was certain she would. She felt she was already there and Teddy was the prince of blood and pain, her eternal torturer and executioner.

Agent Boze ran ahead of his partner toward the faint sounds of panic and terror. He was well aware, in his line of employment, when you hear screaming it usually meant things were only getting worse. The thing beyond the window in Dr. Abileen's lab hadn't left his mind, it was a glimpse into a future he needed to prevent. Desperation swelled inside of him and he fought to keep it in check.

His cellphone rang and he halted. He glanced at the number calling, and cursed. It was his superiors, he held his breath and awaited another grave sign. Answering the phone he wasn't surprised at all to hear what was barked at him. He turned to Agent Jackson who came to a halt beside him. Another short conversation, one he didn't wish to have, but ever since they left the beautiful Dr. Abileen he feared he would eventually.

"What's our orders?" Agent Jackson asked as Boze hung up the phone.

"To contain the problem to this neighborhood at all costs, shoot to kill, until the big boys show up."

Agent Jackson nodded, he already had his pistol in his hand.

"It sounds like Teddy has already suffered the fate of that other doctor. He's spreading that shit to everyone here. The body count is gonna be insane."

"I'm not sure we have enough ammo for this," Jackson said.

"Let's pop the trunk before we walk into this shit," Boze suggested.

They ran for the parking lot, leaving the screaming to carry on like a symphony of pain.

Boze pulled his car keys out of his pocket and hit the button to open the trunk. They ran to their stash of weaponry, the type only government boys were privy to. They stood over the treasure trove of bullets and explosives.

"We can't do this alone and you know it," Agent Jackson said.

Agent Boze nodded and glanced back at the Serenity Canyon management office, "We have a janitorial crew at our disposal?"

"Do you think they know how to shoot a gun? They're just a bunch of janitors."

"It doesn't matter as long as we buy enough time until the Army boys show up and we keep this shit from spreading to the city."

"Alright, let's arm them," Agent Jackson agreed.

Dr. Abileen felt a tingling as the hours ticked by, they felt more like years as the intravenous drugs flooded her system. She unscrewed the lid on a prescription bottle of anthelmintic medication used to kill parasites and tossed two pills into her mouth. She swallowed them painfully down her dry throat, feeling them as they inched their way down to her stomach.

"Let's do this."

She hoped the two agents were equipped to take down as many people as they needed to, with the rapidly mutating parasites she figured the whole damn neighborhood would end up parasite-riddled zombies in no time. She was still uncertain if Teddy was sure of the danger he carried home with him, or if his arrogance was bolstered by a quick blood test which showed no signs of the worms. He was like a walking Trojan horse, a belly and intestine full of an Army ready to destroy all in their path. Just thinking about his stupid face and bald head made her wish she could be the one to mow him down with a blowtorch. She held no remorse for the man who had willingly brought doom to the whole world by playing with worms from a dead woman's frozen brain.

Her gut knotted and she grinned, the drugs were starting to kick in. She hoped they cleaned every squirming invader from her body. Cold sweat broke out on her forehead and she wondered if she might have overdone it with medicating herself but she was ready to suffer the consequences if they got the job done. Her mouth filled with saliva and she awaited the sweet sensation of die-off symptoms, all the extreme vomiting and liquefied bowel movements headed her way would equal annihilation of the invaders in her body, at least she hoped they would. It was the first time in her life she was praying to empty out both ends. She just prayed it would be enough, modern medicine would be their only hope against the ancient worms. Her stomach bottomed out, and she grabbed her IV and ran for the bathroom in desperation. She barely made it to the toilet. Her face went cold, the sweat gathering there ran down her temples as she gripped the steel handicap railing and let her body empty out.

"Soon, I'll know if this was worth it, and it better fuckin' be."

"The phone cut out but Shane was screaming we need to stay away from the club," Carl said.

"Why?" Jason asked.

"I bet you Dr. Reinart is a damn terrorist," Carl said.

"Do you think so?" Larry, the gate guard, asked. He had been silent and wide-eyed during the conversation with the special agents. It was obvious he only applied for a job as a security guard because he believed a place like Serenity Canyon would be peaceful, and it usually was since it was far from town. He swallowed a lump in his throat and looked to Lalo as if he had any answers.

"Everyone shut up. I need to think. How are we going to tell Rosa and Isa?" Lalo asked.

"I have no idea, but Shane was screaming in the background. He was hurt or attacked," Carl said.

"This is some serious shit," Jason said.

There was a pounding at the door, the SCUM crew jumped from their seats.

Sunny cursed under her breath, hiding behind Lalo.

"Open the door!"

"It's the FBI boys," Carl said.

Lalo went to the door and pushed it open.

"First of all, we need a set of keys," Agent Boze said as they rushed inside.

Lalo went to Peter's office and opened a lockbox on the wall. He pulled out two sets of keys.

"These are master keys. They open every Serenity Canyon facility door but none of the houses, obviously."

The agents took them as the crew gathered around them.

"The second thing we need is…your help," Agent Boze said.

"Help? With what?" Lalo asked.

"We have reliable information that Dr. Reinart is infected with a very deadly and contagious disease. He is spreading it to the other residents."

"Do we look like a hazmat team?" Jason asked.

"Yeah, how the hell are we gonna help?" Sunny added.

"Well, we're all in peril. Everyone on this property is in grave danger, and more importantly, we can't let this spread beyond Serenity Canyon." Agent Jackson said.

"Why are you carrying a gun? You ain't gonna shoot a disease," Carl said, but it was obvious to every one of them.

"We may need to kill anyone carrying it. It causes those infected to become violent and try to kill other people," Agent Jackson said.

"Fuck that. Don't count on me for nothin' like that," Carl said.

"What about Shane, Jose, and Rosa and Isabel?" Jason asked

"Jason is right. I can't let anything happen to them," Lalo said and held his hand out.

Agent Boze placed a gun in his palm, "There are more weapons outside in our trunk, we need you all or this won't end well."

"I don't want to be shootin' no motherfuckers who got a disease and are crazy as fuck!" Carl said.

"Listen, we don't have a choice. If you stay here, then you're on your own. The people who come with us will be given guns and ammo," Boze said.

"I'll help, " Larry said begrudgingly.

"I'm in," Jason said.

"Me too," Sunny said, "I'm not getting trapped in here with no gun or anything to protect myself."

"Carl?" Jason asked.

Carl shook his head and held his hands up, "I ain't goin' out there."

"You can't stay here alone, " Sunny said.

"Fuck, okay. Give me a damn gun!" Carl conceded.

CHAPTER 6
OLD JIM

JIM THREW his cellphone against the wall of the small house he shared with Sandy. She hadn't spoken much to him since he lost his job. He was getting sick of the silent treatment. He had downed a cheap bottle of whisky but he knew it wouldn't be enough. Those fucking bastards at Serenity Canyon not only left him without employment but they also screwed up his relationship with Sandy. Jim didn't like to admit the truth, their relationship had always been rocky due to his drinking problem and job hopping. Sandy liked to drink too, but she could maintain. She always told him there was a difference in getting drunk and being a drunk, and he was just a drunk. Sometimes he took it to heart, knowing he was an alcoholic, and other times he'd call her a hypocritical bitch.

Tonight, he felt lonely and desperate. He didn't even know what he would say if she answered the phone. He wanted to cry like a baby and beg her to come home and hold him, but he also wanted to vent his anger all over her for being ignored. He paced the floor, running his hands through his long grey hair. He wasn't a big man but he had lived a rough life in a war that left him wily and tough.

"I'm sick of this shit," He said.

He went to the kitchen sink and ran the faucet. He splashed handfuls of water over his greasy face and buttoned his shirt. His mind was made up, he was going to get his woman's respect back and show those uppity pieces of shit at the Canyon what he was made of, especially that ginger-haired freak Peter. He strutted to the bathroom, feeling the burden lift from his shoulders now that he had made up his mind not to wallow in self-pity anymore. He unzipped his pants and pissed a stinking stream into the toilet.

"These fucks have no idea what's comin' for them."

Jim opened his closet and rummaged through years of collected junk until he located his gun case. He pulled it out and laid it on the bed. He unzipped it and pulled out the rifle his father left for him when the old man died. Jim didn't handle many guns after leaving the service. He had killed enough in his lifetime to want to do it again, but tonight he was pushed to his limit. He meant to blow Peter's brains out the back of his head. A pistol would have been better, it would be easier to hide, easier to use at close range, but he sold his only pistol a couple years prior just to get some money while he was out of a job. For a moment he envisioned himself driving right through the gate at Serenity Canyon in his old Ford truck, Sandy rushing out of the kitchen door, her anger dissolving into passion at the sight of him. It emboldened him. He grabbed his truck keys and headed out the door.

Boze and Jackson led the unlikely gang towards the screams emanating from the clubhouse.

"Larry. Go back to your post, no one leaves this place and I mean no one. Shoot anyone attempting to get past the gate."

The security guard nodded and ran for the gate, the others watched him go and felt a pang of jealousy he was getting to hide in his booth.

The agents halted the rest of the group and looked to each other uncertainly, but the second guessing ended with the clubhouse doors being flung open and a man in a black suit came running frantically at them. He was bloody, covered in vomit, and screaming. His right cheek hung down and flapped as he fled the gala with one arm hanging loosely from its socket and what could have been confused for a chopstick in his functional hand. It was a baton, he was the conductor of the small orchestra hired to play for the residents of

Serenity Canyon. He looked like a penguin who escaped from a polar bear's gut. Hot on his heels hobbled a group of shrieking figures. They were vaguely recognizable, some were dressed like kitchen staff and others as the snooty inhabitants of the upscale neighborhood accept they were all dressed to the nines and covered in blood. They were missing pieces, broken bones protruded through their skin, some of them spitting mouthfuls of bile. They poured out of the clubhouse, twitching and shrieking, an unbelievable nightmare come true. The agents and the SCUM crew hesitated for a split second, their minds coming to terms with the reality coming for them whether they liked it or not.

"It's time people. We gotta hold our ground until the Army gets here, no one can leave Serenity Canyon, " Boze said.

Jason held his pistol out before him but his arms shook so violently he let it drop and looked to his crew mates, and to Lalo for direction. His boss only stood there in wide-eyed terror and racked his pistol to get ready to fire.

"You didn't say they'd be like…this!" Carl said.

"Yeah, you said they were sick. You didn't say they were monsters!" Sunny said, hiding behind Lalo, her hand on his shoulder.

"They *are* sick, it's a disease," Agent Jackson said.

"They're fuckin' zombies!" Jason screamed, waving the gun in his hand every time he lifted it.

"Do I look like a soldier? I don't want any part of this bullshit," Carl turned and strode back toward the management office.

"Carl! Don't go back alone!"

He didn't answer Jason, who watched him retreat. He just kept walking, quickening his pace until he was running back to what he believed to be his only security.

"Pay attention," Boze warned, "they spotted us!"

The conductor fell to the ground on the manicured lawn of the clubhouse. He was immediately swarmed by four sharply dressed living-dead men. Those who once kept their noses in the air, those who refused to dirty their hands or shoes, they were tearing the poor man apart with their teeth. A chorus of flatulence and belching followed showering mouthfuls of vomit being rained down upon their victim.

He had given up fighting after his skull was bashed in by a heavy placard proclaiming the club was built in honor of the rich real estate tycoon who built the community.

"What the fuck are they doing?"

"Spreading the disease," Boze said.

A separate group, three females dressed in expensive gowns, came for the SCUM crew and the agents. They formed a line, weapons ready, their nerves eating holes in their stomachs.

"It's Claudia and her daughters," Jason said.

"I don't give a shit who they are or were, shoot to kill!" Agent Boze ordered.

The skin on Claudia's face and arms were shredded and hanging in thin pieces. Her daughters were close behind her, their necks crooked. Their stomachs were hanging loosely beneath their stained clothing as if they had been stretched beyond what their skin could accommodate. Mothers to ungodly things, incubators of the world's end.

"Shoot them!" Agent Boze yelled.

He pulled the trigger first, and after the first roaring report of his gun, they followed his orders. The SCUM crew fired, pulling their triggers over and over. Bullets cut through the soft skin of the three women, Claudia stumbled back as a shot blew the side of her head open. Her daughters danced as round after round tore into them, but none of them fell. Agent Boze strode forward, his gun lifted. He kept pulling the trigger until their heads were broken shells and their brains were sprayed onto the grass beneath them. His gun was empty, but their bodies kept stumbling forward. Thin white tendrils snaked out of the jagged pieces and reached out for each other, as they conjoined the shattered skulls of Claudia and her daughters slowly began pulling themselves back together to form lopsided heads.

"This is unreal!" Agent Boze said.

"You remember what Dr. Abileen said," Agent Jackson said, his voice twisting with concern, "they're not easy to kill."

"I was hoping she was exaggerating."

"She wasn't. What the hell are we gonna do?"

"We need something more powerful," Agent Boze said, "back to the trunk!"

The group retreated, pursued by the screams of more lumbering creatures. Their first strike had been useless and it was only against three of the things. They had no idea how many more they would have to face and their guns wouldn't be enough to stop them all.

"Why did I stay here?" Sunny wept as they made it to the FBI agent's car.

"It's my fault. I shouldn't have offered you a tour. I'm so sorry," Lalo said.

"No, it's mine. I forgot my driver's license. Like that's really so fuckin' important that I just had to come back here tonight."

Lalo put his hand on her shoulder as she cried, he felt helpless.

"Get your shit together and get over here," Agent Boze shouted as he popped the trunk.

He rummaged through his arsenal and handed them extra ammo and then grabbed a duffle bag and threw it at his partner before grabbing one of his own.

"What is all this? Do all FBI agents ride around with a trunk full of guns and grenades?" Jason asked.

"No, we are a special unit. We're problem solvers, only called when things get out of control," Agent Jackson answered.

"Have you seen anything this bad?"

"We've seen some weird shit but this takes the cake," Agent Boze said. "Jackson, take one of our friends here, post up at the gate. Under no circumstances can any of these things breach the perimeter. They can't make it outta here. The rest of you come with me. We gotta blow these fuckers sky high if we want to stop them."

A chorus of shrieking and groaning silenced them. Jackson tapped Jason on the shoulder and nodded back towards the gate. Jason looked to Lalo, his eyes were wide and confused.

"Good luck," Lalo said to the young man.

"Same to you guys," Jason said and turned to follow Agent Jackson toward the guard booth.

Boze opened his duffle bag and handed a grenade to Lalo and pulled one out for himself.

"Pull the pin and toss it at their feet, do not get near it after you toss it. Just let it do its job."

"Hey, where's mine?" Sunny asked.

"I want you to run to the management office and get the guy who ran away."

"Carl."

"Yes, get Carl and rummage through your custodial supplies, we need anything flammable."

"Okay."

"Go, go quick!" Boze urged.

At the edge of the parking lot stumbled the silhouettes of three stinking, shrieking gala goers.

"Run, Sunny! It's the number seven key, it opens every door. Find Carl, he knows all the closets and supply rooms," Lalo said.

Sunny nodded and took off running back toward the management office. He watched her go and prayed she make it. From what he had witnessed the creatures weren't very fast, but they were almost indestructible.

"Let's take these fuckers out!" Agent Boze said and strode towards the group coming at them.

Shane wiped sweat from his forehead. His skin was clammy and cold, and Jose noticed he had vomit on his shirt.

"Did you puke?"

"No, Sandy did it. She attacked me and barfed all over me. That's when I realized she's a fuckin' zombie."

The custodial closet door was on the outside a small building used by the gardening crew to store their equipment and monitor the timers set to water the golf courses. It wasn't a large space, barley giving the three of them room to stand with a few feet between them. It was filled with sharp tools and gasoline but a brick wall separated them from what was a treasure trove of potential weaponry. If they wanted to scour its shelves for tools to defend themselves, they would have to go outside, round the building and open the door to the grounds shop. The closet they were hiding in held toilet paper, paper towels, cleaning chemicals, mops, brooms, and boxes of plastic bags.

"That thing, I think it was Peter. It killed Rosa," Isabel whispered.

"Oh my God," Jose said, hugging her.

"What are we gonna do?" Shane asked.

"We gotta hide in here and..." Jose said.

A gurgling groan outside the door silenced him, they looked to see the doorknob rattling as the door was yanked from the outside.

"It's gonna get in here, man!" Shane said.

Isabel screamed and covered her face with her hands. The door rattled violently as they cowered in the farthest corner. Jose couldn't believe the power whatever on the other side had. The door hinges wouldn't hold much longer, he was sure of it.

"Find something to fight with!" he said.

The three of them began rifling through the supply closet, looking for anything to force the creature away, to maim it, to destroy it. Shane grabbed a mop handle. Jose armed himself with two broken broom handles they hadn't thrown away yet. Isabel hurriedly found two screwdrivers and a razorblade gum scraper, all were sharp but would put her face to face with the monster outside. She couldn't bear the thought of being so close to it. She scurried to the far end of the closet, hoping Shane and Jose would be able to keep it at bay. The door shook and the sound of scraping metal echoed within the small closet. Shane and Jose turned to face the creature, prepared to fight it with all they had. Nervously, Shane coughed and gagged, he turned away and puked a pool of stomach acid onto the floor.

"What the fuck? Hey, you better not be turning into one of those things!" Jose warned.

"I'm just scared, you asshole. Sandy didn't bite me!"

Shane doubled over, his stomach cramping. Isabel hid behind Jose, afraid to be too near the door and to be so close to Shane too. Jose alternated between holding his makeshift spear out towards Shane and then the trembling door.

"Stop being a dickhead!" Shane said, gripping his stomach.

He dropped his mop handle and doubled over in pain.

"Fuck, I feel sick to my stomach."

"Shane, I swear, man. I'll cut your fuckin' head off if you start turnin'!"

"Don't fuckin' say that! I'm not a zombie, man!" Shane cried.

There was silence, the door went still. Jose and Shane looked to it, hoping the monster on the other side had given up on tearing it from its hinges.

"Oh God, please let it go away," Shane whispered.

"Shut the fuck up!"

Isabel's grip on the back of Jose's shirt eased and she dared to peek around him at the door. A shrieking in the distance sent her back into hiding, and in the night they could hear the pounding of feet on pavement as the thing that once was Peter came charging at the door.

"It's coming back!" Jose screamed.

Shane stood on shaking legs and lifted his mop handle as the door burst in. The bloody thing came tumbling in clumsily, its red hair matted with bloody pool water. Isabel screamed, an ear piercing shriek, Jose pushed her backwards and lifted his broom handle-spear. He lunged forward and jammed it in Peter's vacant eye socket. The sharp tip severed the cord holding the eyeball like a yoyo at the end of its short string, it fell to the dusty floor and rolled to a stop at Shane's feet.

He kicked it away wildly and jabbed Peter with his own mop handle spear, sending it stumbling back on its clumsy feet. Peter fell against the supply shelf but he bounced back, and lunged for them. Jose stepped back until he had Isabel pressed against the wall, her wailing cutting through his subconscious but all he could concentrate on was thrusting his custodial closet spear at the eviscerated abdomen of Peter. He could see his ribcage was picked nearly clean beneath the tatters of the Serenity Canyon shirt he always wore with so much pride.

There was hardly any room between the shrieking undead property manager, and the only thing keeping him from vomiting up loads of parasites into their faces was his stomach and esophagus had been eaten by Teddy and Mrs. Brandon, there was nowhere for the larvae to spawn and grow. He opened his mouth and gagged, but nothing came forth but some frothy, bloody spittle. Shane grabbed a screwdriver from Isa's hand and jabbed him in the cheek with the tip, it went in deeply but wouldn't come out. Shane fumbled with the mop handle and yanked at the screwdriver but it remained stuck in Peter's face. He fell forward and pushed the mop handle aside as he grabbed Shane by his right arm.

Jose darted past dragging Isabel by the hand as he went. The creature which was once their manager was far too busy with his assault on Shane to stop them. The stench of him got caught in their throats in the instant they slid by him, bile, coagulated blood, and pool chlorine, he was far too close to for comfort. Stomach twisting fear gripped them, leaving Isabel in hysterics, as they ran into the night. Jose pulled her to a halt and turned back around at the sound of Shane's agonized screaming.

"I can't leave Shane."

"We have to. Believe me, he's dead already…" Isabel was nearly hyperventilating, "you didn't see what it did to Rosa!"

"Be quiet!" Jose shook her by the shoulders and she fell silent.

"Stay here and shut up. If I don't come back, run."

Jose left her standing beyond the door and went to look inside.

Peter had Shane by the wrist of his right arm, he twisted the appendage in a three hundred and sixty degree circle, a wet tearing was drowned out by Shane's cries. Peter tore his arm completely from its socket. Blood sprayed like a water hose into Peter's face, his mouth opened hungrily but the sustenance did nothing but fall down his throat into an empty abdominal cavity and trickle down his flesh bare ribs.

"Motherfucker," Jose cursed, anger and desperation bubbling over in him.

Jose ran back into the closet and grabbed a fire extinguisher hanging by the door. He screamed as he bashed Peter over the head, heavy thuds smashing into Peter's skull. Peter stumbled and hissed so Jose gave him another vicious blow to his head, stunning Peter. He watched the creature fall over a mop bucket.

"Fuck you!" Jose said, tears spilling from his eyes.

He beat Peter over the back of his skull until he felt it crunch then threw the extinguisher aside. He used his heel and all of his strength to force its bleeding, screeching face down into the ringer of the mop bucket. He yanked the handle with all the frantic, adrenaline fueled, power he had left in him until he could feel bones snapping as he crushed Peter's face. A moist cracking, as satisfying as it was disgusting, radiated up Jose's trembling arm.

He turned to Shane who had fallen to the floor, a pool of blood gathered around him. He was silent and wide eyed, his face white with blood-loss.

"Oh, Shane. Come on, man."

Shane didn't respond, Jose knew his spirit was drifting away.

Isabel came to the doorway and wept. Peter's body lurched and he shrieked as he fought to pull his smashed head free of the mop bucket. Jose turned back and shoved Isabel along. There was no helping his friend, he was gone, there was no way he would survive such trauma and blood loss. Jose shoved her around the side of the building and towards the grounds shop door. There was a large garage door but he skipped trying to open it. If he couldn't get it pulled shut in time then the creature who was once Peter would follow them into their only sanctuary in sight. Plus, it was loud when it came open, and he didn't want to draw any attention to them. He stopped at the steel door, its paint crimson red like the rocks of the surrounding hills.

"¡Apúrate!" Isabel urged as he fumbled with his keys, he hadn't had to open the door in years and couldn't remember which of his many keys would open it.

The night echoed with the sounds of horror, in the distance there was screaming followed by the shrieking of something hungry, something violent. His stomach lurched. His decision not to try to open the metal garage door had been a good one. It would have been like ringing a dinner bell.

"There's more of them! Where is the rest of the crew? We're all fucked!" Jose spoke to himself, his hands shaking as he located the correct key. He was relieved the key still hung next to the others he used every work day. At one point Peter was supposed to take the grounds shop keys from everyone on the crew so he didn't have to worry about them hiding in there and not doing their jobs. Luckily, he must have forgotten to do so or got too lazy to rummage through the whole crew's key rings.

Jose shoved the key into the lock and turned it. He opened the door and dragged Isabel inside. He locked the door behind them, his insides twisted at the sound of Isabel's crying. He knew she would never be able to erase the memory of watching Shane bleeding to death, or the nightmare she lived when Rosa was killed in front of her.

They were met by darkness and two bulky shadows, the silhouettes of the Toro 3000 super lawn mower and the Range Picker. Jose flipped on the lights and his eyes beheld the machines. On an ordinary day they were tools for keeping the grass cut and the driving range clear of golf balls, but with night outside the door and with the air filled with screams of who were more than likely his coworkers and friends, they looked like weapons of war to him.

"These fucks don't know what's comin' for them."

He left Isabel to cry, to empty her heart of some of its building agony. He needed her strong and brave for what he had planned.

Jose began rummaging through the grounds shop, it had a small break room but it was mostly a giant storage room. His heart raced each time he heard screeching beyond the steel garage door. He wasn't a mechanic but on the weekends sometimes he helped his uncle trick out his show cars and trucks, so he had an idea as to how he would make it all work.

Isabel came to stand at his side. He put his arm over her shoulder. She wiped the tears from her eyes and started helping him dig through shelves and toolboxes. It didn't take much guessing on her part to know what Jose planned, how they would attempt an escape. They would make the ride-on mower and the range picker into armored escape vehicles.

Dr. Abileen exited the bathroom on shaky legs. Her stomach growled and lurched, it had been emptied but she still felt the nagging urge to run to the bathroom. She was just outside her laboratory door when the guards came in and behind them walked a short woman in thick glasses. She had a short haircut and black pant suit carrying a small leather satchel. They stopped within six feet and the guards were waved away by the woman.

"Dr. Abileen?" she asked.

"Yes, and you are?"

"Dr. Murphy, infectious disease control. I've been sent to make sure this doesn't get beyond our grasp and, if you're lucky, save you from dying."

Dr. Abileen wanted to protest, to tell the woman she could captain the ship, but honestly she wasn't sure she could do it alone.

"You can call me Sarah, and your expertise would be greatly appreciated."

"Let's not waste time on pleasantries, Dr. Abileen. Let's get down to business before you fall over dead and I have to have your brains bashed in and your body thrown in an incinerator."

Dr. Abileen swallowed the reply she wanted to say and instead led the way into the laboratory to bring Dr. Murphy up to speed on the situation.

"I see you've administered your own regimen of the anti-parasitic cocktail," The short woman said with an amused grin at the IV in Dr. Abileen's arm.

"Yes, it was everything we had that I could think of to destroy them."

"And how's that working out for you?"

"It seems to be cleaning me out. I think I'm experiencing the die-off symptoms, extreme nausea and diarrhea."

"Do you think we have enough time to fool around with checking to see if those traditional treatments will work?" Dr. Murphy asked with a smug grin.

"It's all we have at the moment, unless you have another suggestion?"

"As a matter of fact, I do," Dr. Murphy said and plopped her satchel down on Dr. Abileen's desk. She pulled out a vial and held it to the light, admiring it like she would a painting in an art gallery.

"There are countless parasitic infections going on in the world, many people are disabled from such infections. There have been outbreaks such as this in Russia and other foreign countries, those of course never got leaked to the media. People here in the states don't hear about them, especially those extreme cases swept under the rug.

This situation is going to change all that if we don't act rapidly. I've come baring the solution to this problem."

"What is it?" Dr. Abileen asked.

"In short, an experimental treatment for cancer that was found quite useful in targeting the genomes in worms such as yours. It is highly effective in killing parasites like the ones making a home of your body, and hopefully you'll only need one dose."

"Wait, wait, wait, how did you know this is a parasite?"

"Did you believe the boys in the big offices weren't given daily updates on your research by Dr. Reinart? He gave us all the information every step of the way, and we were preparing for any missteps. When the special agents were sent in, I was alerted and made my way here. They only contact Boze and Jackson when someone shit the bed. Honestly, I worried Reinart would fuck up, and he did."

"By being prepared, you had to suspect this would become one big fuck up and you didn't do anything to stop it?"

"We didn't think it would be unleashed here, in America. We thought *if* anything went awry, it would happen in some place far away, not in yuppie-ville Arizona. Besides, countries effected by such an outbreak would pay any price to get the antidote...don't you think?"

"You were willing to let other countries be overrun by violent walking dead to win wars and to make money?"

"No, we were under the assumption it would be a paralytic, an irreversible one, not turn everyone into," she held her fingers up and made air quotes, "violent walking dead."

Dr. Abileen shook her head in disgust but guilt gripped her, she had her part to play in all of it.

"And yes, our end game is to always win wars and make money. That's the American way, " Dr. Murphy said.

"You sound like someone else I know."

"Theodore. Was an insufferable asshole, but I guess you already know that."

"Was?" Dr. Abileen asked.

"He and his neighbors may be wiped off the face of the Earth by an explosion, a gas line catastrophe. We can't afford any witnesses, you know that, " Dr. Murphy said with a grin.

"You can't do that."

"This is the United States Government. We can do that, and so much more."

"There could be people who aren't infected…" Dr. Abileen said.

"I've been granted complete control over this situation, who gets treated, and who simply disappears. There will be a few, like you, getting the syringe, but there will be those beyond repair. Be thankful you're being medicated and not incinerated."

There was a pinch at the top of her arm as the antidote was pushed into her bloodstream.

"Of course it is, there were signs of it doing so in other corpses discovered near the dig site but our wonderful Dr. Reinart was too enamored by the frozen woman and her brain worm to take it into consideration. The testing he presented was originally in a lab rat, which I suspect he unknowingly burned before the parasite could resurrect it. He believed it would only paralyze those infected, boy was he wrong, " Dr. Murphy said.

"He was blinded by his ego, he thought he could control this. I read his journal. He became obsessed with the parasite. He called it a Goddess and thought her children would become deities themselves, " Dr. Abileen said, rubbing her arm.

"They have in a way, become Gods, they take over the bodies and will of men and do as they please without care of the suffering they cause," Dr. Murphy said as she held a tissue to the tiny pin prick of blood from the injection area.

Dr. Abileen looked to her, Dr. Murphy's words sent a strange chill through her, they were painfully accurate. She was never a religious woman, she always preferred science to the mumbo jumbo of her grandparent's churches and holy books. Even so, comparing the parasitic worms to a god felt unnerving.

"I guess you're right," she said.

"Now, you're going to feel very ill, but do you think you can help me with coordinating a plan around here?"

"I've been sick all day. I think I can handle feeling like hell a little longer if it means we get rid of these things."

Dr. Murphy nodded, "Very good, and we will."

"I'm your guinea pig?"

"Yes. So, keep your fingers crossed you don't wind up being a witness to your own cremation, from inside the incinerator."

"I don't find that humorous. Not after discovering Theodore offered me up as a test subject knowing I would die and come back as a disgusting monster."

"Yes, just take solace in knowing he's probably hobbling around his neighborhood with shit running down his legs and the Army on its way to send him to Hell."

Dr. Abileen grinned, "That does make me feel a little better."

After spending an eternity in the bathroom, Dr. Abileen was laid out on the steel gurney. Her head swam with dizzying nausea, the room spun slowly around her. Dr. Murphy was busy cleaning up the remains of what Dr. Entz had left behind in his battle to spread his progeny.

"How are you feeling?"

"So sick to my stomach, " Dr. Abileen answered.

"Sounds like its working, then."

"I'm sorry. I couldn't help you finish…"

"You helped in the other rooms, it's a miracle you made it this far. Lay there for a while and if you need to puke do it in the trash can."

Dr. Abileen's hand fell to the side of the steel table and felt the edge of the trash can Dr. Murphy had left there. The intense nausea had come on rather suddenly while she worked and sent her falling to the tile floor. Dr. Murphy ordered the guards to lift her up onto the table she just cleaned so she could rest and let the injection do its job within her.

"Soon, you'll be just like new," Dr. Murphy said and stepped outside the door.

Dr. Abileen could hear her talking with the guards but her words sounded far away, muted in her own mind, or was she whispering?

Dr. Abileen felt a surge of fright swelling in her, bells of alarm tolling in the haze of her confused mind. She tried to sit up but Dr. Murphy rushed back in to ease her back down, the guards stood behind her with their hands resting on their guns.

"Take it easy. Everything will be okay."

"What's happening? I feel like I can't concentrate."

"It's normal, just relax."

Dr. Abileen felt cold straps being fitted to her wrists and then her ankles. The guards stood still, watching Dr. Murphy as she secured Dr. Abileen to the table.

"What are you doing?" her voice was weak and distant in her ears.

"Fixing you, making you better, finding the solution to this whole mess," Dr. Murphy answered.

"Help me," Dr. Abileen said, lulling her head to the side to look directly at the guards.

They would help her, they had been through so much. She knew their names, they were loyal to her.

They stood rigid like statues, only their eyes moved or showed any humanity. Behind their respirators she could see their eyes were wide and teary. They didn't want to hurt her, but they also had to obey the woman in charge.

She tried to fight her restraints but her arms felt numb, her legs wouldn't respond to her internal orders to kick like mad.

She had been betrayed.

"Donald! T! Help me!"

"You are going to be fine," Dr. Murphy spoke down to her.

The crowd of twitching, shrieking creatures stumbled toward the door. The night beyond held the promise of meat and warm places to deposit the children inside of them. They went to hunt, to feel the darkness in new skin, and to obey the commands of the worms that were never happy inside one corpse. They were evolving, their young growing faster each time they spawned, they would soon need more than what the neighborhood could offer. A few among the stumbling, finely dressed, horde had flashes of memories of a city not far away. It would hold so many opportunities for their young, so many tasty morsels of fresh meat for them to dine on. Sedona called to the more elite reanimated corpses and the lesser beasts would follow them like a pack of hungry dogs to the paradise amidst the red rocks.

Teddy held Stephi up above his head. Her face was violet. She, his killer, was dying by his hand and he meant to savor it. Her eyes bulged until they both flew from their sockets, her head lulled to one side. He felt the trembling in her entire body, almost orgasmic as her spirit fled her. He would replace it with a new form of consciousness, the pilots in his own brain begged for her flesh. His murderess would become his bride and slave in her new existence. His mind flashed with a memory of her dressed in a white gown, vowing to be his until death parted them. She would now be bound to him even beyond it. He lowered her corpse until she was inches from his face as his wedding day fantasy continued to play out in his mind. He brought his mouth to hers in a kiss of blood. His teeth sank into her soft flesh, her plump lips tore away as he yanked his head back, he chewed on them and delighted in her flavor. He carried her over and laid her out on a table then pried her mouth open. He vomited into her, giving her the gift of his children and waited for her to awaken to their new matrimonial bliss.

Outside a great booming sound rocked the windows of the ball room. Teddy hissed and listened as a group of his kind wailed in defeat and anger. The army of them would not be easily subdued, but somewhere out in the dark, by the pleasant smell of fresh grass, humans were fighting back. He stroked Stephi's cheek before leaving her side to survey the building war beginning to be waged. He came to the ball room door and stood just inside of it. Smoke hung heavy in the air and the scurrying silhouettes of his ravenous children swarmed like ants towards two figures beneath the faint parking lot lights. He only counted two but he guessed there had to be more of them, it didn't frighten him to see their firepower. The humans would claim a few of his kind but they weren't strong enough to resist them all. He shrieked into the smoke filled air and his children spun to look at him, his brain twitched and a signal was sent to the pilots within a group of them while the rest started to move towards their attackers. They came to him, the most elite among them, their father and creator, and awaited his commands. The Gods within him relayed information to those within the brains of his children and they turned back, some rejoining the fray and others to comb the neighborhood. A gurgled screech caught his attention and he looked to the misshapen thing which was once named Peter, it was wretched and weak. If Teddy had his way, he would have just devoured him completely but he granted it a chance at a second life. Its head was smashed and its Serenity Canyon shirt hung from its empty body like a tattered flag. Teddy sent it a command; it would act as a kamikaze among his children, granting them the time to strike their enemy. The old woman came to join the group receiving orders and he realized it was also her time to prove her worth, his first child, his weakest. She too would become a sacrifice in order to protect the most promising specimens among them.

The stumbling horde spun around and headed back toward the club house at a high pitched shrieking.

"They're retreating," Agent Boze said to Lalo.

"What the fuck are we gonna do?"

"Let's get a closer look."

"What? Fuck no!"

"Yes, we are. Come on!"

They ran to the shadows of the shrubs lining the sidewalk and used it for cover to get a closer look at the group of undead yuppies.

Just inside the club house stood the hulking frame of Teddy, his garbled screeches calling the groups of stinking dead.

"He's communicating with the others," Agent Boze whispered.

"That's the asshole you came lookin' for, it's Dr. Reinart," Lalo said.

"If he had kept his ass in his lab this never would have happened, he just had to come home and spread this."

"Fuckin' sonofabitch!"

"He's like their leader or something, look at the way he can communicate with some of them," Agent Boze said.

"A few of them seem intelligent like him, the others are just walkin' shit bags," Lalo said.

"You got that right. I say we take out those mindless ones first, they may be easier to kill, then we'll deal with Theodore and his star pupils."

Lalo nodded, "How are we gonna do that?"

"Hit them with everything flammable and explosive. I hope your crew pulls through, we need all we can get our hands on," Agent Boze said.

Lalo prayed Sunny found Carl and he wasn't too much of a coward to help her gather what they needed. The situation was looking worse by the minute and he worried if they would be able to kill any of them. A handful of them came stumbling over each other, their clumsy, spasming bodies brushed right up against the bushes concealing Lalo and Agent Boze. The smell of them was nearly too much to bear. Lalo recognized them as two younger men who always golfed together, an old preacher who was hard of hearing, and the old widow. At the tail end of the group came a nearly skeletal figure, its abdomen was open exposing an empty cavity. Lalo cursed to himself when he recognized the tattered Serenity Canyon maintenance shirt and wild red hair hanging from a lopsided skull. It was Peter. Agent Boze huddled close to Lalo and they both held their breath as the group went by. They were headed for the parking lot, and the main gate. They were too afraid to speak but their eyes followed in horror as the undead residents and Peter made it to the yellowed parking lot lights and finally the agent whispered, "I hope Jackson and your boys can hold them off or we're royally fucked."

They caught the sounds of distant shrieking, the things were surely returning to the streets and houses they frequented in life.

"Listen, they're spreading out. He sent them into the neighborhood too," Lalo said.

"There's gonna be nowhere to hide."

Larry wasn't too ashamed to climb his ass into his guard booth but Agent Jackson and Jason were left to stand in front of the gate. They watched the explosion set off by Agent Boze and Lalo tossing grenades and hoped it would corral the horde back toward the club house. The minutes passed like hours as they waited, but when the figures stumbled into the yellow glow of the parking lot lights, they knew it was their time to fight.

"Here they come. We gotta do this!" Jason said, more to himself than the agent at his side.

"Save your ammo until they get close and aim for the head."

"That didn't do shit the first time," Jason said.

"Chill, kid. You're gonna hold them back while I toss them a little present," Agent Jackson said, unzipping his duffle bag.

He pulled out two grenades, Jason felt a little relieved to know they would have a little more than just the guns they had but he knew two grenades weren't going to be enough.

"That'll take care of this first wave and maybe another one, but what're we gonna do when more come?"

"We just gotta hope like hell the Army boys get here before that happens," Agent Jackson said.

"Why didn't you bring more? I mean, you have a trunk load of fuckin' guns but you only brought four grenades?"

"Only four? Listen to what you're sayin', kid. We don't usually go to battle with the undead. We really thought cutting them to pieces with bullets would be sufficient!"

Jason's face burned, the agent was right. Who could have ever dreamed the pristine community of Serenity Canyon would become a warzone?

"Now, look alive. They're getting closer."

The shrieking and groaning of the group was only outpaced by their stench, like vomit and dirty diapers collided in a whirlwind of fetid breath and swept across the parking lot to crawl up Jason's nose.

"Larry, get your ass outta that booth!" Agent Jackson ordered.

Larry begrudgingly came out to join them and pointed his gun at the approaching horde who started stumbling faster towards them.

"They spotted us, hold on until they pass the rear of our car and then open fire on their asses!"

Mrs. Brandon was in the lead. Her stained pajamas and distorted face made Jason feel a sickening pity well up inside of him. He wasn't going to try to nurse her wounds or anything, he was still gonna blow a hole in her face, but it still left a scar on his heart. She shrieked and opened her mouth wide. She shot a stream of yellow puke out before her. It immediately numbed the pity Jason was feeling and reminded him of his fate if she got too close to him.

"Now!" Jackson ordered.

Larry was the first to pull the trigger. He had been the security guard at Serenity Canyon for years and never had to fire a gun or use his pepper spray but he had been a hunter his whole life and had good aim. His first shot punched a hole into the center of Ms. Brandon's chest and sent her falling onto her back. There was no time to celebrate, her vile companions were scrambling toward the human's at the gate. Jason squeezed the trigger and blasted the side of the preacher's head off, he spun like a top and tumbled to the black top but shakily fought to get back on his feet. The younger infected were ambling quicker than the two who were blasted to the ground and their wide eyes and gaping mouths were fixed on Jason and Larry.

"You dumbass!" Agent Jackson yelled over his shoulder.

"I'm trying! " Jason said.

Agent Jackson pulled the pin from one grenade and rolled it out in front of them. He jumped back around the gate and crouched, waiting for the party to start. He covered his head with his arms, knowing in the blink of an eye the grenade would go off. One of the young golfers leaped onto the explosive and brought it to its mouth in an attempt to bite it when it detonated. His body was blasted into pieces, his arms and legs went in opposite directions. His guts flew into the sky like fireworks on the Fourth of July and with them rained rancid stomach bile. What goes up, must come down, and they fell like bloody, gooey hail down onto Larry who watched them with childlike wonder until they splatted against his face. He stumbled back and fell over the waste-high gate.

"Get ready to shoot!" Jackson cried.

Jason lifted his gun and shot the second young golfer-bro in the face and chest and sent him falling back onto the pieces of his comrade. He knew it wouldn't stop him but as he was trying to rise, Mrs. Brandon and the preacher came hobbling forward only to slide in the slippery guts of the creature who literally ate a grenade. It was nearly comical the way they slipped and fell over each other.

Jackson stood up and grinned, "Three for the price of one."

He pulled the pin on his second grenade and let it roll. He grabbed Jason by the back of the shirt and pulled him backwards over the gate. They crouched and kept their heads down but Larry was lying on his back, gagging on the shower of guts and bile he had already received. The explosion was nearly deafening, Jason could feel it in his body when it went off. Moments later, sticky hunks of flesh and entrails rained down on them in a microburst of blood and innards. He grabbed handfuls of chunky, red matter and flung it to the ground, Jason and Agent Jackson stood to survey the damage. The whole group was nothing but bloody, charred chunks clinging to cars, parking lot lights, and tree branches. A skeletal figure with red hair spun around and retreated back across the parking lot. Jason and Agent Jackson shook hands triumphantly.

"You did good, kid!"

"You're the one who blasted 'em to hell!"

"We fucked 'em up!"

"We finally found their kryptonite, fire and explosions. Did you see that one pussy out and leave?" Jason asked.

"Jesus fuckin' Christ!" Larry screamed, shattering the moment of satisfaction.

Larry started slapping at his face and arms. He was covered in the blasted juices and blood from the horde, but also the white worms from inside of them. Jason and Agent Jackson panicked. They dropped their guns onto the pavement and started beating at their bare skin. They had no other choice but to strip their clothes off. They tore off their shirts and kicked off their shoes then yanked their pants off. They stood in their underwear, slapping at their skin and hair. The sensation of writhing worms on their skin wouldn't leave them.

"Over here," Larry said and they followed him to the side of his guard booth.

He pulled open the door and ran inside. He came back with a bottle of bleach, "The laundry crew left this in the parking lot when they unloaded their van. I was gonna give it back but fuck them! It's ours now!"

He twisted off the cap and hesitated, knowing it was going to burn his skin and be caustic to his eyes and nose. He looked to Jason, his face looked unsure but he nodded.

"Come on dude, " he urged Larry to do it.

Larry closed his eyes and began pouring it all over his body. He soaked himself in it. It felt like lighting himself on fire momentarily when the bleach hit his wounds but it became tolerable. He didn't dare breathe too deeply for fear of singeing his lung, he held it as long as he could then shuttered and gasped but didn't feel like he would die so he handed it to Jason who did the same thing before helping Agent Jackson douse himself too. Larry then ran over by the bushes and grabbed the end of a hose. He turned it on at a bib on the wall and began bathing in it. Jackson and Jason joined him and didn't stop spraying until they were somewhat satisfied they were clean.

"Do you think we killed them?" Jason asked, shivering not form cold but from the thoughts of being showered in parasites from the bowels of the walking dead.

Agent Jackson leaned over where they had bathed in bleach and inspected a few of the worms which had fallen off of Larry.

"These look dead."

"Thank fuckin' God!" Jason said.

Headlights flooded the three men, they turned, blinded by the high beams. A truck stopped in the tree lined road leading to the gate of Serenity Canyon. Its engine revved loudly, growling like a beast in the darkness.

"Is it the Army?" Jason asked.

"No, they'd announce themselves and we asked for air support," Agent Jackson said.

The truck leaped forward and stopped again, a warning from the driver, he would run them down if they didn't move.

Their guns weren't close enough to show him they refused to let him pass.

"Get outta the way, you needle-dicked bug-fuckers!"

The voice was familiar, a man with a southern drawl and the haggard gurgle of smoking and drinking way too much. Only one man was so well versed in profanity.

"Jim?" Jason asked

The truck was far too loud for the driver to hear Jason. He stepped forward, coming dangerously close to the roaring machine. If the driver took his foot off the brake pedal, Jason would be run down, flattened into a janitor pancake in seconds.

"Jim! It's me, Jason!"

"Get outta my way, dumb sumbitch!"

"You stupid, drunk, fucker! It's Jason from the SCUM crew!"

The engine eased and a head popped out the driver's side window, "Jason, you shit-ass! What the hell are you doin' naked in the road? Was you takin' a bath with them two men?"

"Listen, you can't be here. It's dangerous"

"You ain't seen dangerous yet, boy. Get the hell outta my way."

"No. You can't go in."

"Listen, sissy boy. You just go soap up your boyfriends and let me through. I'm lookin' for my woman."

"No. You listen, you homophobic hillbilly fuck! You can't go in there!" he put his hands on the hood of the truck.

Jason could smell the whisky breath wafting its way on the wind, it mingled with the scent of over-heated radiator. The hood was hot under his palms and through it he felt the engine roar to life again as Jim pressed the gas pedal down. He knew Jim meant business. He didn't want to let him through but he also didn't want to get run over by some over dramatic drunk. Jason looked back over his shoulder at Agent Jackson who had grabbed his gun while Jason argued with Jim. He motioned Jason out of the way.

Jason stepped out of Jim's path and it was a good thing he did. Jim took his foot off the brake pedal and the old truck jumped forward and barreled towards Agent Jackson who rolled and shot three bullets into it as it rammed through the security gate and into the parking lot. Jim was going way too fast and lost control of the truck, he swerved and hit a tree planted in a decorative island separating the entrance and exit lane to the club house. The wreck made a horrendous sound, like a train barreling into a nitroglycerin plant. Jim crawled out of the cab, cussing at the top of his lungs and screaming for Sandy. He had rammed into the tree, a Mesquite, and the force of the speeding Ford toppled it. It came loose from the earth, leaving an open mouth in the ground smelling of damp soil. It fell onto the side of a parked Mercedes, leaving its car alarm screaming. Smoke rose from the hood of the truck, its front end was smashed in leaving its headlights cross-eyed and slowly dimming.

"Sandy!" Jim cried, unaware of the eyes now fixed on him.

Somewhere in the distance a shrieking answered him.

"That asshole is gonna draw more this way and fuck up all our progress!" Agent Jackson said.

"Goddamn it, Jim! Shut the fuck up!" Larry yelled.

"Fuck off, Larry. Ya lazy piece of shit!" Jim hollered.

Jason ran for him. It spooked Jim a bit to see the young man in his underwear charging at him. He squared up, ready to attack.

"Jim, you need to be quiet. They're goin' to hear you!"

"Like I give a rat's ass! These lyin' bastards ruined my life! Fuck you, you yuppie fucks!" Jim turned and screamed towards the club house but froze when he saw a familiar figure.

"Sandy, baby please!" he cried and jogged towards his wife.

CHAPTER 7
HELL UNLEASHED

JASON FELT Agent Jackson's hand on his shoulder, "It's too late. Let him find out on his own."

Jason nodded sadly, he didn't intend to chase Jim down. If he tried dragging the drunk back, he'd only risk his own life.

"I wish he'd shut the fuck up. He's gonna make them shitter-monsters come this way again," Larry said.

"He's right." Jason didn't want to admit it but Larry was right and the last thing they needed was another group of them to come their way after they had no more explosives and were only in their underwear.

"Do you think we can beat our clothes out and put them on again?" Jason asked.

"I don't know if we should risk it," Agent Jackson said.

"Yeah, I don't want those worms in me."

"But what are we gonna do? We can't fight these things in our skivvy's," Larry said.

"I got a plan. I'll be right back," Jason said.

He rifled through his wet pants pockets, carefully avoiding anything squirming, and grabbed his work key ring then hurried into the darkness along the tall gate.

Agent Jackson watched Jason, dressed only in Batman boxers, slink into the bushes and head toward the maintenance shop.

"He better hurry the fuck up," Larry said and motioned to old Jim who fell silent at the shrieking he inspired with his explosive act of love.

The old man stood next to his truck, scratching his head. The sound of the blaring car alarm drowned the odd screech but he knew it wasn't right. It wasn't anything he had heard before. He would do anything to show Sandy he was sorry for being fired and anything to show the bastards who fired him he was not to be fucked with. His mind wandered away from his woman to the face of the kiss-ass sonofabitch Peter.

"Where are you, you red headed motherfucker? I'm gonna blow yer brains out!" Jim leaned into his truck and grabbed his pistol. It was then he noticed there was more than just smoke in his old smashed truck as hot, crackling flames began to grow from the dash. They licked at him like hot tongues, singeing his arm and leaving the smell of burnt hair lingering around his nose when he yanked it out. His pistol was hot; he juggled it for a minute between his two hands, each of them unable to grip it for more than a few seconds until he dropped it in the soft turned soil by the roots of the Mesquite tree.

"Mother fucker!"

He rubbed his palms together. They weren't burned deeply, just left feeling the warning of the fires destructive bite. He kicked the pistol away from the truck and stood back as the flames consumed the entire front end of it. He bent and retrieved the gun. He shoved it in the front of his wranglers and grabbed his cock and balls. He gave the middle finger salute in the direction of the club house. He looked at his smoldering truck, his eyes straying beyond the orange glow and smoke to see three figures frozen, staring at the rising fire. He smirked, the yuppies must be marveling in horror at his entrance.

"You ain't seen nothin' yet, you pig fuckers! I'm gonna show you rich fucks not to mess with a workin' man! I'll burn this whole place down!"

His threats were cut off by an explosion, it sent him flying sideways. For several moments time slowed down, his body was like a rag doll lifted and tossed into the darkness away from the intense heat of the truck going off like a two ton cherry bomb. The dark sky spun above him, the stars obscured by black smoke. He didn't feel the impact of hitting the black top of the parking lot, not at first, anyway, but when time sped back up and became right again he could feel his right shoulder screaming in agony as his body tumbled and rolled. His vision blurred like he was moving at warp speed as the sky and ground went in circles with his movement until he skidded to a stop beside a curb painted red. Above him the lamp post on the other side of the curb and sidewalk was a yellow orb, a tiny star shining down on him. His head swam, not quite recovered from the dizzying tumble he went through. Though he was in pain, he refused to relent until he spoke to Sandy and until he told Peter to go fuck himself. He pushed himself up and looked down at the gun, it was still tucked in his pants hovering dangerously close to his cock. He said a silent prayer it hadn't accidentally gone off in his flight from beside the Mesquite tree, he would have bled to death before he let any doctor try to sew his dick back on. Jim got to his feet and unsteadily looked around. The fire was blazing sky high, his truck was nothing but flames. He knew the fire must've reached his gas tank and sent him superman-ing across the parking lot. He felt a tinge of embarrassment when he realized the group on the other side of the truck fire was still watching him. They couldn't quite get around the blaze, or didn't want to. He figured someone was probably already on their cellphone calling the police so he had to act fast before he was hauled away by Johnny Law.

"Sandy! Get your ass out here!" he screamed and through the flames he could see a familiar silhouette. He knew it was her just by the way her shoulders had hunched with age and her hair was pulled back in a bun. The way her thin arms dangled at her sides, and her breasts were still firm for an older woman. Plus it was obvious whoever it was wore a uniform and not some fancy shmancy dress like the rest of those rich bitches would be wearing. It had to be his woman. She had come to face him.

"Come on, baby! Don't be like that. Come over here and talk to me!"

His anger was fading into a pitiful sadness, one eating him alive inside since the day he had to tell her he lost his job. The disappointment in her eyes was like a thousand knives slowly being pressed into his chest. He couldn't live without her, he needed her to love him even if he had nothing else in the world.

"Sandy? Please!"

The shadow of Sandy took a step closer, even at a distance he could hear a wheeze. He hoped it was her crying for him as he was crying for her.

"I love you, Sandy!"

The wheeze became a gurgled gagging and all at once a spray of vomit splashed onto the black top at her feet.

"Sandy? Are you feelin' sick?"

Jim ran forward, he held his arms up and tried to skirt the fire. He needed to help Sandy, it was obvious she was sick, probably from being so disappointed in him for being a fuck up, like he always was.

"Get back!" a voice screamed.

Jim turned to see Jason running in his underwear, something yellow thrown over his shoulder.

"What the fuck?"

"Sandy isn't herself, man! They're all fuckin' zombies!"

"You crazy little pansy. Don't say stupid shit, get the hell outta here!"

"I'm serious you drunk fuck!" Jason said and waved Jim to follow him.

Jim stared across the fire, his eyes focusing on the crowd gathering. A second shadow leaned over to puke, a third slashed at the flames and hissed.

"What the fuck?"

Jim turned and ran after Jason who was headed for the security gate.

His boots hurt his feet, his shoulder felt like it was on fire, but he ran like he hadn't smoked like a freight train for thirty years. He made it to the gate to find Jason waiting with the other two men in their underwear.

"What the fuck is happenin'?"

"You picked the wrong night for revenge, Jim!" Jason said as he handed plastic yellow suits to his companions.

Sunny crept silently through the maintenance office, afraid to make the slightest sound. Her heart pounded in her ears like a drum. The lights were off, she figured Carl had flipped the switches so he could hide from the hordes of zombified yuppies. Her flight to the maintenance shop was all a blur to her now, she could hardly remember running there and unlocking the door. It was like a waking nightmare her brain had fogged over to help her forget what she saw, what was just outside. She reached Peter's office and tried the door, it was locked. She flipped through the keys and found the number seven key as Lalo instructed her and opened the door.

"Carl?" she whispered, the sound of her shaking voice sent a chill over her skin.

A commotion from under the desk made her heart stutter. She held her breath and backed away until he answered, "That you, new girl?"

"Yeah. I came to get you. I need your help."

"I told 'em. I ain't goin' back out there."

"I know, but I can't do this alone."

"There ain't nothin' we can do but hide. Don't you get it?"

"Lalo needs us, the crew needs us," She said, her voice a desperate whisper.

Carl got to his feet as a series of explosions went off in the distance. He turned to the window and cursed. The last one sounded big and it originated out by the entrance gate, beyond the trees surrounding the maintenance building he could see the glow of a fire.

"We have to help them fight back. Think of Lalo and Jason. Think of Jose and Shane."

"I don't think I can be of much help."

"We have to try," Sunny said.

"What's your plan?"

"Lalo and the FBI guy want us to collect anything flammable, anything we can burn those fuckers with or blow them up. The Army is headed this way, we just gotta do what we can."

"Fuck…okay," He said.

"Where do we start?" she asked.

"The closest closet with any flammable materials is just down stairs but the others, they're on the other side of the club where all them things are."

"We'll start with the stuff downstairs and then we can sneak to the others," She said.

"I doubt this is gonna work." The uncertainty in Carl's voice made her worry he would back out again, but he was all she had.

"We can do what we can. We can't just hide from this."

"Alright, let's go."

Sunny looked out the office window and saw a flash of pale skin in the moonlight. She nearly screamed until she realized it was Jason, only he was in his underwear and over his shoulder was slung a load of plastic yellow suits.

"What the fuck is he doin?" Carl asked.

"I have no idea, but if he can run around in his damn batman boxers then we can sure as hell get out there and help."

"You're right," Carl said, "I should never have left that kid out there. He's my boy."

Their gaze fell on a few figures stumbling their way towards the maintenance shop, ambling in an unintentional way, like a slow-rising tide of death.

"We better be quick," Carl said and pulled his gun from his pants.

Sunny brandished hers and nodded to him in the darkened office, "I'm ready."

Carl was in front of Sunny as they rounded the building, moving as silently as they could. She had no idea where the custodial closets were but Lalo was confident Carl knew them all. They planned to hit the supply closet on the maintenance office building first and then branch out to the others, but they were farther away and in dangerous territory. They hadn't seen Jason again but they hoped whatever he had planned he was still a member of the SCUM crew, a member of the living.

Carl halted beside the door to the custodial shop and motioned

Sunny close to him and whispered as he unlocked the door. They could hear the infected gala-goers in the proximity by their rasping and screeching.

"In here we can find the gas for the leaf blower Peter makes us use to clean out all the doorways at the club. The grounds crew does most of the outdoor work but they gave us one to keep the residents from complaining about leaves blowing in the doors. There should be at least a few glass bottles lying around and some rags."

"We're gonna make Molotov cocktails?"

"Yup," He answered and pulled her inside.

They went to work scavenging what they could and putting together an assortment of explosives, and all the while they could hear the shrieking of voices beyond the door.

"Sounds like we got a crowd forming out there," Sunny said, her attention straying to the shop door.

Carl nodded and started jamming rags down into bottles after she poured the gasoline. Sunny could hear his frantic breathing as he fumbled with the bottles, his hands shook and she noticed she too was trembling terribly. After what felt like hours of gathering jars and filling them they ended up with little to show for it.

"Do you think these will be enough?" she asked.

"We're about to find out," he said.

"You saw how they stood up against bullets."

"Why do you think I hauled ass outta there?" he asked.

Sunny patted her pockets and Carl stuck his fingers in the breast pocket of his work shirt, "Lookin' for one of these?" he asked holding a lighter.

"Should we take a golf cart or something?" she asked.

"We have a quick one in here. It's the cart Rosa and Isabel use for their rounds. Let's load it up. I'll drive since I know the layout, you light 'em and toss 'em," he said.

Sunny took a deep breath and nodded. Her hands were shaking, and Carl's face was drenched in sweat. The picture of desperation, of Hail Mary plays, a team of strangers pitted against an insidious foe.

"Carl, thank you for coming with me, " she said.

"I guess it's better to die like this than in a hospital somewhere."

"We both have a long time before either of those happen. We're walking away from this tonight."

"Not me, kid," Carl said and began depositing the homemade explosives into the back of the golf cart.

Sunny didn't question him. She just hoped if he had a plan of going out in a blaze of glory he at least would give her the choice whether or not she did too.

The garage door slid up on the side of the maintenance shop, the hiding place of the SCUM crew, a group Sunny was now a part of. The air smelled of Arizona summer, of heat radiating off green grass lawns and creosote bushes wet with monsoon rain. Usually, Sunny would take a deep breath and enjoy it, but not tonight. The summer breeze was comingled the scent of distant fire smoke and something rancid… the three walking corpses outside the maintenance shop door. For just a second, all time stilled. Sunny could see their faces, twisted, ravenous visages, unnatural and horrifying. The vile smell of them, it turned her stomach with nervous acid. Sunny's limbs went cold as goosebumps rose on her skin and something in her mind told her this was all futile, death had come to paradise and there was no escaping it.

"Go!" she urged Carl.

The golf cart zoomed forward and when it did there came three shrieking figures at them. Sunny was already prepared since they had already been beating at the door for what felt like an eternity. She gripped a salsa jar filled with gasoline, a strip of towel shoved down into a hole punctured into the tin lid of the jar. She lit the towel and felt her heart leap into her throat when one of the creatures reared back and spit a mouthful of vomit onto the windshield of the cart. Carl screamed and powered the cart forward, knocking the creatures back like waste-covered bowling pins. One of them launched another mouthful of hot vomit as it fell. The puke hit Sunny in the face. She spat and wiped it away with the back of her hand, her anger rising. They were clumsy and still fighting to stand when Sunny tossed her Molotov onto the pile of them. It exploded in a ball of flames. Carl drove away but she watched in horror as the fire ate into their faces, and traced up their backs in a hungry roar. She had never seen anything like it, she just hoped it killed them and left them dead for good.

The whirring sound of the golf cart wasn't loud but it was loud enough to draw the attention of another bumbling pair of undead Serenity Canyon residents. Two old men who were inching close to death before they ever infected with the parasite, making their gaping, violet mouths and wrinkled, snarled faces all the more disturbing, like demonic grandpa's looking to disembowel whoever they got their arthritis-gnarled hands on. Sunny lifted a jar and readied her lighter.

"Here comes two on the right!" Carl said.

"I see the bastards!" Sunny answered.

The old dead men staggered toward the cart as Carl slowed it down to a crawl, giving Sunny a good shot at them. She gritted her teeth and lit the towel in the jar and watched the flames eat at it for a moment to make sure it was good to go. The creature slightly in the lead let out a hiss as she looked him dead in his eyes, they were cloudy and bloodshot. The way his jowls hung and bounced with each awkward, ambling step he took toward them sickened her.

"Go to Hell!" She yelled and tossed the jar and watched the two men go up in flames.

The sight of them, it was so unreal, and brought tears to her eyes. She didn't want to believe it was true. She kept telling herself it was all a nightmare, and that she'd wake up soon. The smell of them filled the air and hit her nose, even at a distance, it reminded her that this was no dream.

Carl sped forward, the cart quickly gaining ground away from the. He made his way along the sidewalk toward the clubhouse and kitchen area.

"Next supply closet is on the other side of the club house and down a ways, get ready. We don't have too many to spare but we'll have enough to cover our asses until we get there," Carl yelled back over his shoulder.

He knew there was a supply room in the back of the kitchen but he didn't think they'd make it back out if they ever managed to get into it in the first place, and he felt a responsibility to keep Sunny from ending up a hippy zombie. He didn't care so much about himself anymore, but the girl, he'd do what it took to keep her alive. She was a part of the SCUM crew now and they stuck together.

Agent Boze and Lalo had to crawl through the bushes, making their way slowly around to almost the backside of the kitchen when a loud explosion halted them. It was big, bigger than the grenades moments before when they knew Agent Jackson and Jason had to be defending the gate. Lalo prayed it was Sunny and Carl, giving the ravenous yuppie zombies an explosive taste of gasoline and BIC lighters.

He crawled up next to Agent Boze who halted at the edge of the bushes, they were either going to have to make a run for the dumpster and take shelter, or hot-foot it for the other row of bushes edging the sidewalk behind it. Frantic screaming put them on edge. It was the cry of someone still human, someone fighting for their life. They held their breath as it drew out long and ragged. The click, click, click, of high heels on concrete came closer and so did the constant scream.

From their vantage point on the ground they could see the lower half of a woman running, a sleek black skirt and pumps. They were impressed how skillfully she could actually maneuver in such shoes but they wished she would stop her endless squealing. She was only drawing the zombies their way, and ruining their escape plan. Behind her rambled the feet of a whole group of the infected residents of Serenity Canyon, twisted ankles in expensive heels, manicured toenails on dead appendages, loafers crusted in feces and blood attached to the crooked legs of men who usually frequented the golf course.

Once she made it to the dumpster the screaming woman did something which could have been helpful if she hadn't been drawing them to her with her cries. She threw the dumpster lid open and started climbing inside of it. She pulled herself up onto the side of it and was about to drop in head-first when one of the creatures grabbed her by the ankle. It yanked her back, raking her abdomen and ribs over the sticky metal dumpster side. She kicked it in the face and pulled herself back to the edge, she went tumbling into the leaking bags of kitchen trash, a plume of insects took flight as she descended inside. It would have been a decent plan if it had been Lalo and Boze, they weren't spotted yet, they could have slipped inside and hid but she was already being pursued, hunted by unstoppable flesh machines. She couldn't close the lid so she was trapped inside the dumpster, flailing in the split open bags of garbage like a toddler floundering in a ball pit of refuse. Two of the well-dressed monsters went in after her and the screams turned to gagging. She would soon join the other hunters.

Lalo pounded the dirt with his fists, they were helpless to save her. The distinct whirring of golf cart tires on the sidewalk was followed by its small tires zooming by. He could see the back of the golf cart, Sunny was hanging on for dear life. It came to a jolting stop and Carl yelled, "Light 'em up!"

She lifted a pickle jar sloshing full of gasoline and stuffed with a microfiber towel they used for cleaning windows and mirrors. There was a tiny spark in her hand and the towel lit. She held it for a few seconds, making sure it was good to go, before tossing it at two women in filthy ball gowns as they lurched for the cart.

"Suck on this, bitches!" she yelled.

The Molotov cocktail impacted the abdomen of one of the creatures and ignited in a glorious wave of orange. Carl didn't waste any time in getting them the hell outta there. When he saw the screaming woman, he hoped he could help her but when she jumped in the dumpster and those zombie bastards followed her he knew it was too late.

"Toss one in the dumpster! She's a goner!" he yelled.

Sunny waited for him to get a little closer and she did as she was told, she tossed a flaming ketchup bottle into the dumpster and watched it go up. The stench was awful and she wasn't sure if it was from the burning bags of trash or the smoldering human flesh mixed in. Tears ran down her cheeks as they drove away.

"Wait!" A voice called and she recognized Lalo scrambling from under the bushes.

She slapped the back of Carl's head and told him to stop.

"It's Lalo and the FBI guy!"

He punched the brakes and he watched in his rearview mirror as they ran for the cart. He put it in reverse and met them half way. The night was full of screeching and the smell of death, he knew they had much more to do.

Lalo and Agent Boze jumped on the cart, Lalo climbed into the back to assist Sunny and Agent Boze rode shotgun beside Carl. They were already spotted by a big group of the infected yuppies, a shrieking, stinking mass of them were moving in their direction.

"Give them a taste of what we got!" Carl said and hit the gas.

The golf cart surged forward and he turned the wheel to drive directly at the creatures. Agent Boze held on for his life, not expecting the golf cart to pick up speed so quickly. Carl jerked the wheel and the cart spun around, Sunny and Lalo were armed and ready. She lit both the explosives and they tossed them onto the crowd as Carl hit the gas and they drove away, fire leaping into the darkness and silhouettes of clumsy dead things stumbling over each other in confusion and alarm at the introduction of the only thing which killed the worms piloting them. Their screams weren't silenced until the flames bit into their throats and lungs like a new invading plague, one which ate the parasites where they slept and bred.

"Fuck all y'all!" Carl yelled as they drove away.

Stephi was now Teddy's bride again. She stood at his side, her wheezing breaths like a sweet love song in his ears, her eyes hung from their nerve cords and bounced on her cheeks. She would be a mother to a million of his children, starting with a zooming golf cart full of human nuisances setting his other children on fire. The worm Gods within his brain sent a signal of concern about the flames, many of them would not survive, the pilots within them would be destroyed and there would be no regeneration of their tattered tissue, there would be no stomach or intestines to hold larvae, they would be dead for good. He stomped out of his throne room, the gala hall, and at his side his bride awaited his orders. His senses told him his weakest children were also being cut down at the entrance gate by explosive-wielding humans. The old woman, his first child, Mrs. Brandon, her pilots were silenced. The useless in life and death, Peter, unable to create offspring, his pilots were somewhere in the distance but a few others, they were gone too. His ire burned hotter than any fire, his anger would rule him soon, and send him into such a blind rage he would tear every cottage in the upscale neighborhood down to the ground just to destroy the living that created so many problems for him and his children. They would flee before him like rats and beg him to give them new life with a mouthful of his vomit. Stephi twitched at his side, anxious to kill and procreate. She was seeing through new eyes now, she was given a new existence with a new understanding of all things, she would soon know the meaning of being a hunter, a killer, and he would guide her. He stepped out into the darkness, his children gathering about him, they would move as one, they would destroy the humans as a family.

"Oh fuck! They spotted us!" Sunny said, pointing to an even larger group of the creatures on the other side of the bonfire they created with the first horde. A hulking beast of a zombie strode between them and they parted for him as if he was their leader, their creator. Carl didn't slow down but Agent Boze glanced back over his shoulder, "Do you recognize him?"

"Yeah, that looks like Dr. Reinart, the guy you came here for," Lalo answered over the whirring of the golf cart tires on the sidewalk.

"Fuck!" Carl yelled, suddenly jerking the steering wheel. It ran off the sidewalk and down a grassy hill towards the golf course pond. Lalo fell from the cart and rolled down the hill, his vision tumbled over and over but in the course lighting he could see a staggering silhouette. He recognized it immediately, it was Shane but he only had one arm. He could hear screaming, Sunny's voice in full panic-mode, and then a loud splash.

Lalo got to his feet dizzily looking about himself. He turned to see Carl and Agent Boze desperately trying to save jars of gasoline from the back of the cart as it sank in the green waters of the pond. Sunny came to his side and grabbed his arm. She yanked him down toward the water.

"Hurry up! He's coming!"

Lalo looked back over his shoulder to the top of the hill and under the yellow light stood Shane. He felt a chill run through him, one of pity and disgust, it ended in a heavy feeling in his heart. Shane was no longer the somewhat lazy, mischievous, guy Lalo knew, but a monster. Agent Boze and Carl came to Lalo's side.

"We got two before it went down," Agent Boze said.

"I dropped the lighter!" Sunny said.

"Fuck, quick we gotta find it!" Carl said.

The three dropped to their knees and frantically searched the grass but Lalo remained on his feet, his eyes glued to Shane who now slowly started to stumble in their direction. It turned his stomach, he was sick with pitiful sadness and terror at what Shane had become. They would never be in this mess if they hadn't had to work the overtime, if the gala had been held one night sooner or later, they would all be home with their families. Fate had cursed them to be there that night, to be plunged into the horror of it all, some never returning from it.

"I found it!" Sunny yelled.

She was standing farther away from them, where she helped Lalo to his feet. Shane was getting closer and closer, his mouth now dripping with either mucus or vomit like a rabid dog. He wheezed and opened his mouth, a high pitched shriek broke the trance Lalo was in and he jumped back into action. Shane gagged a bit and puked down the hill. It missed its mark, fell short of them by many feet, but it reminded them the creature's weaponry went beyond their teeth and hands, they used such emissions to spread the parasite inside them.

"Don't get his puke on you!" Agent Boze warned them though they already knew.

Sunny rubbed her face self-consciously, hoping the few drops she got hit with when they left the maintenance shop wouldn't cause her to become like Shane.

"Light him up," Carl said, his voice cracked and they knew he was holding back tears.

A deafening shriek cut the night like a knife and Shane halted. Behind him, a hulking figure came into view and with it a group of staggering, deformed beings, leaking bodily fluids and screeching cries of war. The mass of them grew by the second until Lalo was sure most of the neighborhood had arrived to drown the last of the SCUM crew in showers of filth until they too grew glassy eyed and became monsters. Sunny hid behind him, he could feel her despair like a heavy blanket on his back. The big one, what was once Theodore Reinart, came to the lead. He was naked except for a coating of black stinking filth, his head and body misshapen. Teddy squeezed his hands into fists the size of cantaloupes and Lalo thought back to the destruction of the Shack, it had to have been Teddy.

"We're fucked," Agent Boze said.

"Look at 'em, the high falutin' fucks. Who's scum now?" Carl asked.

He walked out in front of Lalo and Sunny, gripping an olive jar full of gasoline.

"I'ma need my lighter back."

He held his hand out and Sunny placed a lighter in it.

"Carl?" Lalo said.

"I forgot to tell you, Lalo, but I, in my own way, already told the girl. I gave my resignation to Peter today. I asked him to give my bonus to Jason, the boy deserves it and I won't need it. I planned on calling around for hospice care places tomorrow, but I guess dying here is better than two or three months from now in one of those beds, right?"

"Carl, what the fuck?"

"It's nearing my time. Just tell my boy Jason to quit smokin' while he can."

Lalo didn't know how to respond, "Carl, thank you, man."

Carl nodded sadly, turned back around and walked quickly up the hill towards the horde, a sloshing jar of gas in one hand and a lighter in the other. The crowd came for him, sweeping around Teddy like a wave of walking filth.

"Run!" he called back to Lalo, Sunny, and Agent Boze.

The clawing hands of a woman decked out in a black silk gown reached for him, but before he let them knock the Molotov from his shaking hand, he lit the end of the towel jammed into it. They surrounded him just as the flame contacted the gasoline and in a final shout of resistance, Carl tossed the jar up into the air. It danced there for a second before falling back down on the head of the zombie in the black silk gown, erupting immediately, drowning her, Carl and many others in the vicinity in flames.

Lalo's tears blinded him from the sight of it, mercifully sparing him the memory of Carl standing for a moment completely ablaze before falling to his knees amidst the other corpses. Sunny's screams tore through him, stripping away some of strength he was trying to reserve inside of himself. He was watching all hope die around him.

Agent Boze slapped Lalo's arm and cried, "Let's go!"

The three ran for their lives but as they made their way around the side of the lake they could see shadows stumbling toward them, and shrieks alerting others to their location. They would be pursued relentlessly until the very end. They kept moving, there was nothing more to do than to run and to fight. Agent Boze prayed for the sound of helicopters, the Army was their last hope of making it out of Serenity Canyon. Sunny was a few steps behind him, her screams made him spin around and point his gun at a shadow lurching from the bushes like a rabid raccoon. It gripped Sunny by the arm. He could hear a rumbling in its gut and knew what was coming next. Before he squeezed his trigger, Lalo took a shot of his own. A bullet blasted through the side of what used to be an older man's head. The creature released Sunny and tumbled sideways.

Lalo pulled Sunny away and began pistol whipping the shrieking thing which was once

Pastor Crumm. Lalo never liked him when he was among the living, he always had a fake smile plastered to his face but his eyes portrayed how much of a judgmental prick he was. Lalo's fear had morphed into a blind rage, it urged him to keep pounding the old man's head until it was a broken shell filled with red goo. Agent Boze dragged him away but even in the faint light he could see the old man's brain matter squirming. It made him nauseous. He bent over and plunged his hands into the lake to clean the blood from them.

"They're gettin' too close!" Sunny said, and her companions felt her words in their chests like the impact of a swinging hammer. They were being surrounded and had very few places to run.

"Let's go!" Boze said and they fled once more, not knowing how or if they would make it through the nightmare they found themselves in.

"Go up the hill, there's a couple buildings and I have the keys," Lalo said.

Sunny's heart dropped when Lalo tumbled to the ground, gripping his ankle. She skidded to a stop and went back to where he lay in the grass.

"I twisted my ankle. Fuck, I think it's broken!"

"Calm down, I'll help you."

"Come on! We gotta go!" Agent Boze barked, his eyes darting from them to an approaching group of zombies, then back to the way they came– another large group of them, led by Teddy, who avoided the explosion of Carl.

"Come on, Lalo!" Sunny urged as she helped him up. She wrapped one of his arms over her shoulder and started pulling him along with her.

He grimaced and cried out with each step, but they hurried towards the grounds shop at the edge of the golf course.

"We're never gonna make it," Agent Boze said and pulled his gun and fired into the group, "it won't kill 'em but it will knock 'em down."

They were fifty yards from the grounds shop when a lone zombie came hobbling out of the dark, he held his arms out and the tattered Serenity Canyon shirt caught the breeze carrying the smell of him to Lalo's nose. It was what was left of Peter. Agent Boze raised his gun but only the dry snap of no ammunition registered.

Lalo pulled his gun and fired, "¡Vete a la verga, Pito!"

Peter's body fell back but he twitched, they knew he was only steadying himself to come back for another attack. Lalo handed Boze the gun so he could shoot while Sunny helped him walk the rest of the way to the only sanctuary in sight. The voices of the dead were right behind them, unrelenting, and always hungry. Sunny rushed Lalo along but Peter rolled and snagged Lalo's good ankle in his dead hand. They fell to the grass; the impact forced the breath from Lalo's lungs. Sunny's shoulder jarred against the earth under Lalo's weight and a snap filled her ears seconds before it erupted in hot agony. Agent Boze emptied his clip in Peter's head and pulled Sunny from the ground. She was gasping to catch her breath and Lalo was trying to get his only good foot to move when the screeching of steel caught their ears. Lalo recognized it, it was a garage door.

The grounds shop door pulled upward and inside two sets of headlights glowed. Engines began to rev in the darkness.

"SCUM CREW!" Jose cried out as he drove into sight.

His war machine was once an industrial ride-on lawnmower, a fancy, expensive type with a little cab for the driver to sit in surrounded by Plexiglas to keep golf balls from hitting them in the face. He had the decks lifted, a move usually reserved for cleaning or replacing blades, but the guards had been removed from its blades and they had been forced up and angled outward to cut enemies off at the thighs. Since it had a cabin for the driver, Jose had the room to cram at least one more person inside with him. Behind him came a second armored vehicle, it was the range picker. He had removed the arms with the ball pickers then taped and tied to it pitchforks and sharpened broom handles. It had two pole saws strapped to it, their buttons taped down to leave them constantly sawing. Isabel drove it, her face frozen in a mask of terrified determination.

"¡Corre, pinche Lalo! ¡Corre!" Isabel screamed.

Sunny and Agent Boze lifted Lalo between them, draping his arms over their shoulders and running with his feet barely touching the ground. The two zombie-smashing machines met the three in the middle. Lalo was relieved to see two more of the SCUM crew alive, especially after seeing Shane and watching Carl take him out. He didn't see Rosa, his heart sank but he didn't ask about her. If she was alive, she would have been at Isabel's side like she always was, her absence said it all.

Jose helped Lalo and Agent Boze into Isabel's contraption while Sunny climbed into his and sat on his lap like a child pretending to drive their father's car.

"I don't think O.S.H.A would approve of these, but thank God for you!" Lalo said.

"O.S.H.A can suck my dick!" Jose shouted.

"Late, as usual, but I'm happy to see you!"

"What now?" yelled Jose over the sound of revving saws and whirring blades.

"Fight our way to the parking lot. We gotta join forces with Agent Jackson if we wanna have a chance of getting' outta here!" Agent Boze called back.

Screeching startled Sunny and she pointed to the stumbling figure of Peter who had pulled himself up from the grass, his head was being knit back together haphazardly by squirming white tendrils. There weren't many in him, just those in his mangled brain, but they fought to keep him moving out of self-preservation.

"It's Peter!"

"I got this, girl. I've been wantin' to fuck him up for years!"

Jose swung his war machine around and gave it gas, neither of the vehicles was very fast, but it was quick enough to run down a bumbling freak with half a head.

"Fuck you, Pito!" Jose yelled as the spinning blades caught Peter by the arm and dragged him in like a hunk of meat in a blender. Coagulated blood sprayed the windshield and chunks of Peter littered the grass. Jose kept his foot on the gas and they ran over what was left from the blades devouring his flesh. Sunny looked behind them and the ragged stump of Peter was still wiggling.

"Fuckin' gross!"

"Oh shit, here they come!" Jose said, watching a big horde of the creatures coming right for them with Teddy still in the lead.

"Let's get the fuck outta here!"

The two machines took off across the golf course, overloaded with injured humans and pursued by stumbling corpses.

Jason threw the yellow suits at Agent Jackson and Larry the security guard. Jim came running up behind him, breathing like he hadn't exerted himself in decades.

"What the fuck is happenin'? Are they…zombies? Is Sandy dead?"

"You should have stayed home, Jim!"

Jason, Larry, and Agent Jackson were busy trying to suit up in the plastic yellow suits Jason brought back from the supply closet while Jim looked back over the wreckage of his truck to see the group of strangers, one in particular. They were all dead, monsters all of them, his heart sank. The wind blew and he caught the smell of puke and feces and fire, like the gates of Hell had opened and all the sinners inside had eaten a casino seafood buffet and got wicked food poisoning.

Jim felt his heart drop, it felt like he couldn't breathe and it wasn't from running, it was from knowing the love of his life was a dead thing. He pulled the pistol out of his pants and held it to his temple as hot tears bled from his eyes. He was a fuck up, always had been, but Sandy made him feel like he wasn't such a loser. She accepted him as he was, they laughed together, made love, and even when they fought he couldn't imagine being with anyone else, but now she was gone. And not gone like leaving him for two days because he lost a job, they would always make up and get back together in those situations, she was gone for good, forever, and forever was something he couldn't bear.

"Jim, put it down," Larry said.

"I can't live without her, brother. I just can't."

"Come on, man. Use your bullets on those things. It's their fault she is dead," Jason said.

Jim was ugly crying, snot ran out of his nose and hung on his lip, his face was crinkled and red like a constipated baby.

"I can't live without Sandy."

"Then live for her, make the rest of your life one she would have wanted to be a part of," Jason said.

Jim wiped the string of snot from his nose and nodded, "She always wanted me to make our porch into an Arizona room."

"See, you can do those things and in a way she'll still be with you," Jason said.

Jim lowered his gun and looked at the three of them as they pulled on the same masks the SCUM crew wore when they cleaned the Shack and the smell was too awful, "Why were y'all naked, where's your clothes?"

"No time to explain, we gotta blow these bastards sky high!" Jason said.

"How are we gonna do that if we have no grenades?" Larry asked.

"Let's shoot the cars gas tanks," Jason said.

"No, dummy. That shit don't work, especially in these fancy cars, the gas tanks are really protected incase people get in car accidents. I mean, unless you got incendiary rounds?" Jim actually sounded smart for once when he laid out the facts.

"That's a negative," Agent Jackson said.

"That's a shame, those cars would make great bombs," Jason said.

"We don't have time to jerk our peckers, they're getting' brave and they'll come this way. How about y'all Shoot'em and distract 'em and I'll shove some rags in gas tanks and light 'em on fire?" Jim said.

"That sounds like a good plan but those are new cars, you know some of those gas tanks have locks on 'em," Agent Jackson said.

"All's I need is a screwdriver, ya think I ain't stole gas from a rich fucker before?"

"What about your Arizona room, Jim? This sounds like fuckin' suicide," Larry said.

"Larry, it was a beautiful thought but I'm too damn lazy to go buildin' in my porch. You know that. And without Sandy, I'll just drink myself to death or wind up in jail, may as well do something good with my life or die tryin'."

CHAPTER 8
THE AMERICAN WAY

"LET ME GO!" Dr. Abileen cried.

Dr. Murphy huddled over her, shining bright lights into her eyes and testing her reflexes, nodding in satisfaction. Dr. Abileen remembered the cancer patient, Charlie. Her heart pounded in her chest, her lungs tightened with anxiety. She didn't want to die and live again.

"What did you give me? Am I gonna turn into one of those things?"

Dr. Murphy stopped inspecting and looked her in the eyes, "I'm not like your boyfriend, I'm not that fucked up."

"What are you doing?" Dr. Abileen wept.

"Research, Sarah," she answered.

"I don't understand."

"Well, how about this, before I give you a clean bill of health I have to be sure you're not going to change when, say, you have a heart attack, or when you get into a head on collision on the freeway. I've seen you vomit your guts out and heard it flying from the other end, but what about your grey matter?"

"The only way to test that would be to," Dr. Abileen hesitated, thinking it over but knowing damn well where this conversation was going, and said, " to kill me."

"I'm sorry, Dr. Abileen. It's the only way, but I assure you the few we collect like you from that neighborhood won't be given this final test. You'll be proof enough for me. They just get to be monitored for next three or four years before being disposed of, in a humane way. promise."

"Monitored? You mean experimented on like lab rats."

Dr. Murphy stepped over to a cabinet and opened it. She ran her finger along an assortment of saws and forceps and came back holding the skull saw, the same Dr. Abileen opened Dr. Entz head with.

"I'd like to take a look at your brain just to be certain our antidote is doing away with any infestation there. Can you imagine what countries will pay for this? A one-shot parasite destroyer that works in hours and not weeks or months, maybe I'll name it Sarah or Abileen after you."

Dr. Abileen closed her eyes at the whirring of the saw. She clenched her fists and ground her teeth, waiting for the searing pain of her end. Her heart raced in her chest, she held her breath, a million thoughts ran through her mind, all her joys and all her regrets blurring into one long image. A panoramic picture of the course of her entire life nailed to the inside of her eyelids.

A bang left her deaf, hot liquid sprayed across her cheek, and a sudden weight hit her stomach. Dr. Abileen opened her eyes to see one of the guards, Donald. His arm was extended, shaking, the gun in his hand. Dr. Murphy's blood and brains painted Dr. Abileen and the wall beside of her. The guard's partner, T, went to work freeing Dr. Abileen.

"We gotta go, now!"

She sat up, her head was still spinning and her body felt exhausted, but she followed them in a haze, like walking through a dream. She could barely feel her legs and her heart thundered in her chest as she was led out of the labyrinth-like facility and to a black car. She realized when T turned to speak to her that her hearing was muffled, her ears left ringing by the gunshot which set her free of Dr. Murphy.

"Stay here, we gotta clean this up. Is there anything you need from inside?" he asked.

"My black bag, the antidote is inside, " she answered.

They gathered Dr. Murphy's black satchel and Dr. Abileen was sat in the back of a car. Time drug out, painfully slow, her heartbeat drumming in her temples as she attempted to clean the brain matter from her clothing. The guards climbed into the car and they sped away as quickly as the car could drive. A loud boom issued from beyond the car window, loud enough to feel it in her chest and the entire building went up in flames. She unzipped the satchel to find only few more vials of the antidote, the boys in green would have only been able to spare five of the Serenity Canyon Residents, the rest would have been killed. Although those who were "spared" would have ended up wishing they were killed on sight. They would all be put to death now if the Army realized Dr. Murphy was dead. She was certain Dr. Murphy would have to be in constant contact with them, they would call her soon, they would know.

"I need to call Agent Boze," She said.

Donald dialed a cellphone and handed it back to her.

"If you survive the infected, run from the boys in green. Their orders will be to kill everyone, survivors included. I'll contact you when I can," She spoke and hung up the phone.

She handed the phone back to the front seat and let her head lay back against the headrest as the guards drove her away from her life, her career, away from the nightmare she was trapped in. She didn't know what life would be after it was all said and done, but she was glad they decided she was worth saving and she meant to do the same for Agent Boze and anyone he could rescue.

"Did he get the message?" T asked.

"He got it, zombies don't answer phones," She said.

"Where should we go?" Donald asked.

"Head towards Sedona," She answered.

Agent Boze felt his pocket vibrate. He yanked his phone out and answered it. His eyes went wide as he listened to Dr. Abileen impart her message to the last survivors of Serenity Canyon. He didn't get to ask any questions before she hung up the phone. He stared at the phone screen, horrified but not completely shocked. The government would leave no witnesses.

"We've gotta get outta here. The Army won't help us, they're ordered to kill us."

"What about blocking the gate, keeping them from getting to the city?" Lalo asked.

"That's no longer my concern, surviving is."

Lalo looked to him in surprise, "What the hell are we gonna do if we make it outta here?"

"Worry about staying alive, the rest will fall into place."

Lalo nodded, Agent Boze was right, they still didn't know who would even survive.

The FBI Agent dialed his phone and held it to his ear, Lalo knew he had to be warning his partner.

"The boys in green are ordered to kill us all. Get outta here!"

A massive explosion near the parking lot rocked the earth beneath the Range Picker. The sudden burst of hot flames illuminated shadows of the infected, scrambling and shambling with fire eating into them. Isabel was startled and cut the wheel, their front tire dipped into the edge of a sand trap and the world tumbled as it flipped. Screams filled the tiny cab, Lalo and agent Boze tumbled into one another as they were tossed around.

They climbed from the wreckage, Lalo struggling to stand with one broken ankle. Agent Boze reached down for Isabel who was bleeding from the forehead and dazed, laying half in and half out of the range picker. She took his hand and he pulled her but her left leg was trapped under the seat of her war machine.

Jose and Sunny turned around and parked between them and the horde.

"Get her outta there!" he screamed.

"¡Ayudame, por favor!" Isabel cried.

"Lift the fuckin' thing!" Sunny said and the three men joined her as she pushed the side of the range picker upward.

Isabel cried in agony as she dragged her broken leg out behind her. Lalo was balanced on his good foot but he offered his hand and so did Jose.

"Sunny," he said, "you two get in my cart and fuckin' drive!"

"We can't leave you guys."

"Just do it!" Lalo said.

"What about your leg?" Sunny asked.

"We got him! Head toward the parking lot but cut sideways, we gotta find a way out of here besides the gate. We'll lead them to the fire and then escape, hopefully most will die. We need to be gone before the Army arrives, which is any fuckin' minute," Boze said, feeling his pockets for ammunition. He had two clips, one for his guns, one for Lalo's who was now held by Jose.

Sunny climbed into Jose's cart and they lifted Isabel to sit in her lap.

"Go!"

They took off as Teddy and his horde approached, shrieking and gagging out mouthfuls of vomit. Jose and Agent Boze each took one of Lalo's arms and draped them over their shoulders and rushed away with him hanging between them. Their only advantage was the infected moved relatively slow, but their stamina was unending, like an unstoppable apocalypse in slow motion just behind them.

They were about sixty yards from the edge of the parking lot when another blast went up right in front of them, a shining silver car engulfed in fire, and nearly knocked the three of them on their asses. The heat was an unbelievable wave hitting them, stealing their breath and blinding their eyes for a moment before morphing into a black cloud of billowing smoke against the night sky. Random gun shots tore through zombie flesh and split skulls, the horde was falling but they wouldn't stay down unless they were caught in the vacuum of fire with each explosion. Jason and his boys were waging a true war. Car alarms cried in the distance and the screeches of the dead were those of defeat and not triumph. Above the screeches of dismay there rose a familiar voice. Lalo and Jose glanced at each other.

"Suck my dick you pants shittin' fucks!"

"It's Jim!" Lalo said.

"Come on. We gotta cut toward the perimeter," Agent Boze said, following the path of the cart driven by Sunny.

As they retreated toward the side security-fencing surrounding the community, Lalo could see Jim's silhouette against the massive bonfire he was creating from luxury cars in the parking lot. He was tall and thin, his wild hair blowing in the wind, and he dragged someone along with him, someone with half a head.

Jim wasted no time taking the screwdriver from Larry's guard booth. Larry smiled and palmed him a small bottle of whisky.

"I kept that for the cold nights."

"You're a gem, Larry," Jim grinned, unscrewed the lid and downed the small bottle without a wince or a cough.

He then took off his button up shirt and tore it into strips, not worrying about going to battle in a pair of wranglers and a stained wife beater, in his mind he died when Sandy became infested with parasites. Agent Jackson's phone rang and he ran to the pile of shed clothing to retrieve it. He lifted it to his ear and listened, his face grim.

"That was Boze, the Army has orders to kill us all. We gotta get outta here."

"What? They can't."

"They can and they will."

"Alright boys, I'm stayin' here to finish what I wanna do. Just lay down some shots and then run for it," Jim said.

"You don't have to stay. We could all leave," Larry said.

"I'm not leavin' until I finish what I came here for. I wanted to fuck this place up, get my woman, and I'm gonna do that."

Jim jumped the short security gate and turned to Jason, "It was nice knowin' ya, kid."

Jason shook his hand and he ran towards the dying fire of his pickup truck and beyond that, his destiny.

"Give him some cover," Jackson said.

They took aim and started firing all the ammo they had into the lurching, puking residents of Serenity Canyon while Jim juked and jived, a gut full of a little whisky, and a heart brimming with determination. Jason never considered Jim graceful before, more like a clumsy, hungover old fuck, but the way he worked gas tanks open, shoving strips of his shirt sleeves down in them before dashing to the next, while spinning and avoiding groping hands and sprays of vomit, it was like a ballet. After he lit the first strip of shirt and darted away, they watched with bated breath, and when it went up in a massive explosion, they nearly wept. It spread out, a ripple of pure force and fire, leaving all staggering too close swallowed by flames. The dead danced too, with moves of their own, the Macarena of Doom as they tried patting their heads and shoulders out, they tried swiping the flames away from their arms. The vehicles of parasites were being commanded to save themselves, and they were failing, their pilots perishing when skulls were invaded by intense heat, cooking them like ovens filled with brains.

Jim had never felt such heat in his life, he felt his skin being cooked just being in the vicinity of the first flaming car. The pain was something he could bear, it meant nothing anymore, his emotional aching would soon be over too and he would rejoice as it was snubbed out. The second car went up in a bang, he was a little too close and was flung out across the blacktop. He rolled and was on his feet with the grace of an alley cat, his elbows shredded and dripping blood. He pulled another strip of shirt from his pocket but halted there, Sandy was hobbling over to him. Half of her head was gone but he would recognize the eye still left in her face, and her cheek. She was his woman, his love, even after death. White tendrils snaked wildly out of the side of her head, he knew she would try to change him, but he wouldn't allow it. He would go down a man, not a vile, undead *thing*. He yanked his wife beater off and wrapped it around her disfigured head, tied it off, hoping it would keep her from trying to puke on him…if she even could with half a head. He then grabbed her hand, held it in his like he did when they were so in love, when they'd get drunk and dance in the kitchen together before making love on the couch. She didn't fight him. He pulled her along on his next mission. She slowed him down a little bit but he still managed to shimmy around and dodge sprays of stinking waste to light gas tanks up. The firelight was so bright, almost beautiful, now surrounding him, coming too close. He pulled Sandy against him and listened to her zombiekind dying, hissing and shrieking, their bodies burning with flaming gasoline. A low thrumming of a helicopter in the distance caught his attention. Their nuptials amidst the flames complete, he was ready.

"It's time, baby."

Jim grabbed her shirt-wrapped half-head and dared to kiss what he guessed was part of her lips. It was magical, their vows of love renewed, at least in his heart. The sound became louder, it was almost overhead, gun shots rang out, but he kissed her again, and held her against him. He swayed his body, a slow dance, one last time. Another gunshot rang out, his chest seized, blood ran from where his heart once beat, the heart he promised to Sandy. A voice on a loudspeaker was barking out orders but he didn't listen, he couldn't anymore. He was only focused on Sandy, on seeing her soon in the afterlife.

"I love you, always have, always will."

With the last of his strength, he held her and pushed her backwards. They fell into the wall of flames, their bodies burning, melting. Their spirits fused together for all eternity.

Jason felt his heart leap into his chest at the sound of helicopters. Jim had fulfilled his promise. They had fired all the rounds they had at the creatures as he ran and rambled between cars. When they ran out, they watched him for a moment dancing one last dance with Sandy, surrounded by fire, whispering his undying love to her.

"Jim was a good man. A true SCUM crew member."

It was time for them to retreat, to escape death at the hands of their own military. Machine gun fire cut down the entrance road to Serenity Canyon and they were dressed in bright yellow suits, sitting ducks. Larry caught a bullet in the eye socket, the impact spun him around and for a moment his good eye blinked in disbelief. He fell to the blacktop as Agent Jackson tackled Jason. They tumbled into the stickered brush where they bathed the bleach from their skin.

"Crawl!" he ordered.

Jason obeyed, frantically clawing his way into thorny, flowery bushes as bullets zinged by him. The brush clawed at his face, the rest of his skin protected by the plastic suit, leaving trails of blood dripping down his cheeks like red tears. The helicopter stayed on its path towards the golf course but the man behind the gun spun the gun as they flew over and kept his finger on the trigger, blasting holes into the earth beside Jason's head and then an explosion of searing pain in his back sent him twisting and screaming in agony. Agent Jackson was right behind him, powering through the brush. He barely avoided catching a bullet in the head as he crawled over to Jason.

"Come on, kid! We gotta go!"

He rolled Jason over and felt the exit wound in his abdomen, it was big and mean, bleeding freely from the hole in the shredded yellow plastic. Agent Jackson held his hand over the wound, gave it all the pressure he could while Jason wept.

"I can't move."

"Yes, you fuckin' can. Come on!"

"I'm gonna die here. Just go!"

"Fuck no!"

Agent Jackson got to his feet, bent down and hauled Jason up. Jason couldn't walk, so the agent threw him over his shoulder and hobbled into the darkness away from the sounds of war being waged within the gates of Serenity Canyon.

The helicopters weren't a godsend as Lalo originally thought they would be. They weren't a relief as he had been telling himself. Instead, they filled him with dread. The whole ordeal since they were stopped in the parking lot by two FBI agents hadn't lasted more than a couple hours, but it felt like eons of panic. The help they were praying for had turned into their doom. The cart driven by Sunny was riddled with bullets, it went wildly running off into the bushes at the edge of the community fencing. It flipped on its side and rested in a cloud of dust. The gunmen turned their sights on the three men outpacing the horde behind them and as it flew over them it cut them down on the way to battle the undead. Lalo fell alongside Jose and Agent Boze, a bullet tore through his shoulder and exited in a hot line to burry itself in the soft green grass. Lalo rolled his head to look at Jose, he had a hole in his throat. His eyes were wide and his mouth was opening and closing in wordless speech. Agent Boze coughed and drew a breath, "Are you alive?"

Lalo pulled his sad eyes away to look at the FBI agent, the side of his head was bleeding, his ear was gone, but it looked like the bullet had only grazed him and took a piece of him with it.

"Jose!"

Agent Boze got to his feet. His legs were trembling so bad he could hardly help Lalo up. Jose was still, his eyes gazing into nothing. He was dead.

"Fuck."

"We have to move," Boze said and helped Lalo hop along on his good foot.

A second helicopter was approaching. Boze and Lalo fell to the ground and lay completely still, hoping they were mistaken for dead. It passed over them but still they waited and watched. The first helicopter landed out on the golf course and the second was following its lead. The men exiting it were dressed for chemical warfare, and brandishing flamethrowers.

Stephi stumbled blindly in their direction. Shrieking and vomiting at the soldiers. Her eyes bounced from their nerve cords. She was joined by a large group of shrieking dead, unleashing showers of vomit in defense of their father, Teddy. The soldiers didn't hesitate in letting their flamethrowers spit streams of flame at the approaching creatures. The horde walked directly into the hungry fire, igniting their reanimated bodies. Their cries were loud but in their minds the screaming of the squirming Gods within them roared like storm winds, the howling of defeat.

Teddy came for them, enraged his children were burning, the offspring of the Goddess were being cast back into oblivion. He was the elite among them, the most intelligent, the most powerful, but he was nothing against the hungry flames spit from the end of the human's weaponry. His muscular body was no match for napalm burning at a thousand degrees Celsius. He stumbled back and opened his mouth to shriek, to spit a shower of larvae filled vomit, but his throat was burned. The excruciating heat had traveled into him in a fraction of a second and turned his insides to smoldering blackness. The fire ate through his eyes and into his brain. Those sacred Gods birthed from a frozen Goddess were scorched to nothing, roasted within his grey matter. His body fell to the soft green grass and broke into blackened, smoking pieces. The soldiers paid him no mind and went on about their deadly business, leaving him there as a message to all those who fled from them. They came to kill the invader, and they wouldn't stop until they were victorious. Those men dressed in alien suits of armor, carrying weaponry spitting the flames of Hell, they were ten thousand times more unstoppable than any worm.

Lalo and Agent Boze should have been cheering them on but they knew they would be burned to black chunks on the golf course if they didn't move. They snuck away while the boys in green battled Teddy's children.

They made it to the overturned golf cart, Jose's war machine. It had crashed in a bush and knocked a section of fencing down, making an exit for them. Jose had saved them by making the crazy contraption. They felt so victorious watching him run Peter down with it, like they actually had a chance. Now, Jose, the hero, was cut down by a more prolific killer than any parasite, a monster known as man.

"Sunny, Isabel?" Lalo said as Agent Boze pushed through the bushes to the wreckage of the ride on lawn mower.

He fell over the bushes, trying to get to the cart. His shoulder and leg were screaming in agony. His hand felt a long shaft of metal. He pulled it free and looked at it, an old golf club, probably tossed there by some disgruntled player. He searched the bushes and found another one. He used them to help himself stand back up and gripped them like a cane to steady him as he waited for Boze. Blood ran down his arm and dripped from his fingertips, he worried he might bleed to death.

"¡Aqui!"

His breath caught in his throat, Isabel was alive.

"¿Y Sunny?"

"Esta viva pero muy grave, Lalo."

"Hurry, Sunny is hurt badly," He urged Boze.

"I'm gonna pry the door open. Hold on."

The agent managed to get his hand on the bent door and force it upward to open it.

"Can you climb out?"

"I think so but Sunny needs help," Isabel answered.

She grunted as she reached up and pulled herself to sit on the edge of the overturned lawnmower. Agent Boze helped her down but she needed him to carry her out of the bushes. Her broken leg was swelling, causing tremendous pain. Lalo waited with her while Agent Boze climbed down into the war machine, its blades were twisted and broken, like a fallen beast. Sunny's body was forced out the dented door and Agent Boze followed her, his breathing labored from dead lifting her over his head. She slid down the front end of the lawnmower and rested there unconscious. Agent Boze hurried to examine her.

"She was shot through the side. I can't tell in the dark if it'll kill her or not."

"Can you carry her?" Lalo asked.

"I'm sure I can, but what about her?" He motioned to Isabel.

"She can use one of these," Lalo tossed one golf club in Isabel's direction and she grabbed it.

"How could they do this to us?" Isabel asked, looking out over the destruction and pausing at the sight of Jose's body in the distance.

"Take no prisoners, leave no witnesses. Sickening, isn't it?" Agent Boze said.

The four of them took off into the surrounding high deserts beyond the hole in the decorative fencing surrounding what was once one of the most exclusive luxury communities in all of Arizona, behind them the entirety of Serenity Canyon was going up in flames, every cottage, the club house, the pool house, the maintenance and grounds shops, they were all being destroyed.

Agent Jackson stumbled across the uneven ground, sand, rocks, scrubby brush, all seeking to bring him down. He was breathing heavily and completely exhausted so he made his way to a grouping of thick sage bushes and laid Jason down. He was still alive but barely. Tears stung Agent Jackson's eyes, he had been through some bad situations but this one topped them all and he truly thought this was the end for him. He sat in the dirt beside his bleeding companion and took a few deep breaths.

There was smoke in the air, carried to him on the wind blowing across the golf course, the warzone of death and destruction. The sounds of it in the distance reminded him he still needed to keep going. If he was caught he would be shot and burned before anyone thought to examine him, it was far too risky. He knew it, and didn't really blame the government boys after witnessing all he had in the last few hours within the gates of the luxurious neighborhood called Serenity Canyon.

Jason coughed, sending a mist of blood into the air which hung there for a split second before raining lightly back into his face.

"Easy now, " Agent Jackson said and squeezed Jason's shoulder.

They needed to keep moving but Agent Jackson couldn't bring himself to hoist Jason up onto his shoulder, he didn't have the strength anymore and he knew it would be agonizing for Jason with his gaping bullet wound. He got up and dragged Jason back further into the brush to try to conceal them. He sat for a while, it felt like an eternity, the scent of blood and smoke clinging to him, thinking of what he should do. He knew the Army would send men out to be certain no one escaped the containment zone, he would be killed on sight. But he couldn't bring himself to leave Jason there all alone to die.

"Go, " Jason wheezed.

"No...I can't."

Jason stammered, he couldn't speak anymore, he settled into rough, shallow breathing.

A groaning startled Agent Jackson. He looked around frantically, expecting at any minute to see a twisted face and feel a shower of infectious vomit hitting him.

"She's fuckin'heavy, " a strained whisper filled Agent Jackson with hope.

He shot to his feet, his head popping up out of the thorny brush to see a group of shadows moving.

"Boze, " he said.

"Jackson?" the familiar voice was filled with relief.

The staggering, bloodied crew crested a hill and below them on an unpaved desert road sat a pickup truck. The driver was sitting on the tailgate, finishing off a can of beer. The radio was blaring and he sang to himself, off tune and the wrong lyrics, some country song. In the distance the sounds of helicopters reminded them of the urgency for an escape.

"Ladies and Gentlemen, our Limo awaits, " Agent Boze said.

"I've never been so happy to hear country music!" Agent Jackson said.

Behind them, Lalo and Isa sat with Sunny and Jason. Sunny was in better shape but both were on the verge of dying.

"You guys wait here, let me and Agent Jackson handle this. Be ready to haul ass."

Lalo crept away from Sunny and Jason to watch them go. He held his breath as he watched two shadows moving in stealth down the small hillside, using the taller brush as camouflage, until they reached a ditch at the side of the road. The man in the truck pushed himself off the tailgate and walked and uneven path toward a tree and was busy relieving his beer-filled bladder when he was taken by surprise. The two agents didn't have any trouble subduing the drunken man and even wrapped his wrists and ankles with a roll of his own duct tape they found in his truck before hurrying back to Lalo and the rest of the group on the hill.

The ride in the truck bed was a rough half hour for Agent Jackson and Jason. He let Lalo and the women ride inside next to Agent Boze where Sunny would be more comfortable. Jason was slipping away, Agent Jackson knew it, he hadn't moved or opened his eyes since he was placed in the truck bed.

They slowly rolled by an old trailer sitting back off the road. Agent Jackson braced himself against the cab of the truck as it came to a quick stop and backed up.

"We're slowing down, looks like Boze found a place for us to hide and Dr. Abileen can come patch us all up!" He said down to Jason and patted the young man's hand. It felt cold.

"This is it…the best we can do, " Agent Boze said from the driver's side window.

The guard, Donald, answered the phone, nodded, and then threw the phone on the ground and crushed it. He picked up the broken phone, pulled the back open and fished out the SIM card, he snapped it and tossed it to the sand. Dr. Abileen sat in the back seat, still recovering from her treatment for the parasite.

"Was that Agent Boze?"

He motioned to T and they climbed back into the car, "He gave me his location and told me to destroy the phone."

"Good. Let's go."

They arrived at their destination, an abandoned trailer somewhere near Cottonwood, Arizona. Agent Jackson met them at the door.

"Is this a secure place?" Donald asked.

"Secure as we could find after stealing a truck on a desert road, we couldn't risk being out searching for a place too long. We woulda been made," Agent Boze said from inside the trailer.

The bloodied and traumatized group huddled in a small, dusty living room which was connected to an open kitchen, only separated by a thin island made of fake wood paneling. There were holes in the walls, like someone had gone on a bender and started punching holes through invisible enemies. The room with sparse furniture, a single dark hallway leading from it with two small doors on each side of it, it was their only sanctuary. It felt more like a tomb than a home and Dr. Abileen wondered if it ever really did, even when it was new and belonged to someone. A musty smell, like cigarettes and moldy carpet hit their noses.

"We got an injured girl in here," Agent Jackson said, stepping aside for Dr. Abileen.

"I'm not really equipped to treat her but I'll try my best."

Sunny was on a broken down couch, Agent Boze had a crimson Serenity Canyon shirt held to a wound in her side. Dr. Abileen felt a sadness grip her heart, what a place to be so close to death? A dirty, old trailer where people probably went to shoot up, on a filthy couch which was probably crawling with bedbugs-it was the girl's only source of comfort now.

"Gun shot?" the doctor asked.

"Yup."

"Did it go through?" she asked, leaning closer to Sunny.

"Yeah, this is the entrance, it exited out the back. She's bled a lot," Agent Boze answered, revealing the wound to Dr. Abileen.

Dr. Abileen took the place of Agent Boze at Sunny's side and pressed the dressing to her bullet hole. The young woman was unconscious, barely breathing, and had bled far too much.

"I don't think she's gonna make it," Dr. Abileen said sadly.

"Fuck, first we lost Jason, and now Sunny?" Lalo said.

"We barely made it out. Look at us," Jackson said.

Dr. Abileen's eyes went to a body covered in an old blanket, then to the injuries Lalo, Boze, and Isabel sustained.

She lifted the shirt under her hand to get a look at the bullet hole. Deep in the wound, something moved. Dr. Abileen froze, her eyes caught a hint of something pale and thin. Sunny took a ragged breath and exhaled deeply, she never inhaled again.

"Did she come in contact with any vomit or feces from the infected?"

"I'm not sure. I don't think so," Lalo said.

"She's dead. She'll need to be burned."

"What! Why?" he asked.

"She's infected," Dr. Abileen answered.

"No, no, that can't be," Lalo cried.

"Get my satchel," she said to T, "the rest of you are getting the treatment."

"No, give it to Sunny too," Lalo pleaded, unwilling to accept her fate.

"I'm sorry, it's too late. She's gone, she'll come back as one of them, we have to…"

Dr. Abileen's sentence was cut short by a gurgling deep in Sunny's gut. Her reaction time was still slowed by the exhaustion she experienced after being given the antidote. She turned back in time to receive a face full of infectious vomit. Sunny screeched and leapt from the couch. The trailer erupted in gunfire and screaming.

Dr. Abileen fell back as Sunny jumped from the bloodstained couch. She rolled away and scrambled around a recliner beside a dusty coffee table to see the dead girl scurrying like an animal across the floor.

T screamed while firing at Sunny, who tackled Isabelle and savagely bit into her throat. The bullets tore through her shoulder and back, dark blood misted the air. She fell forward and wretched into Isabelle's opened throat, a load of yellow bile squirming with tiny worms. Isabelle choked, her hands went to the gaping hole feebly attempting to hold it together. T's aim was truer with his next round of shots, he sent one through the side of Sunny's head and one straight into Isabelle's left eye. Sunny fell over Isabelle and all was still for a moment.

The whole trailer smelled like vomit and gun smoke, Dr. Abileen gagged as she wiped her face clean but she didn't have the time to worry about being disgusted or the luxury of finding a sink to clean up.

"Shoot them again!" she demanded.

Donald joined T and they stood over the women and emptied their pistols into them. The carpet beneath the two corpses was crimson and it the gathering pool, Dr. Abileen could see the blood writhing.

"We have to get outta here, there's too much contaminates, grab my bag!" she ordered Donald.

He bent to retrieve her satchel when the Jason's corpse sat up from the floor, the blanket covering his lifeless face fell away. His eyes were clouded with death yet looked around wildly.

"Jason!" Lalo yelled.

Lalo pointed at his former employee and backed away into the tiny kitchen of the trailer. Jason forced the blanket away and got on his hands and knees, he bared his teeth and shrieked at Agent Boze who was only feet away and unarmed. The agent took a step back but stumbled over a side table, sending the lamp sitting on it crashing to the floor. Jason lunged forward, going for the FBI agent. Agent Boze screamed and kicked at Jason, his foot connecting with the dead man's teeth. It didn't stop Jason. He was stunned for a moment and redoubled his attack on Agent Boze.

T and Donald fought to jam clips into their pistols and Dr. Abileen screamed, "Shoot him!"

Jason leaped at Agent Boze who had found the broken lamp and brought it up as his only weapon. The jagged edge of the broken lamp plunged into Jason's abdomen and still he fought like a rabid dog, bloody froth dripping from his mouth. His hands like claws, scratching at the face of Agent Boze. Jason's nails raked into his cheeks, leaving jagged red lines behind. Jason's abdomen spilled out of his wound and onto Agent Boze, blood, intestines, and dancing parasites seeking a new host.

"Fuck!" Agent Boze screamed but in a beat of his terrified heart Jason's head exploded on one side with a shot from Donald's gun.

Lalo ran to Agent Boze and dragged him out from under the twitching corpse of Jason.

Lalo watched the trailer go up in flames while Dr. Abileen

administered the treatment for the parasite to him. T and Donald fanned the flames, making sure the hungry fire consumed everything.

"We need to move before the Army finds us. Sooner or later they'll do the math and realize there were survivors, which means witnesses," Agent Boze said.

"I'm goin' to find my wife and disappear," Lalo said, rubbing his arm and praying silently Dr. Abileen's medication kept him from becoming like Sunny, Jason, and he rest of Serenity Canyon.

"You're all set, none of us should be carriers," She said.

Agent Boze squeezed Lalo's shoulder and said, "Disappearing sounds like a good idea. Sedona is going to be ground zero and we can't be certain other infected didn't escape, I'd say get as far from here as you can."

"Let's go!" Dr. Abileen said as the sounds of helicopters echoed on the horizon.

Anthony had his rig pulled over to the side of the road, the fire in the distance had drawn a large crowd of people and already the government had sent a team to help fight the flames.

"Looks like livin' in such a fancy place don't protect you when a gas line erupts," a woman commented, smoking a cigarette.

"Yeah, ain't that the truth. This ain't the only fire, there's one out by Cottonwood at a trailer too. Probably some meth heads did that one though."

He wanted to keep watching the blaze but he had been on the road for seven days and was anxious to visit his sister Adriana and his niece Sunny. He nodded to the nosey woman and hopped back in the cab. He glanced over to the gift he meant to give Adriana. She'd have to forgive him not calling her for Christmas when she saw what he had.

The fuzzy little dog slept in the front seat. Anthony had a hell of a time catching it when he saw it running down the side of the highway, but he managed to tire it out and grab it. It was filthy and stinking but he planned to give it a quick bath at the truck stop before heading to his sister's house. It looked like a Pomeranian, an expensive little show dog under the crust of excrement in its fur.

"I can't wait to see her face when she sees you buddy."

He rubbed its back and scratched its neck, his fingers found a collar with a little tag on it. He flipped it over, it too was crusted in crap. He spit on his finger and rubbed it clean, "Puffkins."

"What kind of a name is that?" he laughed.

He started up his rig and thought out loud, "We'll have to rename you. My sis loves Teddy bears and you look like one, so how about we call you Teddy?"

ACKNOWLEDGMENTS

We wrote this novel as tribute to our days in the custodial arts. Many nights spent cleaning schools, reading horror, and dreaming of writing horror…

Thank you to our idols and the friends we've made along the way for all the inspiration- Jeremy Wagner, Steve Wands, Paul Goblirsch, Tod Clark, Brian Keene, Ronald Kelly, Mary SanGiovanni, Stephen Graham Jones, Paul Tremblay, Gabino Iglesias, Cina Pelayo, V. Castro, Somer Canon, Laurel Hightower, and so many more!

All of our love and appreciation to our readers, we couldn't do this weird shit without you!

WE ARE THE SCUM CREW!

ALSO BY THE SISTERS OF SLAUGHTER

Novels/Novellas

The Abyssal Plain: The R'lyeh Cycle – Journal Stone 01/29/2019

Tapetum Lucidum – Death's Head Press 10/01/2019

Isolation – Crossroad Press 01/18/2022

Mayan Blue – Crossroad Press 02/22/2022

Pandemonium, Arizona – Journal Stone 06/19/2022

Hell's Cargo – Death's Head Press 08/13/2024

Short stories

Wishful Thinking (wishes book 1) – Fireside Press 10/29/2014

Double Barrel Horror: Just a Few/Tenants rights – Pint Bottle Press 01/27/2016

Splatterpunk Forever – Splatterpunk Zine 11/23/2018

Other Voices, Other Tombs – Cemetery Gate Media 06/23/2019

Her Black Wings – Kandisha Press 01/12/2020

Splatterpunk Bloodstains – Splatterpunk Zine 12/06/2020

Were Tales: A Shapeshifter Anthology – Brigid's Gate Press 09/21/2021

Comics

Resurrection Hill (Michelle Garza)– Dead Sky Publishing 01/24/2024

ABOUT THE AUTHORS

Michelle Garza and Melissa Lason have been dubbed The Sisters of Slaughter for their blood-soaked writing. Their debut novel, *Mayan Blue,* was nominated for a Bram Stoker award and they have contributed to Splatterpunk award winning anthologies. They have been published by Thunderstorm Books, Dead Sky Publishing, Polis Books, Cemetery Gates Media, and many more in their more than ten years of publishing. Working both as a team and separately, they have written novels, novellas, and short stories spanning the horror, sci-fi, and dark fantasy genres. They live in Arizona with their husbands and kids and enjoy all things spooky.